Dara and David, Inextricably Bound by the Curse of Their Evil Ancestors . . .

"I'm sorry, David, to get you here with me. Because we are—not like other people. You can see in the dark now, and there are other things both of us will be able to do later. . . .

"Because of this we are of use to the man who killed your wife. He took me away from my grandparents when I was very young . . . but he couldn't prevent them from giving me this—"

She held up her left arm so I could see the nine-headed cobra twisted around it. It shone with a subtle, almost imperceptible, blue radiance, paler than the silver cave-glow, while its eyes—red by day—shone golden like Dara's own.

"He brought us here so he could make use of us to defeat his enemies, and they know it. Once he's safe from them, I'll get my memories back and he'll free both of us. But if they defeat him, my death will pass from his hands into theirs and they . . . hate me, David, and they're evil, what they want to do is evil. . . ."

DHAMPIRE

SCOTT BAKER

A TIMESCAPE BOOK
PUBLISHED BY POCKET BOOKS NEW YORK

This novel is a work of fiction. Names, characters, places and incidents are either the product of the author's imagination or are used fictitiously. Any resemblance to actual events or locales or persons, living or dead, is entirely coincidental.

Another *Original* publication of TIMESCAPE BOOKS

A Timescape Book published by
POCKET BOOKS, a Simon & Schuster division of
GULF & WESTERN CORPORATION
1230 Avenue of the Americas, New York, N.Y. 10020

ISBN: 0-671-44666-5

First Timescape Books printing December, 1982

10 9 8 7 6 5 4 3 2 1

POCKET and colophon are registered trademarks
of Simon & Schuster.

Use of the trademark TIMESCAPE is by exclusive license
from Gregory Benford, the trademark owner.

Printed in the U.S.A.

*This book is for my brother John,
who endured rattlesnakes and bats
to help me research it,
and for Suzi,
who improved it.*

He who would enter the Kingdom of God must first enter with his body into his mother and there die.

—Paracelsus

DHAMPIRE

Chapter One

"WE'D BEEN HOPING YOU'D BE ABLE TO GIVE US A hand with the inspection," the chief customs officer said. He was thicknecked, overmuscular, about thirty-five: he reminded me of a wrestling and tennis coach I'd particularly hated at St. George's Academy. His assistant—taller, older, visibly nervous—was standing a little behind him, as far away from the unopened crates at the other end of the small cold room as possible.

"Excellent," Alexandra said, giving him her Dragon Lady smile. Her features were beginning to take on that blue-gray blurriness, almost as though I were seeing them through a thin mist, that they sometimes had for me when I'd been too many days without sleep. "If we handle the snakes ourselves there's much less chance of an accident. And many of the snakes are too delicate to survive rough handling."

"All the better, then. Did you bring all the equipment or whatever you're going to need with you?"

"In this suitcase," I said.

"Good. Then let's get it over with as fast as we can." He

picked up a list. 'It says here you've got fifteen Columbian rattlesnakes, eleven fer-de-lance, two sea snakes, species unknown—" He glanced up. "Poisonous?"

"Very," Alexandra said.

."Ah. Then, an anaconda, seven eyelash vipers, one bushmaster, nine emerald tree boas—"

An unexpected piece of luck. "That should read four emerald tree boas," I said and he made the correction.

"And three Columbian coral snakes."

Which meant that the time had come to complicate things. I frowned, said, "There should also be a crate with a half dozen different kinds of small boas and some burrowing snakes in it."

"It didn't arrive with the rest of your shipment."

"You're sure?" Alexandra demanded. "You couldn't have misplaced it or something?"

"I doubt it. You don't lose crates stamped 'DANGER!! POISONOUS SNAKES!!' in bright red letters. It's probably been bumped to the next flight. Are the snakes dangerous?"

"No, not at all," Alexandra said, "but the burrowing snakes are very delicate. They can't take rough handling or cold and if somebody rerouted them to L.A. or San Jose by mistake— David, can you take care of things here without me while I go check with the airline, put a tracer on it or something?"

Fuck. Not again. "I guess, if you're not gone too long. Do you have the ticket stubs?"

"I should. Be back in a few minutes."

I caught the chief inspector staring at her ass as she walked out the door. Which was only to be expected: Alexandra's idea of what the well-dressed lady snake handler wore consisted of cream-colored boots halfway up her thighs, skintight French jeans, an equally tight red top. Part of her Bread and Circuses theory of getting through customs.

"Your wife's got lovely hair," the inspector said as soon as she'd closed the door behind her.

"Very," I agreed. "Where do you want to start?"

"What's in that crate there?"

"Two sea snakes."

"How are they packed?"

"Separate cloth bags inside a larger insulated bag. If you'll give me a second to get ready I'll open the crate for you."

"Please."

I opened my suitcase, took out my folding fence and set it up: a ring a little over three feet in diameter, about two and a half feet high. I screwed the two parts of my snake stick together, took off my suit coat and put on my gray leather vest and long gloves.

"Will that fence hold them in?"

"No. At least not for long. But snakes aren't very smart, and if anything goes wrong it should take most of the smaller ones long enough to escape for the two of you to get out of the room. Put the crate in the ring and give me a pry bar and I'll get started."

I took the boards off one side of the crate, lifted out the insulated bag.

"They're both there?"

"I think so. The bag's still sealed—" I ripped it open, carefully lifted out the two cloth bags, taking care to keep them away from my body and arms. "They're both here."

"Good. Could you hand out the crate and the insulated bag?" He nodded to his assistant, who came up and took them from me, gingerly sorted through the Styrofoam chunks in the crate.

The chief inspector picked up the insulated bag, examined it.

"What's this foil lining for?"

"Insulation, though I had to perforate it to keep the snakes from suffocating. Like those space blankets they use for arctic survival—you know the ones I mean? They sell them for camping now."

"I've seen them. Can you open the cloth bags and pass them out to Jim? One at a time?"

"Sure. Could you hand me some of the spare sacks from my suitcase? It's safer if I rebag the snakes as soon as possible."

He examined the sacks, handed them in to me. I loosed the drawstrings on the first bag with the hook on the other end of my snake stick, waited until the sea snake poked its tiny rounded black and yellow head out, then snared it with the stick. It writhed feebly a bit, hardly protesting as I got it behind the head and dumped it in the other sack. I handed the empty sack to the assistant, who looked in it, shook his head.

"Can you turn up the temperature in here?" I asked. "It's too cold for the snakes."

"I'm sorry, but the thermostat's preset. An economy measure, to keep us from wasting energy."

3

"Then let's hurry. I don't like the way that sea snake looked."

"What's in that crate?"

"Rattlesnakes."

Only two of the snakes rattled when I lifted their cloth sacks from the insulated envelope and none of them tried to strike at me through the cloth. I had to push the first one with my snake stick to get it to leave the open bag; two of the others were dead, as was one of the coral snakes in the next crate.

The emerald tree boas were all alive, as were the fer-de-lance, but they were all sluggish. Had any of the snakes been a little more active I might have hesitated to take the bushmaster out without Alexandra around to back me up if something went wrong—it was a magnificent specimen, almost thirteen feet long, with four-and-a-half-inch fangs—but as it was I had no trouble getting it behind the neck and immobilizing it before it could strike at me or damage its delicate neck with its struggles. Bushmasters are slender-bodied snakes, and even my thirteen-foot specimen was no heavier than a six-foot eastern diamondback rattlesnake, but I could feel it slowly coming alert as my body heat revived it and I was almost as relieved as the two inspectors when I had it safely back in its sack.

Which left only the anaconda. And Alexandra still wasn't back. Which meant either that she'd locked herself in a toilet cubicle in one of the women's bathrooms or that she was gone altogether.

"I'm going to need a lot of help with the anaconda," I said. "It's not poisonous but all anacondas are pretty evil-tempered and this one's nineteen feet long and close to three hundred pounds. We'll need at least another four men to help hold it while you check out the crate."

Alexandra made her entrance while the chief inspector was telephoning. Her face was flushed and excited, even through the blurriness. "They claim they don't have any record of the shipment," she said. "So I called Richard and had him tell them that we were going to sue them for some enormous sum if they didn't produce the snakes alive and in good condition very soon. Are the rest of the snakes OK?"

"We haven't gotten to the anaconda yet," I said. "Two of the rattlesnakes died, and so did one of the coral snakes, but I think the others are going to make it, at least if we can get them somewhere warm pretty soon."

The anaconda was stout and ugly, a muddy olive green with

4

black splotches. About ten feet behind its relatively small head the goat it had eaten in Bogota had produced a huge bulge, half again as big around as the snake's body. I was holding the head, Alexandra had it by the neck, and the four new customs men were holding its body while the chief inspector and his assistant went through the packing material in the crate.

"Why's it all swollen like that?" the man holding it just behind the bulge asked.

"It ate a goat a while before we shipped it," Alexandra said. "Snakes can dislocate their jaws to swallow things much bigger around than they are. They have to, since they mostly eat their prey alive and don't have any way to chew them up into smaller pieces. Their teeth aren't made for it."

"Thanks." He didn't seem particularly pleased with the information.

"That's one reason it's so sluggish," I said. "That and the cold. Otherwise it would be giving us a lot more trouble."

"I'm afraid we're going to have to x-ray that snake," the chief inspector said when he'd finished going through everything else. "I want to examine that bulge."

"It's a goat," I said. "We've got pictures of the snake eating it, if you want to look at them."

"No thanks. Just put it back in its sack and we'll take it into the next room—"

He stared at the x rays for a long time, finally admitted that the pictures showed the goat's skeleton, still partially intact, inside the anaconda.

"Can you give us some help loading the truck?" I asked. "It's pretty hard to find porters who'll agree to handle crates full of poisonous snakes and a few of these crates are too large for Alexandra and me to handle, even with our dolly."

"We're not supposed to," he said, "but after the cooperation you've shown us I don't see why not."

The truck was a lemon-yellow Dodge van with the scarlet head of a cobra flanked by the words "BIG SUR SNAKE FARM" and "Specialists in venomous reptiles" painted on the sides. The little cobra in the glove compartment cage raised its head and spread its hood when I opened the side door.

"All the other cages are empty," I said. "Just put the anaconda's crate about halfway up front and the rest of the crates behind it."

Alexandra waited until we were on 101 South, then put on

her gloves and took the vial of coke out from under the rock in the baby cobra's cage. She held the spoon to my nostrils four times before snorting any herself. The blue-gray vagueness began to dissipate. Another eight spoonfuls and it was gone altogether.

She was smiling—white teeth, tanned skin, long soft blond hair—but behind the smile her jaw was knotted and ugly with the tensions that never left her, that ground her teeth together while she slept no matter how many sleeping pills she took, that turned on her and tried to destroy her the instant she stopped moving, stopped pushing, stopped striking out.

But for the moment she was riding her tension, using it without attacking herself or striking out at me, and I welcomed the respite, the chance to go inside my head with only the coke for company, and play with my thoughts and hopes for a while.

Chapter Two

WE MADE IT BACK TO THE COAST ABOUT TWO-THIRTY. The sky was black and gray and out over the Pacific you could see ball lightning but it hadn't started raining again. Alexandra got a stack of letters out of the mailbox while I unlocked the gate and drove the truck through.

"There's another letter from your father," she said after I'd locked the gate again. "Marked 'Reply Urgent.' What do you want me to do with it?"

"Save it till we get back to the cabin, then stick it in the fireplace and forget it. Like all the rest."

I put the truck in low and started up the road. It was little more than an oversized jeep trail and the spring rains had left it in bad condition: I'd had to have special shocks and springs put in to keep all the bouncing and vibration from panicking the snakes I carried.

"What about this? Somebody calling themselves CET-VER LABORATORIES in New Mexico wants five hundred dollars' worth of rattlesnake venom as soon as possible."

"Excellent. I don't think we've got that much venom on

7

hand but—how long's it been since we last milked the pit vipers?"

"About three and a half months."

"That should be long enough."

"If John hasn't killed them all."

"He said they were all doing OK when we talked to him on the phone last week."

"When *you* talked to him. And that was last week. Anyway—David? Why don't I milk the rattlesnakes this time while you and John put away the new snakes? OK?"

"You sure? It's my turn, remember?" Alexandra was as competent with the snakes as I was but she'd never learned to feel comfortable working with them and we both preferred to have me take care of them whenever possible.

"Yes, but—a couple of things. The first is that I'd like to get the venom centrifuged tonight so we can send it off UPS tomorrow and you're going to be too busy with the other snakes to have the time to get it done."

"What's the second?"

"Something felt really wrong at the airport today. As soon as we get home I want you to get all the drugs and paraphernalia out of the house. Put them in the hollow log just off the property."

"You think we're going to get raided?"

"I'm sure of it. That customs man, the one in charge—it was like he was watching us through a one-way mirror. Studying us all the time, even at the end, when he should have been satisfied."

"If you thought there was something wrong, there was something wrong. You don't make that kind of mistake."

"No. Look, why don't you and John go swimming after you get the snakes in their cages, maybe smoke some mushroom spores and relax. You look tired. I'll join you when I'm done."

Which meant that she wanted to make up for having deserted me at the airport without having to admit anything.

We'd made it up out of the clouds, a gray-black plain stretching away to the western horizon behind us, and onto the ridge: sloping sunlit meadows filled with fuzzy blue lupin and vivid orange California poppies. A few minutes later and we were making our way down through the thick oak and madrone forest on the inland side. The sky overhead was cloudless but the trees blocked out most of the sunlight and little brown mushrooms grew in damp clusters by the sides of the road.

John's Volkswagen was parked just outside our second gate. There was a painting in the back seat, hundreds of tiny black and white portraits against a violet, yellow and pink background that made the clustered faces look like the dark centers of pastel flowers. It was better than a lot of the stuff John had done—and I'd always liked his work—though it had that same uncomfortable amphetamine precision to it. I recognized some of the portraits, Alexandra's and mine among them. Most of the portraits were quite good—he'd gotten me down perfectly, as far as I could tell—but he'd put Alexandra in the center of his canvas and then completely missed the tension in her expression, turning her into just another of those unmemorably pretty girls who work in health-food stores or as cocktail waitresses all up and down the coast.

Or maybe not. I'd just noticed the four other portraits of Alexandra, one in each corner, all of them stark, grim and exquisitely rendered, when I heard John's voice.

He hugged us both, then unlocked the car and took out the painting. He propped it up against the windshield, steadied it with his right hand.

"Do you like it? I finished it four days ago."

"Very much," Alexandra said.

"You, David?"

"It's beautiful. Maybe the best thing of yours I've seen so far."

"Good, because it's for the two of you. A homecoming gift."

John had brought the dolly up from the cabin. We loaded it with the crate of buzzing rattlesnakes and the bushmaster's crate, then started down the path to the herpetarium.

I'd set up my herpetarium in a natural limestone cavern I'd discovered in the cliff behind the cabin soon after I inherited the property from my aunt. The entrance was low and you had to stoop to enter but about two feet past the mouth the cave opened up. The ceiling was high and for most of its fifty-foot length the cave was at least thirty feet wide. At the far end it narrowed suddenly, then ended in a wall of purplish red rock. An eight-inch fissure split the red rock from floor to ceiling, but though my flashlight had given me tantalizing glimpses of further caverns the red wall was at least two feet thick and there was no way I could break through it at present, though I'd had vague thoughts of someday renting a jackhammer or miner's drill.

But for the moment I was well satisfied with what I had. The floor was almost perfectly level and I had as much space as I'd need for a long time to come. I'd installed fluorescent lights and tiers of heated snake cages along the walls, all running off the power generated by our water wheel, windmill, and small solar plant, while in the center of the chamber I'd placed some of the larger cages, the tank in which I'd originally housed my turtles but which I was planning to use for my sea snakes, and all the apparatus I needed for milking the poisonous snakes and preparing their venom for storage and shipment.

The rattlesnakes were happy enough to be out of their bags and into their cages but the bushmaster coiled and struck at the glass whenever I came near. I finally covered its cage with a tarp to keep it from hurting its nose.

John went back up to the truck for another crate while I checked the snakes he'd been taking care of.

"They all look healthy," I told him when he returned with the sea snakes. "You didn't have any problems?"

"Not really. The green mamba refused to eat the first two months and I was afraid I'd have to try to force-feed it but I finally got it to take a mouse."

"Excellent. And thanks. I can give you half an ounce of coke now but we'll have to wait until the anaconda finishes digesting the goat to get the rest. You should have seen us trying to shove the goat down the snake's throat. And for that matter it was pretty grim getting the five kilos of coke into the dead goat."

"No problems getting through customs?"

"Nothing overt, but Alexandra thinks they're still suspicious. I'm getting everything off the property as soon as I've got the sea snakes in their tank. Do you have anything with you here they could bust us for?"

"Nothing I don't have a script for."

The sea snakes were as graceful underwater as they were clumsy on land. John watched them swimming back and forth investigating their tank for a while, then went back up for more snakes while I hid the drugs. When I got back Alexandra was standing at the milking table holding a squirming five-foot western diamondback and massaging its poison glands to get more venom into the beaker on the table.

"Are you sure you chilled that snake long enough?" I asked, making sure I didn't startle her. "It looks pretty active."

"Probably not," she admitted, making a face, "but it's too late to do anything about it now. I'll keep the others chilled a bit longer. But I think we're going to run short. Is it all right if I milk some of the South American rattlers?"

"No, the venom's not quite the same. If you want I can go try to catch some new snakes as soon as I'm done unloading. With any luck we'll have a half dozen or so in the woodpile."

"No, wait till tomorrow morning. I might be able to get just barely enough."

John and I saved the crate with the anaconda in it for last. Alexandra took a break between snakes to help us get it onto the dolly and down to the herpetarium. It glided listlessly around its new cage for a while, then coiled up in a corner.

"Ugly," John said.

"Mean too. You still want to go swimming? I rolled a joint with some freeze-dried spores in it while I was hiding the rest of our stuff."

"Sure. Nothing would please me more, as a matter of fact. What with the painting and cleaning up my mess and getting your truck to the airport for you and all I haven't had any sun for at least a week."

Chapter Three

For a while after we smoked the psilocybin everything was gentle luminosity, an inexhaustible succession of drifting silences. Neither John nor I spoke. When the rocks got too hot for me I'd dive in, angling deep, and chase the small trout in the pool through a few zigs and zags before they darted away from me, then come up under the waterfall until my head was just beneath the surface and I was lost in the icy-white dazzle that was the waterfall exploding into foam where it hit the surface of the pool.

It was perfect: peace at last after the months of cocaine and tension. When I felt myself starting to come down I wandered out into the woods to look at the mushrooms and wildflowers and wash the scent of pine sap through my lungs.

John joined me after a while. With his beard and hair he looked like some small woodland animal—a chipmunk or woodchuck, maybe, or perhaps some sort of small bear that ate nothing but pinecones and berries.

"David, why do you like snakes so much?" he asked me

after a while, and because he was a friend and he trusted me I tried to tell him.

"It's because—it's complicated. Look, one of my ancestors was a man named Vlad Dracul. His son was the historical Dracula. 'Dracula' means 'Son of Dracul.' OK? Anyway at home they always told me that 'Dracul' meant 'Devil' in Romanian but when I went away to school I learned that it really meant 'Dragon.' Because King Sigismund made Vlad Dracul a member of the Order of the Dragon. And where my family came from people thought of dragons as winged snakes and thought that even normal snakes could protect you against evil and—I don't know. I can't explain it any better than that."

Talking about my past had given it the reality I always tried to deny it. I'd grown up in Illinois, in a dark silent house more like a medieval castle than a conventional rich man's home. I was told my mother had died when I was two; I'd never known her and my father never mentioned her. He was a cold, closed man, immensely rich, with no time for my brother Michael or myself; as soon as we were old enough we were sent away to St. George's Romanian Academy (named after the Russian, and not the English, St. George, for reasons that were never really clear to me).

From the academy Michael had gone first to Yale and then on to Harvard Business School; I, two years later, to Stanford for a year, then to Berkeley for a semester, after which I dropped out and drifted around for a number of years—San Francisco, Boston, Florida, and Mexico, where I'd met Alexandra—before my Aunt Judith, the only member of my family I'd ever loved, committed suicide and left me her property in Big Sur.

"Was Dracula really a vampire?" John asked, which was so stupid that it ruined what little chance I might have had of getting my head back where I wanted it.

"No. He got a reputation as a bloodthirsty monster because he killed something between fifty and a hundred thousand people, mainly by impaling them. That's all." I was tired, too tired; there was a dry scraping behind my eyes and my jaw muscles ached. I needed Alexandra.

I remembered our first day together here in the woods, remembered grabbing a projecting rock and pulling myself up out of the water, my whole body tingling, feeling newly awakened, newly alive, as the warm dry breeze and late-spring sun began to steal the water from my back and shoulders.

Alexandra was lying on her back, her legs slightly spread, her tanned body glistening with sweat and cocoanut oil. Her eyes were closed and she was smiling, totally relaxed for the first time since we'd met. She looked very young and innocent, almost gentle, and that was the first time I'd ever seen her look that way.

I stood over her and let the cold water drip from my outstretched hands onto her body. She started and opened her eyes, staring wildly up at me an instant before she recognized me, her eyes wide and deep and intensely black. Then some of the tension went out of her and she smiled at me, a relieved, inviting smile.

She spread her legs and I knelt between them on the smooth white stone. I ran my hands up the insides of her oil-covered thighs and over her slippery stomach to her breasts, then down again between her legs. She took my still-cold, still-soft cock in her hands and held it between them, rubbing gently until her warmth passed into it and it grew hard. I rested my elbows on the rocks and she guided me into her.

Later we'd swum for a while, holding each other beneath the waterfall until our lungs were bursting, then returned to the rocks and the sun to make love again.

"John? I think I need to be alone with Alexandra for a while. We haven't slept for a couple of days and it's getting to me. Do you mind just heading back to your car without stopping by to say good-bye to her? You can come by again tomorrow afternoon, maybe about five."

"Sure. No problem. You look like you could use some sleep."

We walked back to the cabin together without saying anything. I shook his hand, thanked him again for what he'd done for us, then made my way back to the herpetarium.

I bent low to enter the cave, straightened:

Saw Alexandra lying dead or unconscious on the floor, her right arm swollen huge and purple. And on her chest, coiled, its head raised and swaying like a cobra's as it tasted the air with its tongue and vibrated its rough scaled tail in warning against the bright fabric of her top, the bushmaster.

I grabbed a long snake stick and tried to get the snake to move away from her but it avoided my clumsy attempts with a contemptuous intelligence I had never before seen in a snake, struck at me whenever I got too close. It was guarding Alexandra's body like a jackal with its prey and that was impossible, something no snake would ever do.

And I couldn't get to her, couldn't even get close enough to her to find out if she was still alive. If she was still alive there was a chance I could save her by cutting open the wound and draining the poison from it while giving her a shot of the right antivenin but with every instant the chances of saving her grew slimmer.

If she was still alive, if there was any chance at all. And I couldn't get past the bushmaster.

At last I gave up, retreated, hoping somehow that now it would begin to act like a normal snake and attempt to escape. It stayed where it was, head raised, watching me, its tongue flickering in and out of its mouth. Guarding her body.

I couldn't tell if she was still breathing. Her arm had swollen to almost twice its normal size; she hadn't moved since I'd first seen her. I hung back, watching her for any sign of life, trying to think of a way to get the snake away from her.

The fluorescent lights flickered. Alexandra's skin was steaming, misting: she was evaporating, dissolving into a blue-gray fog that thickened and spread, hid her from me. I could see shapes forming in the fog, things moving with a horrible liquidity that made me think of rotting flesh melting from disintegrating bone, of maggots swarming in the empty eye sockets of not-yet-dead birds. . . .

The cloud was a door opening into red-lit shadow where obscenely mutilated figures danced and capered and coupled around a gigantic man-goat who stood fondling an erect cock like a great legless centipede. I could smell the faraway sweetness of rotting flesh. The chill shadows reached for me, wrapped themselves around me as the black flames in the man-goat's eyes drew me to him through the thickening dark—

The bushmaster: I could hear its rough scales, impossibly loud, rasping the limestone floor as it glided towards me through the shadow. I wrenched myself free of the goat-man's eyes, turned and stumbled out of the cave.

Just outside two men in gray suits grabbed me.

"Federal narcotics agents," the one holding my right arm told me. "You're under arrest. We have a warrant to search your house and grounds and it's our duty to tell you that you have a right to remain silent and that anything you say may be held against you."

I began to laugh, couldn't make myself stop.

"What's in the cave?" the other agent asked.

"A snake. It just bit my wife and she's dead and it's coiled on top of her guarding her and I can't get her away from it because—"

"Because what?"

I started to cough, choked. "She's in there."

The agent holding my right arm nodded and the other one stooped down, started into the cave.

"Watch it, Mark," the one still holding me yelled after him. "There might really be a poisonous snake in there."

Mark came out a few minutes later. "He was telling the truth," he said. "There's a dead woman on the floor in the back."

"Any sign of the snake?"

"Yeah. It got away through a crack in the wall. It was a fucking monster, sort of pink and black."

"Alexandra's dead?" I asked him. The agent holding me let go of my arm.

"Yes. I'm sorry. Do you want to take a look at her? The snake's gone."

I nodded and they escorted me back into the cave. But when I looked down at her body, at her frozen contorted face and dry staring eyes I felt nothing.

Nothing at all.

Chapter Four

THE AGENT WHO'D FOUND ALEXANDRA'S BODY phoned Salinas to report her death, then sat across the kitchen table with me while his partner and the six other agents who'd accompanied them searched the cabin and herpetarium.

There was a leather-bound manuscript, one of the grimoires from my aunt's collection, lying open on the table: Alexandra must have been glancing at it while she waited for John and me to get out of her way so she could start work with the snakes. She'd been after me to sell the collection for a long time.

The agent picked it up, started to leaf through it. I recognized it as *The Grimoire of Honorius the Great,* considered for centuries as the most diabolical of all sorcerer's manuals because it contained a forged papal bull demanding that all Catholic priests add the summoning and control of demons to their sacerdotal functions. Not being a Catholic priest myself, I hadn't found the book very diabolical, or even very interesting.

"Is this in Latin?" the agent asked.

"Yes."

"What is it?"

"A grimoire. Means grammar. Supposedly written by Pope Honorius III."

"Oh. I see." He looked at the other books and manuscripts in the glass-fronted case against the far wall. "You collect books?"

"My aunt did. I inherited them from her when she died."

"I see." He carefully closed the book, put it back on the table. "I'm sorry about your wife."

"It's not your fault." Around us the other agents on his team were sifting through bags of flour and cutting open pieces of soap, checking for things taped to the backs of drawers and making sure nothing was hidden in the float tank of the toilet. All they found were our bottles of prescription drugs, in plain sight on the kitchen counter, and those they left where they found them—proof, I suppose, that they were going out of their way to be no harder on me than the minimal performance of their duties required, since the more normal procedure would have been to confiscate everything for laboratory analysis.

I watched them without interest, and if through some fluke they'd chanced across the drugs in the hollow log I don't think I'd have been greatly disturbed. I felt nothing, no grief for Alexandra, no curiosity about the blue-gray cloud and the things I'd seen in it, only a thirst that glass after glass of water did nothing to satisfy, that scraped the backs of my eyeballs raw and made my skin itch intolerably.

The agent in charge saw me scratching myself and came to the conclusion that I was going through withdrawal. He checked my arms for tracks, then made me strip naked so he could check the insides of my legs. Finding nothing—I'd never been into shooting things, or using heavy opiates in any way whatsoever, for that matter—he let me put my clothes back on.

When the coroner's deputy arrived with the men from the mortuary the agent sitting with me was glad to surrender me to him.

The deputy was delighted with Alexandra. I watched him prodding and pinching her swollen and discolored arm, probing the two large puncture wounds with his fingers.

"You said she was milking your rattlesnakes for their poison when you left her to go swimming with your friend?" He couldn't keep his eyes off her.

"Yes."

"And you don't think that was a strange thing to do?"

"No. We always worked like that."

"Ah. But she was killed by that South American snake, that bushmaster. The one that got away. Was she trying to milk it too?"

"No. The venom's too different."

"But the snake couldn't have escaped from its cage and attacked her on its own?"

"No."

"Then either she took it from its cage herself despite the fact that there was no reason for her to do so, or somebody else let it out and then closed its cage afterwards. Is that right?"

"I guess."

"And you can't think of anything she might have wanted to do with the snake, or anyone else who might have opened its cage, or any way in which the snake might have escaped on its own?"

"No. I'm sorry."

He questioned me for perhaps another hour, then surrendered me back into the custody of the narcotics agents, who in turn booked me into the Salinas jail on suspicion of possession of narcotics with intent to sell while they waited for morning to search the field and woods.

I filled out the forms I was given (David Pharoh Bathory, twenty-nine years old, five foot eleven, hair and beard brown, eyes green, no distinguishing marks or scars, no previous record) and let them fingerprint and photograph me, then fell asleep in the booking cell.

When they awakened me the next morning they told me I was free to go. It didn't seem very important. I hitched a ride to a friend's house in Monterey and he drove me the rest of the way back to my cabin.

There was a note on the door from John, telling me to call him as soon as I got back. I called him.

"How are you doing, David?"

"OK, I guess."

"You don't need any help?"

"I don't think so, but thanks."

"You don't even care, do you? She's dead and you don't even care."

I was suddenly angry. "What are you trying to tell me,

19

John? That she'd still be alive if I'd cared for her just a bit more? That it's my fault she's dead?"

He hung up on me. Over the last few years I'd watched him falling more and more hopelessly in love with Alexandra. But we'd both been his friends and he had a strong sense of honor where his friends were concerned: he'd said nothing to either of us, done his best to keep his feelings concealed. I owed it to him to call back and apologize.

"Just promise me you'll tell me when her funeral is, David? Just promise."

I promised, and three days later stood next to him holding him by the arm as they lowered the coffin into the ground and began shoveling dirt in on top of it. He was smiling to himself, so loaded on some combination of psychedelics and animal tranquilizers he could barely stand.

"That's not really her," he whispered. "She's not really dead. She'll come back and when she comes back she'll be in love with me. I know she will, David. I know she will."

I dropped him back at his cabin after the funeral. The ceremony had been for him, not for either Alexandra or myself: anything I might once have owed him I had more than paid, and I had no desire to ever see him again.

The next day I put my aunt's collection of grimoires in storage and put my cabin up for sale. Some of the snakes, the local specimens, I freed; the others I arranged to sell to zoos and private collectors. Finally I called an old friend in Provincetown, on the tip of Cape Cod, and arranged to sell him the coke.

The anaconda finished digesting the goat and excreted the surgical fingers of coke with which I'd stuffed the goat's body a week later, leaving me free to sell the snake. The new Orange County Zoo had ambitions of surpassing the San Diego Zoo's snake house and I was able to unload the anaconda, the sea snakes and a number of other specimens to them at good prices.

From Orange County I left for the East Coast. The cages in the van were filled with snakes for zoos in Boston and Chicago: I'd put the mattress that Alexandra and I'd used when we went camping in the back. Most of the coke was in two false-bottomed cages of South American rattlesnakes but I had a vial containing a little over two and a half ounces of coke for the trip hidden beneath the glove-compartment cobra cage.

I was in no hurry to get anywhere. Selling off what remained of my former life at a profit seemed the logical thing to do but held no great interest for me: Alexandra had always been the businesswoman, the hustler, the one fascinated by the status and money our coke dealing brought us. I had no plans for the future and no desire to make any, only a vague curiosity about some of the more inhuman geologic formations of the Southwest. Something about them—the bare dry rocks, the hot wind, the empty landscapes—felt as though it would be right for me.

Chapter Five

I WAS SITTING EATING A BURRITO IN A TACO STAND just off the freeway when I saw a slim, dark-skinned girl with shiny black hair streaming out behind her in the hot desert wind walk up to the freeway on-ramp.

She was wearing a long dress of dusty black velvet and carrying a green nylon backpack by one shoulder strap. She leaned the pack up against the freeway entrance sign and stood in front of it with her thumb out. I'd passed dozens of hitch-hikers since leaving Big Sur but something about this girl broke through my deadness, made me notice her. I left what was left of my meal on the table and walked over to her.

Her face was strong but finely drawn, without trace of blunt-ness or heaviness, and her eyes were large and strange. They were golden—not yellow like the eyes of a cat but a true metallic gold, soft and shining, with strange shimmering depths, alive with an intelligence that made them seem for all their unexpectedness neither freakish nor bizarre.

"Would you like a ride?" I asked. "I'm going east."

"How far are you going?" Her voice was fluid and unhurried, with something odd in the way she pronounced her words.

"The Grand Canyon first, for a few days, then on to Carlsbad Caverns and a few other places like that, finally to Massachusetts by way of Chicago."

"Good. Is it all right if I ride with you all the way?"

"Yes, but—do you see that van over there? The yellow Dodge with the cobra painted on the side? I'm carrying a load of poisonous snakes. It's perfectly safe, they're all in cages, but a lot of people don't want to ride with them."

"I'm not afraid of snakes."

"Are you sure?"

"Yes." She pushed her left sleeve back so I could see a spiral of dull gold in the shape of a nine-headed cobra, an Indian Naga, twisting halfway up her forearm. The Naga's eyes glittered red with what looked like rubies; her skin was smooth, deeply brown, yet almost translucent.

"Is it real?"

"Yes."

"You're Indian? East Indian?" I picked up her backpack and we began walking back to the truck.

"My mother was, a long time ago."

"And you feel safe, hitching with something like that?"

"Very safe."

I unlocked the passenger's side door and let her in, then went around to put her pack away. When I climbed in on my side I saw her with her face pressed to the glass of the baby cobra's cage. The cobra was just on the other side of the glass, its head raised and its hood spread, absolutely still, seemingly as fascinated by her as she was by it.

She straightened, looked away; the cobra retreated to the flat rock in the rear of its cage. "He's very beautiful, your little cobra."

"Very beautiful," I agreed, somehow uncomfortable. "I'm David."

"I'm Dara."

I started the truck, let it warm up a bit before pulling out onto the on-ramp. "Do you drive, Dara?"

"No. I'm sorry."

"It's not important. I don't mind driving."

"Thank you."

We fell silent then, neither of us speaking for the next few hours. I was intensely aware of Dara, excited by her presence in some way that only began with my consciousness of her beauty, her sexual attractiveness, and yet the excitement took me, not exactly away from her but somehow back into myself. Into the past that had only hours before been so dead and distant.

And yet nothing was the way it had been before. My whole life with Alexandra—the years of coke dealing and lovemaking, everything seemed false, empty. A desperate search for something we'd had at the beginning and then lost, yet looking back I could find no beginning, no time when we'd ever truly shared what we'd spent the rest of our life together trying to regain. The beach in Acapulco where we'd met, the two perfect months together in Yucatan—I remembered the sun and the landscape, the drugs and the sex, but beyond that, behind it, nothing. No one. Only the need to believe in something that had never happened.

And before Alexandra, only my family. The Bathorys. Not so much my aunt and uncles, my father and brother, but our history, our inheritance, the tradition that had shaped and marked them as it had shaped and marked me.

One of my ancestors had been a seven-year-old girl when her denunciation of her mother had resulted in the woman being hanged in the Salem Witch Trials. An earlier ancestor had been a Scottish "witch finder" who confessed on the gallows to having fraudulently accused and caused the deaths of some two hundred and twenty women. He'd been paid twenty shillings for every woman he'd accused. And there'd been crusading priests and ministers, sin and heretic hunters aplenty in our family tree.

But the family's previous history was far grimmer, despite the comic-opera names of many of its Central European protagonists. Some of them—Mihnea the Bad, Peter the Lame, Radu Mihnea, Vlad the Monk, and others—though well known in their day were now almost forgotten, but at least two of my ancestors were still famous: Vlad Tepes—Vlad the Impaler, the historical Dracula—and the Countess Elizabeth Báthory, whose fame was the result of her practice of luring young peasant girls to her castle on pretext of employment, then torturing and killing them, and finally bathing in their blood, supposedly in the belief that by so doing she would be able to retain her youth and legendary beauty. To which end she sacrificed an estimated twenty-five hundred girls before she was arrested and imprisoned.

And they were real to me now, all of them, in a way I had denied for as long as I could remember. Real not in any stupid storybook way but in the fact that their cold crazy cruelty had shaped me as it had shaped the rest of the family, had been one of the elements making me who I was, limiting who I could become, determining who I would never allow myself to be.

It was getting dark. I felt lighter, somehow. Not free, but relieved at last of some of the strain that my lifelong refusal to see myself as who I was, as a Bathory, had put on me.

But relieved or not, I was tired and I wanted to make it a lot farther that night. Which meant cocaine.

I pulled off the road, turned off the motor. I hadn't spoken to Dara since I'd begun driving, respecting her silence, though I'd never lost my awareness of her presence. Now, reaching across her to get the coke out of its hiding place beneath the cobra's cage, I felt awkward, even apologetic, as I asked her if she'd like some.

"No, thank you. I don't like drugs."

For a moment I hesitated, almost returning the coke to its hiding place, then went ahead and snorted six quick spoonfuls.

But then, back on the highway and driving again, I began to feel ashamed of myself, lost, as though the silence that Dara and I had shared with each other before I'd snorted the coke had been in reality a strange and perfect communion, an intimacy without reservation, that I had violated and then discarded. I started talking, going faster and faster as I tried to tell her everything, all about Alexandra and coke dealing and my family, but she reached over and brushed my cheek with her fingertips and when I looked at her, saw her eyes golden and shining in her dark serious face, all my shame and desperation were suddenly gone.

When at last we'd driven far enough for the night I pulled into a deserted rest stop and parked.

"You can share my bed with me, if you like," I said. "Or I've got a tent and an extra sleeping bag, if you'd prefer that."

"I'd like to share your bed."

We undressed in the darkness of the truck, slept naked but untouching, keeping to the outside edges of the bed. There'd been no sexual tension to resolve, no need to establish ground rules or make promises: the silence we shared was more precious than any back-seat coupling could have been and I would have done nothing to endanger it. Yet when I awoke for a moment in the middle of the night I found we were in each other's arms.

Chapter Six

THE SUNLIGHT SLANTING IN THROUGH THE PANES OF the stained-glass window in the right rear door of the truck—the one window Alexandra had completed during her brief fascination with stained glass—lit Dara's face and shoulders with rich mustards and rust-oranges. When she opened her eyes they shone like tiny suns.

I'd awakened huddled in the far corner of the bed, my back pressed against the empty snake cage in which I kept my clothing, as though I'd been trying to escape from Dara in my sleep. Yet as we lay there, I in the shadow and she in the light, I remembered awakening in the middle of the night to find her in my arms. I wanted to reach out for her and take her in my arms again, but something restrained me, held me back, as though I had awakened from my dreams to find myself in the midst of a dance as measured and stately as the unfolding of a flower or the slow drifting of clouds across the moon, a dance which could not be hurried in its inexorable progression towards completion.

"Good morning," I said, feeling awkward, not knowing what else to say.

"Good morning," she said and within her voice, behind her grave smile, I felt again the silence, the intimacy, the communion.

"I'd like to start driving again in about fifteen minutes," I said, relaxing a little when I found that the banality of what I had to say didn't seem to matter. "I've got enough food in the cooler to last us till lunchtime and we can shower and wash your clothes if they need it when we get to the Grand Canyon. OK?"

She nodded. I put on a pair of jeans and a heavy turtleneck—the morning was still cold—then slipped into my sandals and pushed past the curtain into the front of the van.

The sun was just breaking free of the horizon. There was only one other car in the rest area, a station wagon, and it was parked at least a hundred yards away. I got out the coke and snorted my breakfast ration.

"David." Dara's voice surprised me. She pushed back the curtain and joined me. She was wearing the same dress she'd worn the day before but it no longer looked dusty: it clung to her, emphasizing her breasts, her narrow waist, and her hair fell black and silky down her back.

"What, Dara?"

"If you hadn't taken your cocaine you would have known I was going to speak to you before I said anything. Like you knew that I was going to open my eyes before I opened them this morning."

It was true: I *had* known.

"And I knew you were watching me. But you've cut yourself off from me now."

"With the cocaine."

"Yes." Her eyes were luminous and strange, beautiful.

"And you don't want me to cut myself off from you? It's important to you?"

"Very important. It—doesn't matter that much now, while we're still here on the surface of the earth, riding in this truck. But it could be very dangerous for us to lose each other later."

"You mean, in the Grand Canyon? Or Carlsbad Caverns?"

"Yes, and afterwards."

"Why?"

She started to say something, decided against it. "I can't tell you, David. Not yet."

I shook my head, said, "I don't understand, Dara. Please tell me what you're trying to say. What you really mean."

"I can't, David, not yet. When I can tell you, I will. I promise."

"And until then I just take this—whatever it is—on faith?"

"Yes."

It would have been easy enough to explain away the little she'd said, implied: she was another chemical casualty or a follower of the new messiah in Fresno, or perhaps just a young girl driven touchingly schizophrenic by the pressures of parents and society. I could have explained it away, but only by denying what I'd felt behind her words, what I'd known. I didn't try.

I started the truck, concentrated as best I could on my driving. There were no other cars on the highway. Every few minutes I glanced over at Dara, trying to read her expression, trying to figure out what she wanted from me. In the distance I could see mountains like rain-smoothed heaps of gray slag, on either side of us rippling scrubland where only scattered gray-green bushes grew. Dara was as alien and inaccessible as the statue of some twelve-armed Hindu goddess.

The countryside had begun to take on a stark beauty, the gray-green scrub giving way to occasional trees and green bushes, while the ground itself was breaking into delicate beiges and red-oranges. I was beginning to come down from the cocaine. As the excitement, the sense of unnaturally extended alertness, faded to a dull headachiness I found myself becoming more aware of those things I wasn't looking at or paying attention to. Concentrating on the road or looking at Dara I found the granulated surfaces of the dead mountains and foothills, the sound of the wind whistling in through my half-opened window, the smell of the sun-heated dust the wind brought with it, all coming together, becoming part of what I felt and knew. When a trucker honked at me to let me know he wanted to pass the sound was as much part of the landscape as the trees and hills, no more jarring or intrusive than they were.

And Dara. We sat without speaking, without needing to speak. Without having to watch her I was becoming aware of her slightest movement, beginning to anticipate even the most imperceptible gesture or change in her expression. And with

29

this anticipation came the excitement, the sense of your life opening onto a new and unexpected future, that always accompanies the discovery of another person, yet at the same time it was as though I were remembering things I'd known my whole life, as though I were an old man reunited after a long separation with his wife of seventy years, an old man who finds her every action reawakening long forgotten familiarity. Yet I did not feel old. I felt young, full of energy, excited.

I was driving deeper and deeper into a dream, into a new reality that obeyed its own strange imperatives and owed nothing to the world that had ended for me with Alexandra's death. A reality in which everything that Dara and I shared—a flock of birds wheeling by overhead, two cacti by the side of the road, the horizon huge around us and a car passing us on a blind curve—had a resonance and a meaning that it had never had before. A reality in which I was beginning to feel the hope and fear behind Dara's silence, to know them and share in them without understanding or needing to understand the reasons behind them.

I remembered the way Dara and the baby cobra had stared at each other, sharing something I'd been unable to perceive, remembered the way the bushmaster had stood guard over Alexandra's body until it was too late to save her. I wanted to ask Dara about the blue cloud, the satanic man-goat and his dancing worshipers.

Instead I said, "You were waiting for me there, by that freeway entrance."

There was no need for her to say anything: the answer was there, in her silence, in her eyes. I didn't understand the necessity driving her, couldn't even guess at its nature, but I shared in her acquiescence, in her submission to a purpose not her own.

And I trusted her. There was no way I could have not trusted her.

We made it to Grand Canyon Village by eleven. We did our wash, showered and ate, then arranged for hiking permits and campground space, finally repacked our packs for the next day's hike.

The rest of the day we spent studying the canyon.

It was not just a piece of landscape, a pretty view, a monument to blind erosion. It had spoken to me in Big Sur, drawn me to it despite my paralysis. And now, looking out on its immensity, looking down on its malachite green domes, purple temples, colored spires, down to the dirty ribbon of rushing water a mile below that was the Colorado River, I knew that the canyon was alive, an entity, a potent force, and I respected it.

I could feel Dara's longing, her fear, and not knowing why or how I shared them.

We held hands, Dara's palm dry in mine, as we watched the sun setting over the canyon. We were lost in the canyon and each other, paying no attention to the gawking tourists around us, but just before the sun vanished completely and the tourists began to drift away I heard a woman exclaim:

"Jim! Look at her eyes!"

"Don't stare, Mary. Probably contact lenses."

We stayed staring out over the canyon long after the trace of the sunset was gone. There was a half-moon and in its light the canyon was shadowed and strange, blue and mysterious. Yet its nighttime visage was less terrifying, less threatening, than its daytime grandeur, and for all Dara's fears I felt that it was not only alive and powerful beyond imagining, but something I could trust.

We returned late to the campground, undressed in silence in the darkness of the truck. We reached out for each other, tentatively explored each other's bodies with our hands, yet even as we touched we knew that the time had not yet come for fuller sexual union. The desire was there but we sidestepped it, yet as I stroked her hair and held her breasts cupped in my hands, as she pressed herself against me and I kissed her gently on the lips, I knew the time would come when our lovemaking would be complete, and I knew that that time was coming soon.

Chapter Seven

I AWAKENED KNOWING THAT SOMEHOW IN MY SLEEP I had grown gigantic, so gigantic that I contained worlds, whole stellar systems, yet I contained nothing, it was I that was contained, supported, cherished. Dara sleeping in my arms contained me as I contained her, both of us grown immeasurably vast there, in the back of the truck, between the clean sheets.

I must have dozed off again because the next thing I remember was Dara shaking me awake.

"Get up, David. It's late."

We dressed and ate some fruit from the cooler, then drove to the rim. I locked the truck. We shouldered our packs and started down the trail, Dara leading. She was wearing a pair of jeans and one of my T-shirts, plus a pair of tennis shoes we'd picked up for her in a supermarket the day before. I was shirtless and barefoot: I'd done a lot of barefoot backpacking in the woods behind Big Sur and my feet were tough.

There were only a few clouds in the sky and as we worked our way down the morning temperatures climbed rapidly through the nineties. But it felt good to sweat, good to be walking down the trail with a pack on my back, good to be with Dara. I felt in harmony with all creation. The only problem was avoiding the puddles of mule piss and the piles of mule dung, but even shoeless as I was it was not a problem to be taken seriously. Occasionally we had to flatten ourselves against the wall to let a mule train pass us.

We walked slowly, letting the other hikers pass on. There was an unhurried, dreamlike quality to our descent that the weight of my pack, the tourists and the mules somehow only intensified.

It was well past noon and immensely hot—I'd heard one of the people passing us say the temperatures had already hit a hundred and thirteen degrees—when the day began to cloud over. We'd worked our way down through the layers of yellow limestone and pale pinkish sandstone into the brick-red hermit shale and below that to the slightly paler red of the Supai formation. Thick clouds were sweeping out of the northwest to cover the sky and the hot canyon air was growing thick and muggy.

And suddenly I was an ant dangling unsupported over the abyss: I could feel the trail shifting beneath me, feel the rock splintering and cracking, crumbling away from beneath my feet, and I knew that I was going to fall, that nothing could save me from the abyss. Dara was somewhere immeasurably distant from me; I could see her only a few feet away from me but I knew I was alone, unsupported, beginning to fall—

But Dara turned, reached back and brushed the center of my forehead with her fingertips and the trail was solid beneath my feet again. We continued on, switchbacking deeper and deeper into the canyon.

It was almost dusk by the time we reached Indian Gardens, which we'd planned as our halfway point. Somehow it didn't seem to matter that we'd never reach the river or Bright Angel Campground by nightfall.

But there was no question of staying at Indian Gardens. People were everywhere; mules were tied to all the hitching posts and brightly colored sleeping bags littered the ground; there were long lines for the drinking fountain. What we had come for was elsewhere.

We were a long way past Indian Gardens and it was getting dark before it started to rain. Though the air had begun to cool it must have still been in the eighties and the first raindrops felt good on our sweat-soaked bodies. But as the temperature dropped and the rain increased to a cold torrent we began to shiver. We were soaked through, and since the weather report had been for three days of clear skies I hadn't thought to bring any rain gear—we had no tent, no jackets, not even a ground sheet to put under our sleeping bags, nothing with which to dry or protect ourselves.

We continued on in the twilight and then in the darkness, using my flashlight. The storm showed no sign of letting up, was if anything getting worse; water ran in little rivulets across and down the trail. We hugged the wall, afraid of losing our balance on the slippery rocks.

Lightning flashed two, three times. By its light I could make out what looked like a small cave some ways off to the left.

It might provide us with the shelter we needed for the night. I took the flashlight from Dara and scrambled off across the loose, slippery rocks and up to the entrance.

At first I thought it was too shallow to be any use to us, but when I shone the light into it I detected an oval hole big enough to crawl through in the back. I knelt down and aimed the light through the hole.

Inside it was unexpectedly beautiful. Delicate crystalline formations grew from walls, ceiling and floor, like an intricate three-dimensional lattice of glass lace. The formations were totally unlike anything described in the Grand Canyon guidebooks: instead of the crushed and flattened roots of long-buried mountains I'd found fairyland. The air inside was fresh and the floor near the entrance was not only level and free of crystals, but dry. We could sleep there.

"It's not only perfect, it's beautiful," I told Dara when I returned for the packs. "We can sleep in there, safe from the rain."

She lit my way back to the cave with the flashlight but stopped just inside the outer entrance, refused to go any further.

"No," she said. "It might not be safe."

"Why?" For some reason the fear I could hear in her voice, see on her face, was suddenly contemptible, irritating. "Do you want to stay outside and get wetter?"

"No, but—David, we *can't* go in until we're sure. They're stronger in caves."

"Who are?" She wouldn't answer me. "There's no reason not to sleep in there, nothing to be afraid of."

"Nothing? David, can't you *feel* it?"

There was only the noise of the storm, the tattoo of the rain on the rocks outside, the cold wet wind cutting into my back and neck. And yet—

I tried to reach in through the opening, felt something like a greasy membrane resist the forward motion of my hand. Before I could pull it back the membrane had given way, stretched without breaking to hold my hand like a tight glove of flabby lung tissue.

And suddenly I was afraid. Afraid of the dark, afraid of the closed confines of the cave, of the millions of tons of rock overhead. Afraid of the unknown. Afraid even of the Grand Canyon rattlesnakes, the pale pinkish rattlers found nowhere else in the world. This cave would be perfect for them.

And then Alexandra lay newly dead on the floor of the cave, hundreds of flesh-pink rattlesnakes squirming over her body like maggots or the boneless fingers of dead children.

I yanked my hand back. The membrane clung to it an instant, reluctant to release me, and then I was free and Alexandra was gone.

The cave was empty. All my fears seemed absurd. Grand Canyon rattlesnakes? I had far deadlier snakes in my truck. But the membrane, that had been real, that was something to fear—and Alexandra had been killed in a cave.

"There's something stretched across the hole," I told Dara. "Like a flabby membrane. When I touched it it made me afraid, and I saw my wife lying dead—"

But she was smiling, shaking her head. "No, it's all right then. I hadn't dared hope they'd still be so weak. I was afraid—" She caught herself, said, "Here!" as she stepped forward and reached past me to thrust her arm, the one with the Naga coiled around it, into the hole. There was a brief flash of light, like a spider web burning, then nothing.

"Let me go first, just in case. There may still be some traps left inside."

She climbed in through the hole, sweeping the air in front of her with her Naga-wrapped arm. After a few seconds she smiled and gestured me in after her.

I put the flashlight down on a rock and handed the packs in to her, then picked it up again and followed them in. It was warm inside the cave, much warmer than it had been outside.

"Dara—"

"I still can't answer your questions, David. Not yet."

"When, then?"

"Soon. I promise. Very soon."

We spread the sleeping bags out, undressed and crawled in between them. And then, without warning, the tension that had kept us apart for so long was gone and I was reaching for her, pulling her to me, and she was holding tight to me, kissing me. As I touched, tasted her, felt her hesitant fingers exploring my stiffening cock, I was diving into a sea of light, into the center of some unknown sun, yet at the same time I was being caught up in a gossamer web, encased in sheath after sheath of darkness.

"Please, David. Make love to me." With Alexandra lovemaking had been all prowess and technique, all pride and control; with Dara I regained a simplicity I'd never known I'd lost. Her flesh against mine, the taste of her mouth, her skin, the curve of her thigh beneath my hand, all were new to me, new and exciting in a way that Alexandra's expertise had never been.

When I entered her there was a momentary resistance—she was a virgin, I realized—and then we were moving together, joined in a rhythm at first quiet, almost languid, but swelling, accelerating, beating faster and more powerfully until finally I exploded into total synesthesia, into an orgasm that blasted my eyes with color and my ears with sound, a total experience like nothing I had ever known before, claiming all of me, destroying me and re-creating me out of nothingness.

And then it was over and we lay together in the still darkness of the cave, our arms around each other, my limp cock still in her, still joining us as we kissed.

Her face was wet. I put my hand to her cheek. She was crying.

I kissed her softly beneath her eyes, held her until her breathing changed and I knew she was asleep, watched over her until I too fell asleep.

Chapter Eight

THAT MORNING WE PASSED FROM SLEEP INTO WAKE-fulness and from wakefulness into lovemaking so naturally that there was no sense of transition: we were asleep, and then we were making love. We were tender, gentle, almost shy with each other; there were no pyrotechnics like there'd been the night before, and yet for all our shyness we met and merged and were changed.

When it was over we lay side by side in the cool darkness. I was at peace, content for the moment to lie on my back and feel the warm sage-scented breeze from the entrance blow across my body, yet I felt alert, awake, full of energy, with none of the torpor or dullness that so often follows sex.

I slowly became aware that though the only light in the cave was a dim glow filtering through the entrance hole, I could see the ceiling above me, its delicate crystal stalactites glowing with a ghostly silver light, the dark stones from which they hung shimmering faintly, as though coated with moonlit spider webs.

But what I was doing was not exactly seeing, or not just

seeing, for I had become aware of the roof in the same way you feel the heat starting to go out of the air just before the day begins cooling off, and now, looking up at the ceiling, I could *feel* it in much the same way as, blindfolded, you can *feel* the pressure of a wall you're groping for against your fingers just before you touch it.

"David." I rolled over on my side to face Dara. Her skin shone with the palest of silver glows but her eyes were still golden, small suns in this place of the moon.

"David, you just realized that you can see in the dark now." I nodded. "And you want to know why."

"Yes."

"Because making love with me has changed you, just as making love with you has changed me. You are no longer the same person you were yesterday. Nor am I."

Her voice was very tired, very sad. I didn't understand. I put my arms around her, felt her shoulder muscles knotted tight with tension. I tried to work the tension out of them, felt her relax slightly.

"I believe you, Dara. But—who are you? Why are you here, with me?"

"I don't know anymore. I—agreed not to know, and I let them take my memories away from me so I could be here with you now and so we could make love with each other, but—"

She shook her head, forced herself to go on. "David, all this was planned for us. By someone else, for his own purposes. I was put by that highway to wait for you. Everything was arranged in advance."

"Everything. . . ." I remembered feeling suddenly hungry, looking for an exit, deciding I had a better chance of finding something without meat in it at the taco stand than at the hamburger stand across the road. Everything.

"Alexandra?"

"Yes." A whisper. "I'm sorry, David."

"Why?"

"To get you here with me. Because we are—not like other people. You can see in the dark now, and there are other things that you—that both of us—will be able to do later, when we've learned what our abilities are and how to use them.

"Because of this we are of use to the man who—arranged all this. Who killed your wife. He took me away from my grandparents when I was very young and brought me to live with him in a huge cave underground, but he couldn't prevent them from giving me this—"

She held up her left arm so I could see the nine-headed cobra twisted around it better. It shone with a subtle, almost imperceptible, blue radiance, paler by far than the silver cave-glow, while its eyes—red by day—shone golden like Dara's own.

"He brought us here so he could make use of us. But, David, the . . . what we are together, we really are. The way you feel about me, the way I feel about you—none of that was forced on us. It could not be forced on us. This is vital and you must understand it, you must believe it. Our love, our lovemaking, was planned, yes, but only because he knew it to be inevitable if we were brought together. He did not create it or force it on us; he only makes use of it."

"But why do you let him—use you?"

"Because I had no other choice and because he is—I don't *remember* him, David, not who he is. They took that away from me. All I remember is what I thought about him, what I believed and what I knew was true, but not . . . why I believed it or how I knew it was true. But he isn't, I remember that he isn't, altogether evil, and he—owns my death. Controls it. Not how I'm going to die, or where, or when, but what will happen to me afterwards."

"But you don't remember what that is?"

"No, but—I used to know and it frightens me, David. It terrifies me."

"Do you remember, not who he is but *what* he is, if he's even a human being, or—I saw something when Alexandra was killed, like a blue cloud with demons and . . . *things* inside it—"

"No. He's a human being. But those things you saw, those were some of his enemies, and not all of them are human. Though the ones you saw might have been human, and keeping their true forms hidden from you. But they're our enemies now, because he wants to use us to help him defeat them, and they know it."

"Use us how?"

"I don't know how, but I know that—once he's safe from them, and he no longer has to worry about them or be afraid that they'll be able to use us against him, then I'll get my memories back and he'll free both of us. But if they defeat him my death will pass from his hands into theirs and they . . . hate me, David, and they're evil, what they want to do is evil. . . . That's why I let him take my memories away, so that his enemies can't use me against him, because he's the only chance I have. That either of us has. But if he succeeds in defeating them we'll be safe."

"If what he's told you and what you remember are true."

"Yes."

"Dara, do you remember—when you got into the truck for the first time, the way you and the baby cobra stared at each other?"

"He didn't use me to make the bushmaster kill her, David."

"Are you sure? He couldn't have made you do it, and then made you forget it?"

"No. I remember that he . . . didn't force me to help him."

"I'm glad, but—he's still set it up so that right now you don't know enough to do anything except what he wants you to do. No matter what that is. And if I believe any of what you've told me, I have to, maybe not believe all of it, but act as if I did, as if the only hope for either of us was to help him get what he wants—"

"And you believe me."

"You. Not him. But—Dara? Why *me?* Is it because of my family?" I was afraid of the answer, didn't want her to say that I'd fallen into the world of vampirism and eternal damnation that all the books I'd sought out, all the historians who spoke of Elizabeth Bathory as pathologically insane, Vlad Tepes as a "cunning Renaissance prince" and a "technician of terror," had enabled me to deny.

"Because of who we are, and what we are together. That's all I know, David. I'm sorry."

I put my arms around her and held her, not questioning her, letting her know as best I could that I still believed her, that I still loved and trusted her. Not her hidden master, nor his plans for us, but her, Dara, the girl I was holding.

"His enemies," I said a while later. "Why did I see them there if he was the one who killed Alexandra?"

"Your wife had something to do with them, was maybe one of them, and what you saw was them trying to protect her."

"They failed." I could summon up no bitterness, no sense of loss.

"Because they're still weaker then he is. But his power is

waning, and they're growing stronger. Soon they'll be more powerful than he is, and then they'll try to destroy us or gain control of us. That attack they made on you on the way down, the membrane they put across the entrance to the cave—those were just ways of testing us, finding out how strong we were. But as long as we keep them from separating us or turning us against each other our powers will keep on increasing, and we should be strong enough soon to protect ourselves without his help."

"Again, if what he told you—what you remember him telling you—was true."

"Yes."

"What does he want me to do?"

"Just continue driving and visiting all the places you'd planned to visit, while our powers grow and we wait for his summons."

His summons. Right out of *Robin Hood,* or *Le Morte D'Arthur: And the King summoned his courtiers and bespake them, saying—*

The shocking thing was how easy it was to accept.

"I don't have any choice, do I?"

"No." She kissed me gently. "Neither of us has a choice."

We dressed and repacked the sleeping bags, then climbed out through the entrance hole and into the light.

The sky was clear and the day already hot, though the rocks were still glistening with the previous night's rain. We made our way to the path, started up it.

Climbing out of the Grand Canyon is like climbing a mile-high mountain. But though we had to rest from time to time, we were never as tired as my backpacking experience told me we should have been.

"Why were you so afraid, before we found the membrane?" I asked somewhat later, while we were resting and eating some of the fruit we'd packed in.

"Because they'd attacked you on the path down, and because both the canyon and the cave are places of power. And where power is concentrated like that his enemies can use it against us.

"Look." She pointed to a spot far below us on the canyon wall, where even in the bright morning sunlight I could see a faint cool shimmer totally unlike a heat mirage. "There's the cave. Even from here you can feel its power."

We soon began meeting hikers on their way down from

Indian Gardens. Many of them seemed to be staring at us with unusual curiosity but I didn't pay any attention to them until a heavyset man of about fifty in a too-tight red nylon bathing suit stopped me and asked, "Excuse me, but is that the latest thing?"

"The latest thing?" I repeated stupidly.

"You know. Your eyes." He gestured to include Dara. "Gold and silver."

So my eyes were now silver? "Contact lenses," I told him confidently.

"But the dark iris?"

"One-way glass, to make them look natural."

"Ah. Thank you. I must say the effect is startling."

I waited until he disappeared around a bend in the trail, said, "Dara?"

"I'm sorry, David. I've always been able to see the silver there, in your eyes and under your skin, and I didn't realize that there'd been a change in your eyes that people like that could see. I just thought I could see the power in them better now. But you handled him well."

"My years of experience as a part-time dope dealer. But are there any other signs of, of my transformation?"

"Not that someone like that could see, no."

"But that you can see?"

"I can see the power in you a bit more clearly, as though it were closer to the surface of your skin than it was before, or shining a little more brightly, but that's all."

We reached the rim by midafternoon, spent the rest of the day sitting looking over the canyon while we explored Dara's fragmentary memories together, looking for something that would be of use to us but finding nothing.

Watching the sunset over the canyon through the window of the restaurant in which we'd decided to eat dinner, I found myself wondering again about the matter-of-factness with which I'd accepted the new terms of my life. How could I be sitting eating a restaurant dinner here with the other tourists, knowing what I now knew?

As if to emphasize the changes taking place in me, the gathering darkness revealed that almost every rock formation in the canyon shimmered with its own spectral light.

"A place of power," Dara said. And that was that.

It seemed the most natural thing in the world to follow my

original plans and spend the next day at the Petrified Forest and Painted Desert. Dara and I behaved like typical tourists and I even bought her a piece of petrified wood.

We spent the night at a campground just past the New Mexico border and arrived at Carlsbad Caverns late in the afternoon, after driving all day through the most monotonous country I had ever seen. We took our places in the small stone amphitheater facing the caverns' entrance, watched as the bats, ten thousand of them a minute, came spiraling up out of the ground, their hundreds of thousands of beating wings creating a wind rank with the smell of bat guano as they angled off to the southwest in a cloud that stretched from us to the horizon.

The entrance to the caverns blazed like a door opening onto a cold subterranean sun and I could feel the power of the place twisting and burning in my spine.

Chapter Nine

THE CAVERNS HAD CLOSED TO THE PUBLIC AT THREE and would not reopen until eight in the morning. We stayed a while longer, trying to find our way to the feeling of personal contact with a living entity we had had at the canyon, but the forces twisting at us were unbearable and we had to leave.

We rented a room in the town of Carlsbad, some miles away. Even there the caverns were a rasping agony that was all the worse because it was almost pleasurable.

We tried to make love but as soon as we'd touch each other the caverns would reach out to us through our interface, would try to draw us to them. We had to stop and lie side by side without touching on the bed.

And then something interposed itself, shielded us from the caverns' energies.

"They're outside the window," Dara said. I got to my feet, threw back the curtain.

Hundreds of tiny albino bats were clinging to the window screen and shutters, their naked wings wrapped tight around them, their blind red eyes glinting in the light from the room.

Hundreds more were darting around in the air outside, like a cloud of impossibly quick moths. Their dirty white fur shimmered, gleamed with power.

"They won't hurt us," Dara said in a taut, overcontrolled voice. She had joined me at the window. "Not while they're still his to command. They've been sent to help us."

His to command. Not Vlad the Impaler, Renaissance prince inhuman only in his cruelty, but Count Dracula. Bram Stoker's invention. Bela Lugosi in his black cape and feelthy foreigner accent, the rubber bat with the strings you could almost see.

"Are they vampire bats?" Keeping my voice as calm as I could.

"Yes." Dara's voice was impossibly distant, as though she were reading a grocery list to me over the phone. "That's all I know, David. All he'll let me remember."

The bats clinging to the screen never moved. At last we closed the curtains on them and went to bed. Eventually we slept.

When dawn came we were sitting waiting in the stone amphitheater. At first there was just a low buzzing, the sound of thousands of paper-thin wing membranes, but with the first light we could see the bats as they flew high over the entrance, folded their wings and dived straight down into the interior.

There were no silver-shimmering albinos among them, nothing to indicate that any of them were anything but the useful, harmless insectivores they were supposed to be.

When the caverns opened for the day we had to walk back up to the Visitor's Center, pay our fees, and then be fitted with the radio receivers that took the place of tour guides. They dangled from our necks like bulky toy telephones.

A man in a ranger's uniform examined our fee receipt, waved us on.

Once past the stench of the bat cave we began to see the giant stalagmites and stalactites, the limestone formations that resembled fossilized squids or Portuguese men-of-war, the helictites like the roots of impossible trees, pushing their way sideways out of the rock, twisting and gnarled and interwoven, the cave coral like clusters of stone barnacles, the drapery stalactites like folds of hanging fabric, the pits, pools, columns and chasms—but for us the sculptured rock was only context for the living energies of the caverns. Columns shone with the light of silver suns; networks of flaming lines the color of

45

burning aluminum ran across the roof, walls, floors; blinding lights shone through the solid rock as through murky glass, burning at us through the asphalt of the path.

We tried to maintain what we thought was a normal pace, never taking our radio receivers from our ears. Our eyes were almost always drawn to blank walls, unimpressive columns, small boulders. Only rarely did we find ourselves looking at the same formations as the other visitors, and then we might stare for long moments at something no one else had given a second glance.

We made it as far as the Green Lake Room before attracting anyone's attention. We were standing half blocking the path, lost in a thousand-petaled flower of silver blue flame pulsing just beneath the surface of the asphalt, when the guide stationed in the chamber noticed it. When we finally realized he was watching us, we—I don't know how to describe it exactly, but we turned his attention away from us so that he ceased to be aware of us.

It was as natural and effortless as blinking your eyes to get rid of a cinder; in the confusion of forces and powers through which we were moving such a feeble manifestation of personal power seemed so totally insignificant that it was not until much later that I realized it was in any way unusual or out of the ordinary.

At last we moved on to the next chamber, the so-called Queen's Chamber. And found the source, the center, the heart:

Within and between and around the interlocking helictites, projecting from every side powers complex and alive flowed and changed, sang through shifting spectrums. And from a hole in the wall hidden high behind fluted drapery stalactites like the fossilized mantle of a great jellyfish, a waterfall of suns burst, fell soft and shining through air and stone.

We wrapped ourselves in concealment, climbed the rough cave coral to the hole, wriggled through it into a long, low tunnel, the energies singing through us growing ever subtler, ever purer as their intensity increased, as we crawled deeper and deeper into the radiance.

At last we came to a large chamber, its far end covered by a pool of water. Bubbles rose from the bottom of the pool, burst with a soft plopping sound.

And here, at the center, there was only clarity, only silence.

A slab of rock by the edge of the pool drew us to it, pulled us down onto its rough surface to make love, to merge ourselves with that vast grid of living energies which coexisted with the caverns, which sent tendrils of itself out to every part of the living earth.

We were lost to ourselves, making love with bodies forgotten, when a sudden glaciality, an invading tension, froze us into our separate selves and I saw, superimposed on the scene before me, a hand mounted on a wooden rod, bone fused to wood, jutting from a basin of thick yellow liquid into which nerves and tendons, arteries and veins, dangled like roots. The fingers curled slightly inward, the skin was weathered and rough, and to the tip of each finger an eyeball glistening with moisture had been sewn. The eyeballs gazed inward, down at the palm, each burning with a different color flame—green, orange-red, pink, blue—and in the center of the palm a sigil the color of a livid bruise had been drawn or stamped, and I was there, in the palm, trapped within the lines of the sigil.

And then the hand melted, was gone, leaving me poised above Dara, trapped in her sucking mucous membranes by the impersonal lusts of my body, feeling my substance draining out of me and into her. And yet even as she leeched my essence from me I was one with her, sharing her violation, feeling my cock penetrating and rending her, but though I knew she was as aware of what was happening to me as I was of what was happening to her, our mirrored awarenesses did not cancel each other out but only reinforced each other, resonated and grew stronger as I felt myself building towards a dark orgasm which I could not stop but which I could not survive, as I felt myself losing control, dying—

I was crawling naked through blue-white tunnels, dragging myself over ridges and spines of knife-edged ice, leaving behind me a trail of frozen blood. Light shone through the tunnel walls. Ahead of me fat hairy ice spiders spun their brittle webs but I always managed to break through the half-completed webs before the spiders could fasten themselves to my body. I kept on crawling, crawling toward the cleansing fire that waited for me at the end of the last tunnel, the fire I knew I would never reach. . . .

He was me and he was not me and though I knew him they had hidden his name from me. Four men in black held him down on the long blue-white table while the fifth severed his head from his body. The head was wrapped in dark cloth; the blood was saved.

There was a garden beneath the earth where giant fungi grew in moist white rows. The men in black planted his head at the end of the last row as I watched terrified, unable to move, unable to turn my head away to protect my staring eyes from the dirt raining down on them.

They watered the ground over his buried head with the blood they had saved.

Something was growing, pushing its way up through the sticky black earth—

And I was lying naked on the cold rock and Dara was gone.

Chapter Ten

I TRIED TO GET TO MY FEET, COULD NOT, LAY sprawled and helpless in the center of the caverns' pulsing heart.

Dara had been taken from me, summoned back to her mysterious master or taken prisoner by his enemies, and without her I was only a crippled fragment of myself, voiceless and blind, my thoughts and feelings as unreal as the pains an amputee feels in his missing limbs.

I could hear the distant voices of the tourists in the Queen's Chamber. I reached for my clothes, could not force my fingers to close on them.

And pulsing through me the energies of the caverns, lulling me and soothing me, making it almost impossible to hold on to my thoughts, to drive myself on.

The visions of the ice tunnels and of the man who was me and not-me's death were losing definition, fading into each other, like the dreams that begin to slip away from you as soon as you're completely awake.

But I hadn't been asleep and dreaming, I'd been forced into unconsciousness by whoever had used the hand of glory to take control of Dara and me. My visions could have been manufactured for me, spun around me to keep me distracted and helpless while Dara was being stolen from me—or while she was being compelled to leave me and surrender herself to whoever had used the hand against us.

Whoever had used the hand against us. If what I'd seen had been real, some sort of clairvoyant vision made possible by my new powers or by the energies of the caverns, then Dara's master was dead and Dara was in the hands of his enemies. If it had been Dara's master that I'd seen killed. If the vision hadn't been designed by either her master or his enemies to make me think that he'd been killed when in fact he had not.

But the hand—I had *seen* it: there was no way it could have been a hallucination or an illusion. It reminded me of the hands of glory described in many of my aunt's grimoires: the hands of hanged men, specially prepared and dried, the fingers set aflame when the sorcerer who had created the hands wanted to use one of them to render someone unconscious. But I had at one time or another read every grimoire in my aunt's collection—and her collection was reputed to be one of the best in the United States—and none of her grimoires mentioned the yellow fluid, the sigil on the palm, the eyeballs sewn to the fingers. And this hand had done far more than just render us unconscious. How much more I could only guess.

Dara had been taken prisoner. Either forced back to the master who she had believed meant her no harm but who had used me to violate and torture her just as he had used her to violate and torture me, or in the hands of the man-goat and his dancing worshipers.

(Dara chained naked to the altar, two of the mutilated dancers holding her open to the man-goat, his huge segmented cock a hungry bronze centipede, the other dancers watching and waiting, skillful knives cradled in playful hands—)

And after she was dead, when they finally let her die, they'd do to her what she'd been so terrified they'd do. And I didn't know what it was they could do to her, didn't know how to find them, how to recognize them if I found them, didn't know what I could do to rescue her from them if I found her.

But I was beginning to feel stronger. I tried to stand, had

to grab a stalagmite to keep from falling. I got my pants on, had to sit down for my shirt and sandals, finally hung the radio receiver around my neck and crawled back through the tunnel to the Queen's Chamber.

And maybe she hadn't been captured yet, maybe she was hiding from them and from me somewhere in the caverns or out in the desert, still gripped by the fear and the horror of me that the hand had forced on her. Hiding somewhere where I could find her, could let her know that I still loved her, make her believe that I wouldn't hurt her, wouldn't betray her.

Find her before they found her. Find her before she fled the area altogether, hitched a ride out with any of hundreds of people going almost anywhere.

And even if she was a prisoner they might have had to keep her here so they could use the caverns' energies on her or so they could force her to use the energies for them.

The drapery stalactites blocked my vision of the Queen's Chamber but I could hear people talking somewhere off to my left. Half remembering the means Dara and I had used to make ourselves unnoticeable I tried to shroud myself in concealment again before dropping to the floor.

I must have succeeded because dozens of tourists passed within a few yards of the spot where I lay half stunned without seeing me.

When at last I felt strong enough I staggered onto the path and took my place among the tourists. All I'd been able to think of to do was to make a thorough search of the caverns and the desert around them: I remembered reading that the whole area was honeycombed with caves.

And if she fled from me again, if I couldn't find a way through the fear and horror to the part of her that still knew I loved her?

They could have taken her away, taken her anywhere.

She was not in the Papoose Room. Not in the Boneyard or the Lunch Room or the Big Room, not back at the truck, on the nature trail, sitting in the amphitheater, in the Visitor's Center, the main corridor, the bat cave, Devil's Den, the Green Lake Room or the Queen's Palace. I crawled for hours through dangerous side tunnels closed to the public. Nothing.

But perhaps she'd broken free of the hand, was looking for me, not finding me because we were both moving around looking for each other. I sat down at a table in the Lunch Room, an untouched cup of coffee in front of me, waiting until long after the lights had been turned out and the caverns closed for the night, then made a final search and returned to the surface.

People anticipating the bat flight were beginning to fill the amphitheater. I sat down among them, let myself fade into noticeability.

The caverns were blazing with ever-increasing brilliance and their energies soothed me, pulsed through me and carried away my weakness and confusion. I accepted the strength they gave me as I had accepted the power to conceal myself, without questioning it.

The bats came swirling up out of the caves in counterclockwise spirals, flew away. The tourists left. In the gathering darkness I could see the landscape burning with what looked like thousands of silver bonfires.

I wrapped myself in my unnoticeability, returned to my truck for a length of rope and a flashlight. After a second's thought I discarded the flashlight—with my new sense of vision I could see without it and its beam might give me away to anyone able to penetrate my concealment—and got my knife out of my tool kit.

As a weapon it was a joke—a Boy Scout-type jackknife with a two-inch blade, a corkscrew, can opener, nail file and screwdriver—but it was all I had.

Most of the caves I found were insignificant guano-stinking holes or ended in sheer drops of up to hundreds of feet. I explored every cave I could, the silver powerflame with which they burned always giving me all the light I needed to see by; I used my rope when necessary, sometimes jumped crevasses or worked my way around the edges of deep pits when what I could see beyond them looked like it might conceal something.

It was almost dawn before I found a cave with a different feel to it. The powerflame with which its entrance burned looked no different from the silver fires marking the entrances of the other caves I'd tried, but something about this cave twisted at me, rasped me, yet with none of that undercurrent of almost pleasurable attraction that had been so much of what had made the main caverns so unbearable at first.

The entrance was free of brush, the ceiling high enough so I could make my way in without stooping. The cave slanted down for about twenty yards, then angled sharply off to the left, ended a few yards further on in a long vaulted chamber.

Just inside the entrance to the chamber a young couple—both park rangers by the evidence of their discarded uniforms—lay dead, their bloodless bodies covered with hundreds of small dry wounds. There was dried blood on their clothing, on the small khaki blanket on which they must have been lying when they were attacked; blind cave insects swarmed over their bodies as they would have swarmed over baby bats fallen from the roof, crawled in through the small dry wounds to feed on what remained of the muscles and internal organs.

Ignored by the insects, nine albino bats lay dead and crumpled on the cave floor, their dirty white bodies still shimmering with a faint residue of the power that had been theirs in life.

They'd only been able to kill nine of the tiny bats before they died. Nine, out of the hundreds we'd seen outside our motel room window.

There were two sets of footprints in the thin layer of guano covering the cave floor. Small shod footprints skirting the bodies, leading back to a shallow depression where someone might have lain on the guano for a while, then the prints of one shod and one bare foot leading out again.

And by that shallow depression, Dara's left shoe.

I searched the rest of the cave, found nothing, no other footprints. Dara had been alone, then, following orders or under compulsion—her fear of me could never have driven her to hide herself here, lying in the rank guano within yards of the dead lovers' desiccated bodies—and now she was gone, could be anywhere.

I went back to the truck, searched her backpack for something that would tell me more about her, tell me where she came from, who she was. Everything was new, unused; her sleeping bag had never been slept in; I could have duplicated the clothing and camping equipment in twenty minutes at any of a hundred stores.

When the tourists began arriving for the morning bat watch I asked all of them if they'd seen a black-haired girl with golden eyes and a missing shoe. No one had. Which proved nothing.

I searched the caverns again, drew strength and support from their vast heartbeat but learned nothing, gained no new powers or abilities.

At the Grand Canyon Dara had told me that I was supposed

to continue with my trip exactly as I'd planned it while waiting for her unseen master's summons.

He'd killed Alexandra, killed the couple in the cave, and if he wasn't dead he'd probably been the one who'd used the hand of glory to turn our lovemaking into something altogether evil. But I couldn't think of anything else to do.

Chapter Eleven

BUT THE OTHER GEOLOGICAL WONDERS I'D PLANNED to visit proved to be just wind- and erosion-sculptured stone, dead and meaningless. I conscientiously looked at everything a tourist was supposed to look at, hoping for I didn't know what— a message that I alone could see or read on the surface of some boulder, a fat man in a checked suit with a collection of dirty postcards he'd insist I examine, a rabbit with a pocket watch who'd tell me to follow him down his hole. But there was no one, nothing, and at last I'd exhausted my list of national monuments, state parks and natural wonders.

I drove straight through the rest of the way to Chicago. I took no breaks, felt no need for sleep or rest, didn't even bother to get out of the van to stretch at gas stations.

A quick stop in Chicago to deliver some snakes to Loren Beldon, a herpetologist known for his work with African cobras and mambas with whom I'd kept up an occasional correspondence over the last few years, then on to Boston to drop off the other snakes, and from there to Provincetown, the end of

55

the line, where Larry was waiting to buy my coke. And if no one summoned me, no one contacted me—

I'd have to find them, track them down. Work my way past the neurotics and the sadists and the showmen to the real black-magic underground, if there was one. Maybe join the Church of Satan in San Francisco to show people I was interested, then let them know who my ancestors were, hope someone would try to recruit me for something. My dealing experience would keep me from giving myself away in all the obvious ways that most of the undercover narcotics agents I'd encountered had given themselves away.

Try to work my way through my family's self-indulgent and pretentious morbidity to whatever reality might have at one time preceded it. There'd be nothing to be learned from my brother Michael, a social Darwinist whose imagination was limited to schemes for getting his while the getting was good, and even less to be learned from my father, but there might be something in the house itself—some of the old privately printed books in the library, maybe diaries or records hidden away in a trunk in the attic, something like that.

My Aunt Judith would have known what I needed to know if anyone in the family did, but she was dead, a suicide. Perhaps I could find a way to parlay her collection of grimoires into contacts of some sort.

My Uncle Peter had spent a year in a Catholic seminary before retreating to his Pennsylvania hermitage; from what little I could remember of him he was slow and stupid, pathologically timid, but perhaps his shyness and stupidity were only pretexts for his solitude, only masks behind which he hid something far more sinister.

And my Uncle Stephen—he was just an exhibitionist, a publicity-seeking poet of very minor talents who would have traded his obsessive treatments of decadence and decay for rhapsodies to spring and eulogies of the honored war dead in an instant if he'd thought it would bring him more public attention, but perhaps he'd learned something real while re-searching his image. If not, there might be some way I could put his morbid reputation to use.

I could go to Romania, waste months checking out Snagov's Monastery, Castle Bran, Visegard, the palace at Tirgoviste. A sentimental pilgrimage.

And if none of that got me anywhere, back to zero. Research, card catalogs and cross-references while they had Dara, could be torturing or mutilating her. With about as much chance of finding her as a the average graduate student researching his thesis had of being taken on as apprentice to a black magician.

I could hide myself from people, I could see in the dark, and I didn't seem to need sleep or rest anymore. All of which might have been useful if I'd found out where Dara was and was going after her, none of which would help me find her.

I didn't get to the zoo where Loren worked until long after it had closed for the night but I'd called ahead and he was waiting for me outside the gates.

We shook hands and introduced ourselves. He didn't notice my new eyes: I'd experimented with my power to turn people's attention away from me on my way from the caverns, found that I didn't need to use the caverns' energies to make it work and that I could fine-tune the ability, keep people from noticing my silver eyes or, say, that I was holding my hand up in front of their faces while carrying on an otherwise normal conversation with them.

The gatekeeper unlocked the gate for us and we drove the van up onto the sidewalk in front of the snake house, then worked together bagging the snakes and transferring them to their new cages. Without the theatrics for the customs inspectors it was dull routine, work I'd done a thousand times before, and I wasn't paying much attention to what I was doing.

Loren had just gone inside with the emerald tree boas and I was reaching into a cage for a Sonoran coral snake when I realized that Dara was there in the truck with me. I couldn't see her or hear her but I could feel her presence, could sense a change not in my surroundings but in myself, in who I was, no longer just the David Pharoh Bathory I'd been reduced to but David/Dara again, a single entity once more. There was no telepathy involved; I couldn't read her thoughts, but she was alive and she healed and completed me, made me once again that which I should never have ceased to be.

"Dara?" I asked aloud. Then the coral snake struck. It had slithered up onto my glove while I was distracted and now it held onto the flesh of my inner arms with its short fangs, its delicate red, yellow, and black banded body balanced precariously on the end of my glove while it worked its jaws back and forth so as to get as much poison as possible into my flesh from its stubby grooved fangs.

And Dara was a dead weight in my mind, smothering me, paralyzing me and keeping me from calling out for help. I stood there, unable to move, looking down at the coral snake, feeling the wound burning, the flesh whitening, a great welt beginning to form—

At last I broke free of her, refused her, thrust her from me. I yelled to Loren to get the antivenin out of the drawer in back, lost his reply as the dizziness and confusion hit me. The coral snake had lost its perch on my glove, but was holding on with its teeth, dangling unsupported in the air like a short length of bright-banded clothesline. I grabbed it with my other gloved hand, ripped it from my arm and dropped it back in its cage, managed to close the lid on it before I fell.

My vision was going, everything fading into an unfocused blur, and I couldn't breathe. The first cramps had begun in my muscles and abdomen and my backache was getting worse and worse.

And I was in a ruined temple. Great blocks of rough stone, the roof open to the sky, grass and weeds growing in the cracks in the floor. A bare-breasted priestess with smooth dark skin who listened to the whispered words of a green-eyed serpent that coiled itself around her, merged with her as she became a green tree, became a golden Queen with the head of a cobra on a throne of ivory in a palace of burning diamonds.

The Queen looked down on me as I lay there in my agony, reached out to touch my wounded arm with a long golden finger that spread its hood and struck—

And I was lying on the floor of the truck, Loren bending over me still holding the syringe with which he'd injected the antivenin.

There was no pain, no dizziness. I tried to sit up, found I could.

"I think I'm OK now," I said.

"You shouldn't be." He put down the syringe. "Lie down."

"No, I'm fine. I've gotten bitten before and I've built up an immunity."

"If you'd had any real immunity it wouldn't have hit you like that. You're lucky you're not dead."

"No, really, I'm fine. Look." I held out my arm so he could

see that the welt was going away, stood up to prove that I could. "I think the whole thing was psychosomatic. Hysterical. I just panicked."

"I saw the way it was hanging on to your arm—what happened, exactly?"

"I don't know. I got distracted for a second and the next thing I knew it'd slithered up onto my glove and was attacking me."

"Snakes don't do that. Not coral snakes, anyway, even if it seems that that's exactly what this one did. There's got to be some other explanation for its behavior."

I considered telling him about Alexandra, decided against it. "I know. I let myself get distracted and I must have missed something. But I'm glad I'm getting out of the business anyway. I've just got a few more snakes to drop off in Boston and then I won't have to worry about any more mistakes."

"Do you have a place to stay tonight?" he asked. "We've got a spare bedroom now that Jim's away to college and you probably shouldn't overexert yourself. . . ."

"Thanks, but I've already made arrangements to stay with some friends. They'll be expecting me soon."

"Look, why don't you come inside with me and drink some coffee with me in the office for a while, then I'll drive you over to their house and drop you off. I'll put your van in the back parking lot and pick you up on my way in to work tomorrow if you feel up to driving. If not you can leave the van in the lot until you need it again."

"Thanks, Loren, but—why don't we finish with the snakes, then I'll sit and drink coffee with you for an hour or so and then if I still feel up to driving you can follow me back to my friends' house and make sure I get there all right. Otherwise I'll do it your way. OK?"

"OK, but I don't want you taking any more risks tonight. I'll take care of the rest of the snakes for you."

I agreed, watched as he bagged and transferred the Gaboon viper and the two Australian tiger snakes, as well as the now docile coral snake.

While we were sitting in his office waiting for the coffee to get hot I asked him if he'd ever been bitten by any of his venomous snakes. He said yes, twice, once by a green mamba and once by one of his cobras. Which gave me an opportunity to remind him of the fact that not only are most snake bites not fatal but that most of the people bitten are snake collectors, and to go from there to a discussion of the exaggerated fear most people have of snakes, and from there on to talking about the various kinds of folklore and superstition surrounding snakes. I don't think he was very interested in the subject but he seemed willing enough to talk about it, probably because he wanted to keep me sitting there where he could observe me and make sure I was all right as long as possible.

When I finally got around to asking him if he'd ever heard of a goddess with the head of a cobra he shook his head.

"Not that I can remember. There used to be, let's see, an Egyptian goddess named something like Ua Zit who was portrayed as a cobra with a woman's head. There's a statue of her in one of the museums here. And you've got all sorts of seven- and nine-headed cobras in India, but I don't really know anything about them. Except that in all the pictures of the statues I've seen they've got the heads all wrong and made the teeth look more like sharks' teeth or maybe dogs' teeth than like anything you'd find in a real reptile. You'd do better to check with the reference librarian at the public library if you're really interested."

We talked and drank coffee for another forty-five minutes or so. I told him I'd call him early the next morning to let him know how I was doing, then drove out to one of the nearby suburbs and parked in front of a random house until he drove away.

As soon as I was sure he was gone I took the vial of cocaine out from the compartment beneath the baby cobra's cage and snorted four spoonfuls. I didn't like the way the drug made me feel—it seemed to dull my perceptions rather than heightening them and there was no exhilaration or freedom in its excitement, only increased anxiety—but I knew it was cutting me off from Dara, building me a wall behind which I was safe from her.

Or rather, safe from those who were using her against me.

I found an all-night gas station, refilled the tank and left for Boston. Whenever I started to feel a little calmer I snorted more coke.

Chapter Twelve

SOMETIME DURING THE NIGHT'S DRIVE I REALIZED that, unless there was some sort of magical or ritual benefit to be derived from killing me, whoever had tried to use Dara and the coral snake to murder me must still think I was a threat to them.

Which meant either that they thought I knew more about them than I really did, or that they knew some way I could find them or get at them, perhaps some way to use my new abilities against them that hadn't occurred to me yet. And even if they were trying to kill me because they thought I knew something I didn't, there was a chance I could learn what I needed to know from their attempts against me.

Unless, of course, they succeeded in killing me.

And as long as they thought there was a chance to get at me through Dara they'd have to keep her alive.

If my resistance to their first attack hadn't already convinced them they couldn't use her successfully against me.

If killing me was more important than whatever else they had planned for her.

And *if* she wouldn't be more useful to them against me dead than alive.

(Dara's long slim hand mounted on a wooden rod which merges with the bones of her raggedly severed wrist, the rod jutting from a bath of yellow liquid into which her nerves and tendons, arteries and veins, dangle. On the dark smooth skin of her palm a sigil has been branded and I am trapped within it, staring up at the two naked eyeballs that have been sewn to the tips of her long tapering fingers, staring up at Dara's golden eyes and I can see her there, trapped inside the gold, staring helplessly down at me—)

I called Loren from a gas-station phone booth a little before seven to thank him again for having saved my life and for the offer of his spare bedroom, then told him I was feeling fully recovered and was already on the road to Boston but would phone and try to arrange to meet his wife and him for dinner the next time I was in Chicago.

I made sure I was totally coked while transferring the snakes the zoo in Boston wanted to their new cages. I kept only the baby cobra, the South American rattlesnakes whose cages concealed the coke, and a small shy rainbow boa of which I'd become somewhat fond over the years.

The snake-house keeper had originally been trained as a marine biologist and was far more interested in aquatic salamanders than in the snakes in his collection. As far as he was concerned any religious or devotional interest in serpents could be more than adequately explained in Freudian terms.

I remembered the way Dara and the baby cobra had stared in silent fascination at each other, remembered the subtle blue radiance the golden Naga she wore on her arm had taken on in the cave where we'd first made love. I remembered the golden Queen whose finger had become a striking cobra, a cobra whose bite had neutralized the coral snake's venom instantly, in a way no antivenin could have done, even if I'd had the immunity I'd told Loren I had.

I made it to Provincetown about three in the morning and parked my van in a lot just inside the city limits, where it wasn't likely to attract too much attention, then walked the rest of the way in. The bars were closed and Commercial Street, which in the daytime would have been packed almost solid with gays, tourists, college students, runaways and street vendors, plus the occasional Portuguese fisherman or high-school girl in her letter sweater, was almost deserted. The only people I saw were a few middle-aged gays still hanging around the benches in front of city hall—the Meatrack—and a young kid on some sort of overlarge Japanese motorcycle.

I passed Larry's two junk stores, his boutique, and Second Skin, the leather store with which he'd started, on the way to the bookstore over which he had his apartment.

We'd gotten to know each other at Stanford, where he'd been the graduate student in charge of my floor of the dorms, kept up our friendship when I transferred to Berkeley and he'd dropped out. He'd tried his hand first at painting, and then, more successfully, at leatherworking and handbag design, finally ending up working fourteen hours a day, seven days a week, keeping his shops together during the five-month season, then traveling and playing around with electronic sculpture the other seven months of the year.

Larry was my oldest and probably my best friend but I veiled the change in my eyes before taking the key to his back door out of its hiding place in the concealed zipper pocket in the doormat and letting myself in.

Both his Danes remembered me; I scratched them a bit behind the ears and under the neck before going upstairs.

He was in the front room, sitting at a computer console and playing some sort of game against three color television sets.

"Hi, Larry." He looked like a tired satyr, very Greek and bearded; he'd gotten a lot older in the three years since I'd last seen him.

"Hello, David." He stood up, hugged me. He was a lot taller than I was. "I'm sorry about Alexandra."

Which had a lot to do with why I like him: he and Alexandra had hated each other within minutes and yet he really *was* sorry.

"It's OK. It's not that important to me now." Which was an evasion but not an outright lie.

"Sit down." He flicked off the console. "Do you want something to drink or smoke or snort, maybe even something to eat if there's anything around?"

"No thanks. Not yet, anyway. Larry, has anybody come around looking for me or trying to get in touch with me?"

"No. Was somebody supposed to?"

"Not exactly, but—sort of. Nothing to do with the coke."

"About the coke. I'm not going to be able to buy it from

you after all. A pound or so, maybe, but that's it. We're going to have a really bad season this year."

"You're sure?"

"Completely sure. Sales are already dragging way behind last year and the tourists we're getting don't even buy snow cones for their kids. A lot of people in town are going to go under before Labor Day."

"Are you one of them?"

"No. My junk shops'll keep me alive but you can only sell so many rubber chickens. At least and keep your self-respect. Which is getting harder and harder to do around here anyway. But I've lined somebody up to take the rest of the coke off your hands."

Which meant that there was at least one more chance that somebody was waiting here to contact me. "Anybody I know?"

"No. A friend of a friend, but he's not supposed to be into any sort of heavy-duty violence. Plus he'll be able to give you a lot better price than I could've."

"But you still want a pound for yourself?"

"If you still want to sell it to me. You can get more money for it from him."

"I'll give it to you. Free. No charge."

"You're kidding."

"No."

"How come?"

"I'm getting out of dealing just like I got out of snakes and you're having a bad year. A favor for a friend."

"You're sure? I mean, thanks, but I can't just accept—"

"I'm sure, and yes you can. Drop me off at my truck and then we can meet up at that little lake just off 6 to make the transfer."

There was a police car parked alongside the van, its right door open. One of the cops was shining a flashlight in through the van's side window while the other was radioing in his report.

"Fuck," Larry said, taking in the cobra's head and the lettering on the side of the truck. "You might at least have warned me."

"Sorry," I said. "Most of the time it just makes people want to leave me alone. And anyway, I've got the coke hidden where they'll never find it. In with the rattlesnakes."

"That's OK, then, but you still should have warned me.

Though I don't think we'll have any real trouble with them. I know both of them; they're local and since I'm a property owner and a year-round resident here now they'll probably give me a lot better treatment than they'd give you. This is still a small town in a lot of ways. Let me talk to them."

We got out of the car, moving slowly and keeping our hands in plain sight and away from our bodies until they recognized Larry. He said hello to them, shook their hands and introduced me to them, then said that I was his guest and would be staying with him, not sleeping in my van or doing anything similarly illegal.

Which turned out to be insufficient. They'd examined the truck's interior with their flashlights, seen the baby cobra and the rows of cages, heard the rattlesnakes rattling. And ever since a little girl had lost an eye and part of her face to an improperly trained attack dog the previous summer it was very, very against the law to bring any sort of dangerous animal into Provincetown.

Their report had already been radioed in and was undoubtedly on file not only in the local office but with all the other police stations and law-enforcement agencies they'd have contacted to get information on me and my truck. And while my ability to make myself unnoticeable would have gotten me out of the immediate situation, and would have made the fact that there'd be a report on file about me no more than a minor, if continuing, annoyance, Larry had no such abilities. Any major trouble with the local police, even a minor investigation, and he was through in Provincetown. So I had to find a way to convince the top cops that no crime of any sort had been committed, that the report that they'd radioed in had been mistaken, and convince them in such a way as to make sure the new information would go on file with their original report.

But it turned out to be easy, ridiculously easy, one of those problems whose solution comes to you as soon as you realize what exactly it is you need to get done. I told them that, yes, I was a dealer in poisonous snakes and that I had been carrying a load of poisonous snakes in the van, but that they'd all been delivered to the zoo in Boston and that what few snakes I still had were perfectly harmless. I told them that they'd been mistaken in thinking the cobra was a cobra, that it was in fact a perfectly harmless garter snake just like the ones they sometimes saw in their own yards and gardens, and I invited them to inspect the glove compartment cage while I turned their attention away from all memory of having seen a cobra, away from the cobra plainly visible before their eyes, while I kept them from considering the possibility that what I was telling them might in any way conflict with what they thought and perceived and believed and remembered.

They radioed in their amended report, apologized to us for having inconvenienced us, then drove away.

"David," Larry said very slowly, his voice gone neutral in a way I'd never heard before, "you told me you were getting out of dealing just like you were getting out of snakes. All right. But what are you getting into?"

I started to turn his attention away, make him forget, keep him from being afraid of me. But I couldn't do it. He was the last real friend I had.

"Magic," I said. "I think. Or something like magic."

"You mean real magic. Sorcery and witchcraft, things like that?"

"Real magic."

He nodded very slowly, waited a moment, then asked, "Black magic?"

"No. Not me. But other people."

He let out the breath he'd been holding, nodded again. "All right. I believe you. I wouldn't have believed you, but—you couldn't see your eyes while you were telling them that the cobra was just a garter snake, David. That, and the way they just drove off—could you do that to me? Just tell me anything and make me believe it?"

"I'm not sure. That was the first time I ever tried it. But I think so."

"It's scary, David."

"I'm scared too, Larry. Very scared. But I'm as much your friend as I ever was and you can still trust me as much as you ever could. Let's get the coke out of the truck and back to your apartment and then I'll tell you all about it. I need to talk about it with somebody and you're the only one I can trust."

I started telling him about Dara while I weighed out his pound and he shaved down a rock on a piece of black glass so we could snort a few lines. I was still talking when the phone rang.

It was 6:00 A.M. He reached for the phone, picked it up, listened for a second, then handed it to me.

"Hello?"

"Hello, David." It was my brother's voice.

"Hello, Michael. What do you want?"

"Father's dead. You're needed here at home."

"I've got some business to take care of."

"Drop it and get here as fast as you can. If our sister means anything to you."

Our sister? We didn't have a sister.

Unless—

Dara.

Chapter Thirteen

THE FAMILY HOLDING WAS A ROUGH SQUARE OF LAND four miles on a side. Like the surrounding countryside, most of it was flat prairie, but its center was a geologically unique deformation of the landscape resembling a lunar meteor crater. This was the heart of the estate. The rest of the land, despite its enormous potential value as farmland, had been left undeveloped and served only to insure the family its privacy.

Sometimes when a large meteor strikes the surface of the moon a crater with three distinct features is created. Circumscribing the crater is the ringwall, a circular wall of mountains splashed up by the meteor's impact. Inside this is the crater itself, and at the center of the crater is a single central mountain. At one time I must have been told why lunar meteor craters often had the central mountain and why earthly ones never did, but if so I have forgotten the explanation. What impressed me as a child was how like a lunar crater my home was.

But if it was a crater, it was a fairy-tale crater. There was a great circular hole perhaps three hundred feet deep and a mile in diameter, surrounded by steep hills. The crater floor (I had thought of it as a crater ever since one of my early tutors had shown me a drawing of one such crater, though I had later been told repeatedly that the true explanation of our unique landscape had nothing to do with giant meteors) was thickly forested with maple and oak, elm and birch, but its walls were sheer rocky cliffs except in one place where the cliff wall had crumbled to form a gentle slope.

A steep central hill, a tiny mountain blunted by gravity, rose from the forest almost to the level of the surrounding plains. It was moist down on the crater floor, green with the scent of growing things, but as you climbed the central hill the trees and topsoil grew thinner until you found yourself climbing barren rock.

And it was there, on the bare rock, that my ancestors had chosen to build their house—or rather, their chateau, for though built almost entirely of native materials it was a European chateau in design and execution. Almost all its furnishings and fixtures had been brought from Europe, presumably traveling cross-country in covered wagons.

When the first other people of European descent arrived in the area more than one hundred and seventy-five years ago they found my family already established, their massive mansion complete and fully furnished, their life more that of cultured Europeans in Byronic seclusion than that of American pioneers. The first settler to happen upon the house had been met at the door by a servant, entertained, and then sent back to his sod hut.

Or so, at least, my father had told me, and the story was consistent with what I knew of our family's subsequent behavior. We had never mixed with the farmers who settled near us. Occasionally a Bathory would be seen in one of the small towns that grew up in the vicinity of the estate, occasionally some local official would visit the house on business. But such visits were rare, and discouraged.

I was a member of the seventh generation of Bathorys to be born in that house. My ancestors were buried in the graveyard at the base of the hill, under stone markers so set amongst the trees that one could not tell where the cemetery ended and the forest began. On each grave a shade-loving wild-rose bush of a type I had never seen elsewhere, with tiny roses mottled pink and white, had been planted, and the bushes had thrived and spread, adding to the confusion of cemetery and forest.

It was very beautiful there, the kind of picturesque landscape so many people dream of, and for most of my life my greatest dream had been to escape from it forever, to know that I would never have to see it again.

I had thought I had achieved my dream and freed myself, that I would never have to return. And now I was returning.

"I've got to leave," I told Larry as I put the phone down. "Can you sell the coke for me, take care of everything? I'll phone you and tell you how to get the money to me as soon as I've got things straightened out."

"Sure, if you want me to, but do you have enough gas to make it to Hyannis? The station here won't be open for another half-hour or so and I'd like you to sit and talk a little longer before you get going. If you can. Just until the gas station's open."

I looked at him, saw that for him this was the last time, that he expected me to return—if I ever returned—as someone completely different, someone he didn't know and could never know.

"All right. Until the station opens."

"What happened? Was that the call you were waiting for?"

"I think so. That was my brother Michael calling to tell me my father's dead and that I've got to come home immediately if my sister means anything to me."

He started to say something, closed his mouth, finally said, "Dara's your sister?"

"Yes."

"You're sure?"

"I think so. Yes."

"David, you said she was nineteen or twenty years old. Right?"

I nodded, knowing what was coming.

"But you're twenty-nine years old and your mother died when you were two. We're old friends, David; I know all about you. So she can't be your sister unless she's a lot older than you say she is or unless she's a half sister of some sort—"

"I don't know, Larry. Maybe. Or maybe my mother didn't die when father said she did."

"But it doesn't make any difference to you that she's your sister? You're in love with her anyway? I mean, romantic love? Incest?"

"Yes. It doesn't make any difference."

A slow nod. "All right. Then where's your father come into this? You said your brother told you he was dead?"

"Yes." I told him about my visions of the ice tunnels and of the man who was me and not-me.

"So your father was a . . . black magician who used you and Dara to wage some sort of war against another group of black magicians. What about your brother? Was he helping your father or was he part of the other group?"

"I don't know. If Dara's my sister, then Michael's got to be involved too, but—but then I don't really know who he is. I mean, I thought he was, you know, just a hypocrite, all smiling and friendly and honest outside but sort of small and greedy and trivial inside, just empty, but—"

"But now you don't know."

"No. What time is it, Larry?"

"Just after seven. You better get going."

"I'll be back as soon as I can, Larry. With Dara."

"All right, David. As soon as you can."

It was after midnight by the time I reached the family estate. The surrounding prairie was lit with no more than the faint silver phosphorescence I had come to expect in everything I saw but when I reached the top of the hill over which the road leading to the house passed I had to brake, stare.

The crater pulsed with silver fires and now that I was at the top of the hill, no longer shielded by it, I could feel the power pulling at me, shaking me, caressing me. How could I have grown up in the center of all that without having felt it?

But perhaps I *had* felt it, felt it without understanding what it was I was feeling, without knowing what it was that was making me so unhappy, had forced me to leave.

The road, freshly blacktopped, led down into the crater and through the forest. Every tree, every bush, gleamed with its own silver light. Fallen logs, night-flying birds, creepers and outcroppings of rock—everything shone. The power flowed around and through me, gentle, insistent, irresistible. Even the gravestones in the family cemetery gleamed soft and silvery. The wild-rose bushes burned like white-hot wire.

It took an effort of will to remember how I had always hated it there. But no, I had never hated the forest for itself: it had been my one refuge from the house. But the house, the house I remembered as so cold and dark, even the house pulsed and shimmered like something out of a lunar fairy tale.

And it had been this, it had to have been this, that whoever had tried to kill me had been so afraid I'd find.

Chapter Fourteen

I CLIMBED THE STEPS—NATIVE BLACK MARBLE, quarried in the crater itself—to the house and rang the bell. There was a cross of wild rose nailed to the door and it burned with white light. Even the door, a single slab of European black oak, shimmered in the darkness.

Had Michael been the one who'd tried to kill me?

A moment later Nicolae, a servant I remembered from my childhood, answered the door. He was brittle and slow moving; he had been old when I had moved away twelve years ago. A rare smile lit his face.

"Ah, Mr. Bathory, come in! Come in. Your brother was just telling your Uncle Stephen that he'd been totally unable to locate you. They've been searching for you for five days now, ever since your father died."

Five days ago the hand of glory had appeared and Dara had been taken from me. But—totally unable to locate me? He had known I was at Larry's, had called me and summoned me home—

Without admitting to Uncle Stephen that he'd known how to locate me. Why?

"Father dead?" I asked, trying to sound startled.

"Why yes. His funeral's tomorrow. You didn't know, sir?"

"No."

"Then why don't you wait in the library while I fetch your brother? He'll be able to tell you what happened."

"Of course. Thank you, Nicolae." He hurried off.

The library was more of a reading room and museum than anything else; most of the family's books were kept in a basement annex while the medieval manuscripts were housed in a special room of their own. The library itself only housed two kinds of books: those which had been written by members of the family, usually privately printed and bound in leather, and rare first editions, also bound, for the most part, in leather. The librarian's main task was to keep the books well oiled so they wouldn't dry out and crack.

I'd never taken much interest in either literature or book collecting but the family seemed to produce at least one notable collector in every generation. In my father's time it had been my aunt and now it was my brother, with his collection of medieval German anti-Semitic pamphlets.

The books covered three walls. The fourth wall contained a huge black marble fireplace tall enough for a man to stand in flanked by two uncatalogued Goya paintings that had been in the family since the artist had painted them. The one on the right depicted a witches' sabbat; the one on the left was a portrait of one of my ecclesiastical ancestors, a priest who had visited Spain around 1800.

I sat down in front of the fire, feeling the power of the house and land weave itself into the remembered bleakness of the life I had lived there. My blood was dancing in my veins. I awaited my brother.

I heard his heavy footsteps on the carpet—unmistakable, even after twelve years—and rose to meet him.

"Michael."

"David." We shook hands formally, sat down in facing armchairs.

"Would you like a drink?"

"Please."

"Whisky?"

"That would be fine." He rang for a servant, ordered two whiskies.

Michael was about my height, perhaps twenty pounds heavier, and immaculate. He wore a dark-blue suit, a blue and gold necktie, a white shirt and conservative shoes. Dark-blue socks. His brown hair was cut short, barely long enough to comb. He had no facial hair and he looked out at you from soft brown Dale Carnegie eyes.

He looked exactly as I would have expected him to look, wore the same mask with which he'd fooled me all my life. But the indoor pallor of his skin was overlaid with the silver phosphorescence of power. His skin glimmered, gleamed, flamed. And his eyes—they were still brown but brown with moving pinpricks of light appearing and disappearing in their depths.

I tried to turn his attention away from my suspicions, to reduce the me he could see to the David Bathory who thought his brother's facade hid only the same petty greeds I had assumed it hid when I'd last seen him twelve years before. I couldn't tell whether or not I was succeeding.

"I hear father's dead," I said.

"That's right. We've been trying to get in touch with you since his death. The funeral's tomorrow. It was certainly luck, you stopping in when you did—?"

Which meant what? That I wasn't supposed to tell anyone that he'd been the one to call and tell me to come home?

"Lucky?" I asked. "Didn't you phone me?"

"Me? No. I've been trying to find you for the last five days, David. All anybody could tell me was that you weren't at your place in Big Sur."

"I left right after my wife's funeral."

"Yes. I know. I'm sorry I never got to meet her."

I studied his face. There was a faint air of suppressed triumph about him. For the first time I realized that I was very, very afraid of him.

"And you really didn't phone me?"

"No."

"I thought it was you. It sounded like your voice. But it's been so long since we've talked with each other . . . I must have been mistaken. How'd father die?"

"Suicide. To be exact, he shot himself in the head."

"Why?"

He shrugged. "Who knows? I've lived here thirty years and I never understood him."

"But you must have some idea." Was he afraid somebody else was listening to us? "Business problems? Debts? A woman?"

"As far as I know he had no interest in women, at least after mother died. Debts? His lawyer told me that the estate is worth at least thirty-five million. And business problems—do you know what business he was in?" He was watching me closely, as if hoping for a reaction.

"No," I said.

"Neither do I."

"But after all these years you must have some idea—"

"None. Perhaps I'll be able to find out now that he's dead. You know he was never willing to share anything with us." There was a depth of feeling in his voice that surprised me.

I drank some of my whisky. "You don't have any idea at all why he killed himself? Nothing different about him—"

"Oh, he changed all right. No question about that. Here, I'll show you."

He stood up abruptly, led me into the manuscript room. There was a new door in the far wall.

"What's that lead to?" I asked.

"A room he had added on to the house. Over the years we've always followed the original plans when it's been necessary to enlarge the house. Always. This is the first thing ever built in defiance of them." His voice was thick with remembered anger.

I had never even heard of the plans he was talking about.

He opened the door, waved me through it. "As soon as I've got legal possession of the house I'm going to have this torn down."

It was a large room filled with Orientalia. Tibetan scroll paintings depicting the life of the Buddha, Indian miniatures, books and manuscripts printed in what might have been Chinese or Tibetan characters, books in English, French and German dealing with Oriental philosophy and religion. A small gilt statue of Kali dancing stood on the mantel. Facing it from across the room was a seven-foot statue of Shiva. There were shelves of statuettes, prayer rugs on the floor, tapestries, a display case full of scarlet cords. The windows were open but the smell of some sort of incense still lingered.

76

"That's not like father," I said, startled despite myself. He'd always been the strictest of Catholics, a man so deeply rooted in the European tradition that it was far easier for me to picture him as a black magician than as a dabbler in yoga or Zen.

"Not like he was when you knew him, no. But he got strange near the end."

"I saw a lot of cars in the parking lot," I said, changing the subject. "Who's here for the funeral?"

"Uncle Stephen and Uncle Peter, of course. Then Cousin Charles—I don't think you know him. He's a priest. A few minor relatives. And a Mr. and Mrs. Takshaka. Mother's parents. Why they should show up now, after all these years—"

Mother's parents. My grandparents. Dara's grandparents, who'd given her her golden Naga before she was taken from them by my father with his room full of Oriental religious curios—"

"I don't know anything about them," I said, trying to keep from showing anything beyond a mild curiosity. "Who are they?"

"Indians. Not American Indians, India Indians. But they're Aryan, at least, even if they are almost black. You must have inherited your complexion from their side of the family."

"Are they here now?"

"Not at the moment, no. They'll be back for the funeral." His eyes flicked away from me to focus on something behind me. I turned. Uncle Stephen stood in the doorway. He was dressed, as always, in his almost-clerical black, and his skin shone with the universal silver sheen.

"Ah, David!" he said. "I'm so glad you could make it home for the funeral. We see you so rarely here." He smiled a patently false smile.

As soon as he spoke I recognized the voice that had summoned me home, though it no longer resembled Michael's in any way. But why? And why had he pretended to be my brother?

I shook his hand and told him it was good to be home.

Chapter Fifteen

"WHAT ARE YOU DOING UP, STEPHEN?" MY BROTHER asked with a barely perceptible edge to his voice.

"I couldn't sleep so I came down to look at poor Gregory. Then I heard David's voice and decided to say hello to him instead."

"I was just showing him father's collection."

"Disgusting stuff, isn't it?" Uncle Stephen said to me. "All those cheap prints with their bright colors and those ridiculous statues. . . . I'll be thankful when Michael gets rid of it all.

"David," he said as if the thought had just struck him, "whatever happened to Judith's collection of grimoires?"

"They're in storage," I said.

"Now that you're home you should send for them. They're part of the family collection and should be here where we can care for them properly."

"I don't know how long I'll be staying," I said, "but I'll find out about having them sent for."

"Good." He smiled again.

"When's father's funeral?" I asked Michael.

"Tomorrow evening, around seven-thirty."

"Just before dark. Isn't that a little unusual?"

"Quite unusual," Uncle Stephen agreed, "but that's how Gregory wanted it and Cousin Charles agreed to respect his wishes. It's not contrary to any church rule, and we've even been given a dispensation for a Latin Mass."

"After the ceremony we're going to bury him next to grandfather," Michael said. "We had the grave dug today and the headstone's been prepared, but we could use your help as a pallbearer."

"Of course," I said.

"Good. With you, me, Stephen, and Uncle Peter that makes four. We need six, so I guess we'll have to use two of the servants. William and Alexandru, probably."

"Where's Uncle Peter?" I asked.

"Upstairs asleep, I suppose. You know it's almost three?"

"Really?" Michael said. "Then I'd better get to bed. There are still a lot of details I'll have to take care of tomorrow."

"Where do I sleep?" I asked, though I had no intention of sleeping.

"Your old room. Nicolae had Robert make up your bed as soon as you arrived."

"Good night, David," my uncle said. "I just wanted to say hello to you before you turned in for the night. We can do some real talking tomorrow. It's been a long time. Too long."

"Stephen," Michael said as my uncle turned to leave. Uncle Stephen turned back to face him. "I just thought of something. Can I talk to you privately for a few moments?"

"Of course, Michael."

"Excuse us, David," Michael said. "Good night."

"One thing first," I said. "Is father's body in the chapel?"

"Yes. They did an excellent job of embalming him. You can hardly see the bullet hole."

The chapel was lit by twelve long tapering candles in silver candelabra. Father's coffin was on a low table in front of the altar. The top half of the black coffin was open. Michael had been right: the bullet hole in his head was almost invisible. He must have used a small-caliber gun.

His features were composed and there was a faint smile on his lips. I wondered how the mortician had achieved such a peaceful effect, for father had never looked peaceful in life.

But the longer I stared at him the less peaceful he looked.

It was nothing that would have been visible in a photograph, but I could sense worms of silver light crawling around just beneath the surface of his skin. And he looked stronger than he had in life, as though death had changed his fat to muscle. He also resembled Michael much more than I'd remembered; there was something about the set of his features, some ingrained nuance of expression that not even death had been able to eradicate, that I'd never noticed before and that reminded me of my brother.

I leaned forward, touched a finger to his face. The flesh was soft and faintly moist. I thought about great soft fungi growing in moist white rows, loosened the collar of his shirt to examine his neck. It was unmarked.

Why had Michael and Uncle Stephen been up and fully dressed at three in the morning?

They'd gone into the library. I hesitated a moment, looking down at father, then wrapped myself in unnoticeability and made my way as silently as I could through the house to the manuscript room, through whose thin walls I had occasionally overheard scraps of conversation from the library when I'd been a child.

". . . about the phone call." Michael's voice. He sounded angry. I sat down in one of the armchairs against the connecting wall, started to pick up one of the manuscripts laid out for display so I could pretend to be studying it if someone discovered me, then put it back on its table again: if Michael or Uncle Stephen penetrated my unnoticeability they'd know I'd been there trying to hide myself from them, and not just studying manuscripts.

"And only your word that you didn't call him," Uncle Stephen said. He sounded amused.

"You've forgotten the Nagas." An unfamiliar voice, cold, grim, precise.

The Nagas: Mr. and Mrs. Takshaka. My maternal grandparents.

"But why would they want him here?" Uncle Stephen asked. "*We* want him here."

"It's not important what they want," the grim voice said. "What's important is that they're dangerous to us, and that we cannot tolerate them here. You should kill them now, before they can harm us."

"How?" Uncle Stephen asked. "We don't understand them, and we don't want to understand them. Look what happened to Gregory. Unless you, Michael, perhaps you could tell us—"

"I repudiate mother and her race, and everything they stand for. As you know well, Stephen."

"But how can we trust you," the grim voice asked, "with your mother's tainted blood flowing in your veins?"

"You need not trust me. You need only obey me. I am a Bathory and a dhampire. I am your master."

"Not yet. Not until you master Gregory."

"I am your master *now*, grandfather. I can force you to obey me."

Michael's grandfather, our father's father, had died before I'd been born. Was dead and buried.

Dead and buried and in the library talking to Michael and Uncle Stephen. A vampire.

"For the moment," Uncle Stephen agreed. "Until you confront Gregory. But, Michael, I too am a Bathory and a dhampire, and I remember what your mother made of my brother. Why should *I* accept your dominion?"

"Because father was a coward and a fool, for all his untainted blood. I had to learn to deny him, and to deny my mother's blood in me, and that denial forced me to develop the strength he needed but never had."

"Perhaps. He may have been stronger than you think, Michael. But why would the Nagas want David here, if they were the ones who brought him here? To help rescue Dara?"

"No," Michael said. "If they'd wanted to rescue her, they could have done so earlier, before I'd had a chance to gain any power from her."

"Unless they wanted you to gain power from her," Uncle Stephen said.

"They're here to prevent Gregory's transformation," the grim voice—my grandfather's voice—said. "And they have power over fire: they could burn him in his coffin before he's ready."

"Then they could have burned him earlier," Uncle Stephen said.

"But why now?" Michael asked. "Why are they here, if not to prevent his transformation?"

"The three of you are here again now. Their own kind."

"I am not *of* their kind, Stephen. And you would do well to remember it.".

"Dara, then. Or David."

"We cannot tolerate them here any longer," the third voice said. "You must destroy them or force them to leave us. Tonight."

"How, grandfather?" Michael asked.

"You could kill them. They can die. Your mother died."

"The first time," Uncle Stephen said. "Not the second."

"Gregory will bring her back to us."

"If he survives his forty days," Michael said. "If they don't destroy him first. If Satan accepts her."

"You don't have the strength to master my son alone," my grandfather said. "And should either Dara or David join us before you gain dominion—"

"Then you will have all of us before our time," Michael said. "Perhaps. But they will do what I demand of them, as will you, grandfather, even now, before my dominion is complete. And as will you as well, Stephen. Remember, only I can protect you from father."

"Protect me, Michael? Do you really think I fear my fate? I am only sorry that my responsibilities to my family prevent me from embracing it sooner."

"Then join us now," my grandfather said. "Living as you do—as you all do—you only thwart us. When you join us you will see how wrong you've been."

"When I join your communion I'm sure I will, father. But until then I have duties I must fulfill."

"It's almost dawn," my grandfather said. "I must sleep. Will you nullify the guardians for me?"

"Yes," Michael said. I heard light footsteps, then silence. The door hadn't opened or closed.

"Do you have everything prepared?" Uncle Stephen asked a moment later.

"Almost everything. Unless there's a way I can use one of them to master father without freeing her, now that the Nagas are here—"

"There isn't any way. If they try to interfere we'll have to stop them. No matter what the cost to the family."

"Agreed. But if David and Dara escape I'll know whom to

blame, Stephen. And I'm still not completely convinced that you weren't the one who brought David here."

"To what purpose? His blood bears the same taint as yours and he is even less of a Bathory, even less fit to rule than you are. But it's time to finish readying her for tomorrow."

"I'll be studying everything you do," Michael said. "Your knowledge of the rituals may still be superior to mine in some ways but I'll know enough to know whether or not you're trying to deceive me."

"There would be no point. As you said, with you gone who would I have to protect me from Gregory?"

Once again footsteps, then silence. They hadn't opened the door or gone into the hall. I waited a moment longer to make sure, then went out to my truck and got the vial of coke: psychic self-defense, to keep them from using Dara against me. Back in my room I snorted some, then lay on my bed and pretended to be asleep while I tried to make sense out of what I'd heard. But in the end what was hardest, despite everything that had already happened to me, wasn't so much understanding what they'd said as it was accepting and believing it.

Both Michael and Uncle Stephen were dhampires, and a dhampire was someone who ruled his undead ancestors. His ancestors who were vampires who were my ancestors. Michael had been the one who'd taken control of Dara and me in the caverns, and who'd taken her away from me—and who'd tried to kill me in Chicago?—but he was planning to free her again tomorrow so he could make use of her somehow to gain control of father.

For what he'd done to us, and what he'd made us do to each other, I'd hate him for the rest of my life.

Michael was half Naga, as I was half Naga and Dara was half Naga, and Michael suspected Uncle Stephen of plotting against him—and Uncle Stephen *was* plotting against him, was lying to him and must be planning to use me against him in some way. Because Uncle Stephen hated him for his Naga blood, which was Dara's Naga blood, which was my Naga blood.

My father was dead now but he would be alive again soon, and a vampire. As his father, my grandfather was a vampire, as Uncle Stephen and Michael would become vampires.

As Dara and I would become vampires unless our Naga blood saved us.

Our Naga blood. My long-dead mother was not dead, or not exactly dead, and she was a Naga, was perhaps even the cobra-headed Queen on the throne of ivory who'd saved me from the coral snake's attack—and her parents, my other grandparents, a Mr. and Mrs. Takshaka would be here tomorrow when Dara was freed.

When perhaps we would have our only chance to escape.

And it was strange that there'd been no mention of God, or Christ, Satan's traditional adversary. Only the Nagas.

Chapter Sixteen

ABOUT SEVEN THAT MORNING I DECIDED I'D STAYED
in bed long enough to simulate a night's sleep for anyone who
might be watching me. I rang for a servant and told him to get
my clothes from the truck, showered, then dressed and went
downstairs to examine the books in father's new room.

And realized how stupid I'd been in not looking at them the
night before, because about a third of the books I'd seen on
the shelves were missing. I glanced through a few of the others,
found nothing that would have been out of place in the inspi-
rational section of any West Coast bookshop.

I'd been letting the seeming familiarity of my surroundings
lull me into a false sense of security, treating everything like
a game which I could win if I could outplay my opponents.
Who intended to make sure I never got a chance to learn the
rules.

I went looking for the Takshakas, was told by Nicolae that
they weren't expected back before the funeral. I checked out
the house again anyway, but didn't find them.

". . . sounds a bit like the Manichean Heresy, your idea
that Satan is as powerful as God and is the absolute ruler of

this world while God rules only in Heaven," I heard as I walked into the dining room. Two men were sitting at the end of the long table with their backs to me, talking in low, earnest voices.

"But if a man commits a sin, hates himself for doing it, yet knows that he has had no other choice and that he will sin again in the same way, how can he beg God for forgiveness? What choice does he have but despair—?" The speaker broke off when he caught sight of me. He was a big man, well over six feet tall but stooped, as though deformed by a lifetime spent carrying some too-heavy load. His long black hair and full beard looked as though he'd made an unsuccessful attempt at removing years of tangles with one brushing.

I seated myself across the table from the man to whom he'd been speaking. There was no doubt in my mind that this was Father Charles Bathory. He was a strikingly handsome man, still young, with a smug unthinking look on his face and something to the way his robes fitted him that suggested they'd been discreetly tailored.

"Good morning," I said.

"Good morning," the priest replied. His voice was over-hearty, with a public-speaker's sincerity. His companion mumbled something.

"Don't let me interrupt your conversation," I told them as a servant brought me a vegetarian omelet.

"We were just finishing," the bearded man said with an effort. He was gaunt and colorless, with a fish-belly pallor that made his black eyes look sunken, and he looked like a man who'd been afraid to go to sleep for most of his life. His skin was splotched with silver and he wore a too-large but expensively cut suit.

"You must be Uncle Peter," I said. "I'm David. And you," turning to the priest, "must be Father Bathory."

"Call me Charles," he said. Uncle Peter mumbled a greeting without meeting my eyes.

"We can continue our conversation later if you'd like, Peter," the priest said, dismissing him. Cousin Charles's skin was so lightly tinged with silver that I was sure he could have little or no part in what was happening here, but he monopolized the conversation, to my uncle's evident relief. I was treated to an endless monologue about the good father's parish, in what had once been an upper-class neighborhood in Chicago but was now well on its way to becoming a slum. The loss of many of his well-to-do parishioners had hurt the church financially, it seemed, but the black children sang so beautifully that some of the richest members of the church had continued to take an active part in it even though they'd moved out of the neighborhood, and that, combined with the gas station and butcher shop which two other parishioners had left them . . .

While Cousin Charles spoke Uncle Peter was eating with careful speed. He finished his breakfast steak and got up, obviously relieved at the chance to escape.

"Uncle Peter," I called after him, interrupting Cousin Charles. Uncle Peter froze like a little boy caught stealing money from his mother's purse, turned unwillingly back to face me.

"Excuse me, Charles," I said, "but I haven't seen Uncle Peter for fifteen or twenty years and there are a lot of things I'd like to talk to him about. I'm sure we'll get another chance to talk with each other later."

"It's been a pleasure talking with you," he said genially. I pushed back my chair and joined Uncle Peter, escorted him out into the hallway.

"Where would you like to talk?" I asked. "The library?"

"No," he said quickly. "I don't like the library."

"Good. Neither do I. How about outside? Down in the forest. Of course, if you're afraid of getting your suit dirty—"

"No, let's go outside. I feel better outside. And it's a beautiful day," he added as if the thought had just occurred to him.

We walked down the drive. It was sunny out, with only a few cumulus and cirrus clouds in the sky. Birds sang and hopped and flew in the trees and gray squirrels were everywhere.

Uncle Peter tensed, shrinking into himself, when the first gravestone came into view on our left. He only began to breathe normally again after we were well past the cemetery.

Somewhat further on we found an oak tree fallen by the side of the road. We sat on its trunk and talked.

It was almost impossible to get any information out of him. He volunteered nothing and after the first few minutes I gave up trying to keep up the fiction that what had become an interrogation was in fact a friendly conversation.

He grudgingly admitted that he lived in a cave hollowed out of the side of a hill in Pennsylvania. I already knew that. He told me some things about the forest where his cave was, though not how to find it, but he wouldn't tell me why he had chosen to live there as a hermit. He did his best, in fact, to tell me nothing at all yet he seemed mortally afraid of lying to me or offending me in any way.

He gave each question I asked him careful consideration, like a squirrel turning a nut over and over in its paws while trying to decide just where to bite into it, then answered with a flood of inconsequential or irrelevant details. And after each such trivial or incoherent disclosure—after, for example, he'd revealed that he'd been born two years before my father or that he'd last seen me when I was thirteen—he'd go rigid, sitting with a look of pure terror on his face and refusing to say anything further.

At first I pitied him and did my best to make it easy on him but as the time passed I lost patience with him. I bent the power of the forest to my will, used my ability to focus his attention where I wanted it to don a mantle of spurious charisma but it was no use. He cringed away from me but still refused to answer my questions.

Finally I asked, "What do you know about vampires?"

"Nothing!" he stammered, his face contorted and twisting. "Just what I read in Bram Stoker's book. I can't read in my cave. The light's too poor. I haven't read a book in years. I don't remember what I read in *Dracula*. It's been too many years."

He stared at me a moment longer, then fled back up the hill, leaving me alone on the fallen tree.

Dracula? I hadn't read it since I was twelve. Aunt Judith had taught me that it was just a malicious fantasy but by now it was obvious that she'd made a practice of protecting me from knowledge she thought too dangerous for me. Perhaps there was something in *Dracula* I'd forgotten.

I walked back up the drive to the house, asked if my grandparents had by any chance returned early. They hadn't.

The librarian was anxious to help me but I told him that I just wanted to browse through some books in peace while I waited for father's funeral. He said he understood and left me alone in the library.

I found three listings under "Vampires" in the English-language section of the card catalog, plus a number of cross-references to the Russian, Romanian, German and French collections—all languages that I should have been able to read as a graduate of St. George's Academy, none of which I could actually read, though I understood a little spoken Romanian.

Some Of Your Blood by Theodore Sturgeon I discarded almost immediately: as far as I could tell it was a "psychological study" of a man who'd developed a taste for blood because his mother always bled when she nursed him. *Dracula* gave me a wealth of information about vampires, but I had no idea whether any of it was trustworthy, though the book's preface said that Stoker had been a member of the Order of the Golden Dawn, which it described as a society of serious students of the occult that had flourished near the end of the nineteenth century and had included such people as Aleister Crowley.

Montague Summers's *The Vampire: His Kith and Kin* was an irritating pseudoscholarly compilation of legends, superstitions, rumors and errors—he misquoted one of the grimoires in my aunt's collection—all of which the author seemed to take as literal truth. Some of what he said corroborated Stoker's tale and some was patently absurd, such as his claim that you had only to scatter mustard seeds on your roof and threshold to keep yourself safe from any vampire intent on doing you harm, since the vampire would be forced to spend the time until dawn compelled him to return to his coffin counting the seeds.

But despite its many evident absurdities the book contained some information that seemed to corroborate and clarify things I had overheard while hiding in the manuscript room, including the statements that a suicide will often become a vampire and that forty days must pass before a vampire can rise from its grave. The book also claimed that vampires could not abide wild roses, and though the reason it gave, that the vampires were afraid of becoming caught in the brambles, was another of Summers's idiocies, there was the evidence of the wild-rose bushes planted on my ancestors' graves to lend credence to the idea that there was some sort of connection between vampires and wild roses. But Summers's book made no mention of dhampires.

My reading had consumed most of the day. I had unconsciously wrapped myself in unnoticeability while I read, as I realized when, emerging from the library, I was almost knocked down by a servant who failed to see me until he ran into me.

"Mr. Bathory!" he said. "Dinner's ready and we've been looking everywhere for you so we can proceed."

"I'll be right there," I assured him.

"Excuse me for mentioning it, sir"—he looked disapprovingly at my faded jeans and plaid wool shirt—"but shouldn't you dress for dinner? The funeral's directly afterwards."

I felt like laughing for the first time since my return. "I'm afraid I don't have any proper clothing," I told him. "I've been living in a cabin in the woods, you know."

"Your black suit is hanging in your closet, sir, and Robert shined your shoes for you this morning, while you were out walking with your uncle. If you'll permit me, I'll inform the rest of the family that you'll be down in a few minutes."

There were five people I didn't know at the table: three undistinguished-looking persons with only a minimal silver sheen to their skins—no doubt the other cousins—and a diminutive couple with dark skin and wavy black hair who I knew must be my maternal grandparents.

They were small, neither over five-four, and very slender, with fine delicate bones. Their faces were smooth and unwrinkled, their movements swift and graceful, but the very fact that they showed no sign of old age's degeneration somehow marked them as ancient. They seemed to wear their age like a second skin, a cloak of wisdom and experience, yet they had a vitality surpassing that of anyone else at the table.

Their eyes, startlingly, were the deep blue of a Siamese cat's, and their human features were at times veiled by barely perceptible auras of transparent blue flame that sometimes suggested the heads of giant cobras with spread hoods, sometimes suggested multitudes of smaller cobra heads, each with its own life and intelligence, yet they alone, of all the creatures and things I had seen since Dara and I had first made love, manifested no evidence whatsoever of the silver phosphorescence that I had come to expect of everything I saw.

No. Dara's bracelet, the golden Naga she wore twisted around her left forearm, had had the same blue aura. And these two little dark-skinned people, my grandparents, were Nagas, as I was half Naga.

A place had been saved for me between Uncle Peter and one of the cousins, too far away from the Takshakas· for me to be able to talk to them during the meal. Everybody was standing behind the chairs. I took my place and Michael, who was sitting at the head of the table, asked Uncle Peter to say the grace. Cousin Charles looked offended, no doubt because as a priest he considered it both his right and his duty to say the blessing.

"Bless us O Lord and these Thy gifts which we are about to receive from Thy bounty . . ." Uncle Peter said haltingly while Uncle Stephen watched him with a malicious smile. Uncle Peter stopped, obviously at a loss for words, and Cousin Charles finished triumphantly, "through Christ our Lord. Amen." Everyone sat down. The servants brought the soup.

I studied the Nagas covertly while I ate. After a while I realized that they had been watching me while I studied them and as soon as I realized they knew I was watching them they grinned at me, then resumed their conversations with their neighbors. But I had no chance to speak with them before the funeral and though Uncle Peter sitting next to me drank an immense amount of wine, the more he drank the more tight-lipped he became.

The funeral began with Mass in the chapel. I sat with the other pallbearers in the front pews. Though I hadn't confessed, I took Communion with the others. If Cousin Charles knew about my omission he said nothing. More than twelve years had passed since the last time I'd knelt at the rail and the wafer the priest put in my mouth was so unexpectedly bitter that I almost gagged on it.

Before the Mass ended I'd begun to feel chills and a growing nausea. Helping roll the bier out of the chapel to the waiting hearse, I felt a giant hand clench itself in my stomach and begin twisting. Weak and dizzy, alternately hot and cold, it was all I could do to help lift the coffin into the hearse and make my way back to the car in which I was to ride.

Nicolae drove the rented hearse down the hill to the cemetery. I was in the back seat of the second car; behind us came other cars with more family and the household servants.

The sun had set by the time we reached our destination but there was still a little light in the sky. I staggered out of the car. Around me servants were lighting kerosene lanterns. No one seemed to notice my distress.

I couldn't understand what was going on around me. I knew I was supposed to help carry father's coffin to his grave but I couldn't connect that knowledge with the black box I could see being unloaded from the hearse.

"Hurry up, David. Give us a hand," Michael called and I ambled over to the hearse and helped lift the coffin from it. I was imitating my brother's actions without understanding them. We carried the coffin into the silver-shining woods.

My physical discomfort was going away but my confusion was increasing. I walked along mechanically, not paying attention to what I was doing. Things caught my eye—a glowing leaf, my brother's back, a gravestone with its inscription weathered to illegibility—and held my fascinated, uncomprehending attention.

We lowered the coffin into the ground. Cousin Charles sprinkled it with holy water and began the final parts of the funeral service. People threw sprigs of wild rose into the hole. Two servants began shoveling dirt down on the coffin.

I was standing by the hole, watching the servants shovel the silver dirt, when I suddenly sensed Dara somewhere in the woods behind me.

Acting without thought I turned and walked away from the grave into the woods. I saw Dara. She was walking slowly, moving as if in a trance.

I ran up to her and caught hold of her arm. She awakened instantly.

"David!" She looked around. "Where are we?"

I could only stand dumb, clutching at her arm.

"What's wrong with you?" she demanded. "What have they done to you?"

I could only nod and smile, happy to have found her. The forest was beautiful.

The wind brought Cousin Charles's solemn voice to us.

"We can't stay here. Come on!" She began to run. I followed her, happy to be running.

Finally she stopped. "Can you understand me at all?" she asked.

Her words were meaningless. I smiled at her.

"Here." She twisted the Naga off her arm and forced it onto mine. There was a moment's sharp pain, then my head began to clear.

"Can you understand me now?"

I nodded, not trusting myself to speak.

"What did they do to you?"

I thought about it for a long time. "Dinner," I said finally, trying to tell her about Michael and Uncle Stephen and about the Nagas.

"They've given you some kind of drug. Do you understand me?"

"Yes." The words were beginning to come. "Tripping. Not like—"

"Can you remember things if I tell them to you?"

"Yes." My mind was slowly growing clearer. "Talk slow," I added.

"I am your sister." I nodded. "Our brother Michael is our enemy. Uncle Stephen is our friend. He gave me this ointment."

She took a small metal box out of her dress and showed it to me, then put it in my pants pocket.

"If we get separated lie down in a safe place with your head to the north and rub some of this ointment on your forehead. Then follow the Naga. It will lead you to me. Do you understand?"

"Yes."

"Good. How do you feel?"

"Wonderful."

She frowned. "Can you remember more if I tell you more?"

"Yes."

"We are dhampires. That means our grandparents and now our father as well are dhampires. Michael is a dhampire too. So are our uncles.

"We will not gain our full powers until father has been dead forty days. But when we make love our powers grow. Whenever any two dhampires have sex together, power is generated.

"Michael had been forcing me to have sex with him. There is power in rape, though not as much as in lovemaking. He has been draining me of my power. Do you understand what I've been telling you?"

"Yes."

"You're sure? Don't try to think, just remember."

"Yes."

"Good. Now we must make love. I no longer have enough power to keep us unnoticeable without your help. We need more power to hide ourselves and to overcome the drug they fed you. Take off your clothes. Hurry!"

I began to take off my clothes. There was something I knew I should remember, but I didn't know what it was.

Chapter Seventeen

The woods were silver. A three-quarters moon gleamed through the branches. Dara lifted her dress over her head and drew me down beside her onto the damp oak leaves and pine needles.

Part of me seemed to be watching us from the tannic-acid smell of the rotting oak leaves, yet as we held on to each other, as I fumbled with her breasts and tried to stroke her skin, my cock swelled and stiffened with a need for her so desperate and painful that it pushed the last of the impersonal bliss in which I had been floating out of me.

"I can feel them in the woods all around us and I can't keep us hidden much longer without your help. Hurry, David!" Dara said as she pulled me over on top of her.

I pushed myself into her, tried to make love to her. But I could not match myself to her rhythms or find a rhythm of my own, could not regain that sense of rightness and certainty that would have enabled me to shrug off the clumsy weight of my body and lose myself in our interface, in our lovemaking, and as I grew more frustrated, more desperate, I tried to substitute force for the sensitivity I could no longer find in myself, as though by slamming my cock into her with greater and greater violence I could somehow break through to the missing rightness.

The power swirled through and between us, burned in us, but only in the instant when it leaped the gap between us did we share it, did it unite us. When I held it the woods around us were transparent crystal and it was easy to sense the vampires loosed and searching for us, easy to wrap ourselves in a shining obscurity they could not penetrate. And when the power passed from me to Dara it was as easy for her to make use of it as it had been for me. But the easiness with which I could use it, the ecstasy I felt when it exploded in me, only made it all the more frustrating, all the more agonizing that we could not share it.

But at the same time that the swirling crystal wind was burning in me I was sinking into the rotting darkness that had once been my father. The power that had been his in life was leaving him, a dark sluggish tide flowing from him to us and enabling us to use the luminous energies of the living earth, but he and his power were one and as his strengths became ours we found ourselves trapped with him in his dead unresponding flesh.

He could feel himself rotting and disintegrating, feel parts of himself slipping from him no matter how hard he tried to hold on to them, while new things were springing to life within him, dark cancerous fungi feeding off the man he had once been. He felt a terrible emptiness opening within him, a void he knew instinctively could only be filled with stolen life, stolen blood.

He remembered all those he had loved—Saraparajni, his Naga wife, his brothers Peter and Stephen, his children, Michael, Dara and even myself—with a strange cold petrified love, but while what little remained of the man he had been still hoped for our deliverance, that hope was now the channel through which his new hungers flowed, so that it was we above all others whom he desired to drink and empty, we from whose bodies and beings he needed to gouge empty replicas of himself, hollow vessels to contain the void within.

And at the center of that void, Satan, around whom the other vampires danced a beautiful, terrible dance that moved in my father with ever-increasing strength as Satan molded and

95

pruned and shaped him. A dance my father could no longer fight, that was claiming him for its own and would soon bring him life and blood and love—

And as he was flooding into us, a river of hungry shadows, we were making clumsy violent love, feeling the power building in us, coming closer, ever closer, to the fusion we were unable to achieve.

And then there was a sudden twisting, a wrenching and a falling, and I was no longer in control. I felt, I participated in my body's actions but they were animated by another's will. My brother's will.

Dara knew the change coming over me for what it was and tried to get away from me, struggling in silence so as not to attract the vampires in the woods around us. Michael held her down and thrust my cock which was his cock was a blunt fist gripping a heavy wooden stake a knife-edged shard of broken glass into her again and again. And though I hated him and fought him and would have killed him if I could, yet he was almost me, was the me I had always rejected and refused and thrust from me, and sometimes I found that it was I who was grinding myself into Dara, I who was glorying in her pain and sharing in my brother's laughter. And then Michael had spanned the interface between us, become the interface, so that it was me, helpless, being raped by my brother in Dara's and my interlocked bodies.

And all the time he was bleeding us of the power we generated, taking it into himself.

And then I had pulled myself out of Dara, had turned her over and pulled her to her knees, was gripping her throat tight in my right hand while I alternated strokes between her ass and vagina. Her sphincter muscles were tight and tensed and she cried out with pain each time I thrust myself deep into her ass, yet the strokes in between had become smooth, desperately gentle, futile attempts at transforming what was being done to us, what I was being allowed to do, into lovemaking. And all the power in our love and pain was being drained from us by my brother.

Finally Michael took complete control, pushed me aside to watch from the tannic-acid smell of the oak leaves, to watch and see and know what it meant to be a Bathory and a dhampire.

And then Dara and I were united again and Michael was reaching through our pain and despair into the rotting darkness that had once been our father. He took father's developing hungers and needs and passions for his own, mastered them and broke them to his human will, so that only through him could father feed the void opening within him, so that father could do nothing but what Michael willed him to do. It was cold, brutal, abstract as some sort of chesslike game played with surgical knives in the body of a patient not expected to survive.

Triumphant and tired, Michael began to withdraw from our minds, was suddenly gone. I lay on Dara, exhausted, my softening cock retreating on its own from between her buttocks. We were both too drained to move. Dara was crying softly.

Uncle Stephen stepped out of the forest shadows, holding two flaming dead hands in front of him like torches. He stuck them upright in the ground in front of us and traced a circle around us with his finger. The circle glowed a sullen red. I tried to get to my feet and stop him, found that I was paralyzed, no longer even able to follow his movements with my eyes.

He squatted down in front of the flaming hands and sprinkled something from a vial of shiny black glass onto one of them. The flames crackled and sputtered. He turned to face us. I felt my cock begin to stiffen.

"Dried semen from a hanged man's final ejaculation," he told us, genial and smiling as a furniture salesman approving your taste in upholstery. "It will restore your vitality, so that what you did for your brother you can now do for me. You'll be ready in a few minutes.

"I'm sorry to do this to you," he said with what sounded like genuine regret and I remembered that Dara had said that he was our friend, "but I am fighting for all our lives. When your brother reawakens he will regain control of Dara, and the power I'll have gained from you will be your only hope. I still need Michael's protection—Gregory would kill me if he could and my time has not yet come—but with your help we will soon be free of Michael. And since I need your help and know you will not grant me it freely, I must compel you."

While he'd been talking he'd been taking off his clothes, so that he now stood naked before us, a skeletally thin man whose skin shone a pale silver. He took a human finger bone from the pocket of his neatly folded wool trousers and dipped it in green liquid from a second vial, then traced a complex pattern on each of our foreheads.

He poured the remnants of the vial's contents on the other flaming hand and withdrew, circling around behind us. I could hear his heavy, excited breathing as we found ourselves repeating everything we had done and felt before. There was no third presence in our minds but we were helpless to alter a single action, a single emotion. I hated and fought against a Michael who wasn't there, felt him bleeding us of the power that was building up and up in us, filling us without being taken from us.

I was moving in the same rhythms which my brother had forced on me when he had taken control of father, Dara was crying out again with the pain of her abused sphincter muscles, when I felt Uncle Stephen's hands on me, a sudden tearing pain in my own ass as he thrust himself into me, joined in our agonized rhythm and took the power we had generated for his own, then directed it back through us against my father who, defeated once, was unable to summon up any resistance against him.

Uncle Stephen pulled himself out of me and I lay sprawled once more atop Dara, so exhausted I was unable to see the forest glowing in front of my eyes.

"Sorry again," I heard Uncle Stephen's cheerful voice say as I drifted slowly off into unconsciousness, "but I can't afford to let Michael learn about this just yet. I'm afraid you'll have to forget about my part in this business for the moment."

There was a hissing sound, then I was coughing on thick, rancid smoke. I lost consciousness.

When I awakened Dara was gone. My Aunt Judith, not middle-aged as she'd been when she'd killed herself, but young and beautiful, with great pale eyes and long dark hair, was kneeling over me, her lips pressed to my throat. I could feel the terrible suction as she drained me of blood, was glad somehow, in a childlike way, to see her again after so many years. I tried to reach out and take her hand but didn't have the strength.

I slept.

Chapter Eighteen

MY FATHER'S SHADOW TIDES LAPPED WEAKLY AT MY mind, cold like the ground beneath me. My heart was beating, I could feel myself breathing, but I could see nothing, hear nothing, smell nothing, and my body would not obey me.

I remembered Aunt Judith leaning over me, her eyes dead sapphires, her cold lips pressed to my neck, remembered the way I'd tried to reach out and take her hand.

I tried to touch my hand to my neck, explore the place where she'd bitten me, but my arm was too heavy and I couldn't move it.

Strength was flowing back into me from my father, but too little, too slowly. I forced myself to try to climb the dark tide to him and take what I needed, but I couldn't get to him, couldn't force my way through the spongy darknesses that separated us. I would have to wait, as I had had to wait at Carlsbad.

I tried to reach through the darknesses to Dara, found only emptiness where she should have been.

Aunt Judith's eyes so cold, so empty. So hungry, where

they had once been loving. And they were going to make Dara like that, make me like that. I hadn't been strong enough to protect us, had been too stupid to suspect the Communion wafer Cousin Charles had put in my mouth—

No. I had *participated* in what Michael had done to Dara, could not perhaps have been used as I had been used had I not been as much a dhampire as Michael, had I not had within me the potential to become what he was.

And what if the only way to defeat him was to make myself over in his image, to become everything that I had long ago, before I'd known what decision it was I was making, refused to become?

But there was still the Naga, the tight spiral of gold I could feel clasping my left forearm. Dara had said to follow the Naga to her.

My vision was beginning to return: I could just make out a faint silvery glow, like a cloud of metallic afterimages. And I was beginning to smell the oak leaves again, hear the branches above me moving in the wind.

I tried to move my hand again, managed to inch it to my throat. The skin around my jugular was bruised but unbroken.

I groped for my pants, jerked them closer. The metal box containing the ointment was still in the pocket where Dara had left it. I had to find a safe place, lie down with my head to the north and rub some of the ointment on my forehead, then follow the Naga to Dara.

A safe place. My truck? No, the snakes in it were too dangerous. Where, then?

The silver glow was getting steadily brighter.

But perhaps I was asking the wrong question. What could I do to make someplace safe?

I thought about Cousin Charles's priestly paraphernalia—his holy water, crucifixes, whatever I could find—then rejected the idea. Not after the Communion wafer. I didn't even know if he was a real priest.

Uncle Stephen would know what to do but I couldn't trust him, not after what I'd overheard him say in the library, not knowing that he'd been the one who'd arranged Dara's and my violation for Michael. Uncle Peter was too terrified of everyone—even me—to be trusted. And the Takshakas, my Naga grandparents, had done nothing to help us. Perhaps I had to follow Dara's instructions before they could do anything.

The woods around me were starting to come into focus. I tried to sit up, was suddenly very sick. I would have to wait a little longer.

I would have to try to make do with garlic and wild roses, hope they'd protect me till dawn. My bedroom had a door that could be bolted from the inside and it was as likely—or as unlikely—to be safe as any other room I could think of in the house.

I levered myself up to a sitting position, managed to maintain it despite the dizziness and the nausea. The moon had set but I could see the forest around me, the trees like silver-spider-webbed volcanic glass, the forest floor a dark lake lit from beneath by a trapped moon. And in the distance, but closer, clearer, somehow than the forest that separated me from it, the house blazed, bright as burning metal.

I got my clothes on, half crawled, half staggered up the hill to the house, stopping only long enough to rip some bright-burning branches off a wild rose bush on the way.

The house was deserted. Everyone was gone or asleep. I got what I needed from the kitchen and workroom, then made my way slowly up the stairs to my room.

I shot the bolt on the door, then nailed a cross of wild rose and a clove of garlic to its solid oak. I hung a second cross and another clove of garlic in the window, rubbed garlic around the crack between the door and the doorframe, then did the same for the crack between window and window frame. I strung all but one of my remaining cloves on a piece of twine which I tied tight around my neck, then ate the final clove.

The bed was a massive four-poster and heavy, but I finally managed to shift it around enough so I could lie on it with my head to the north. I put the two carving knives I'd taken on a chair by the bed where I hoped I could grab them in time if I needed them, then lay down on the bed. I opened the metal box and rubbed some of the ointment onto my skin. It felt cool on my temples but warm in the center of my forehead.

Within a few minutes my dizziness and nausea were gone and my sense of urgency had given way to a feeling of relaxed alertness. I began to feel a sort of not unpleasant electrical vibration in my head accompanied by a hissing sound. The vibrations spread to my body, began moving up and down it. My body felt increasingly rigid but the rigidity was comforting, even soothing, as though my previous suppleness had been maintained only by some tremendous unconscious effort which I was at last being allowed to relax. The vibrations slowly increased in frequency.

After what might have been another ten minutes the vibrations died away. I lay quietly a while longer, waiting for whatever was going to happen next, then sat up. I felt something first give and then break as I sat up, twisted back to see what it was.

And found myself staring into my own face. I was still lying there, my mouth slightly open, my eyes closed as if in sleep.

I reached back to touch the sleeping face with some half-formed idea of finding out if it was real—

Only I no longer had the hand I was trying to use. My left arm terminated above the wrist in the nine flaring necks of a Naga.

The Naga was a cool luminous green, like liquified jade. Its nine heads were more like those of sculptured Chinese dragons than like those of actual snakes, with high, almost bulging foreheads, eyes like disks of burning crystal, and flaring nostrils over long sinuous mouths. It regarded me a moment out of its eighteen eyes, then twisted away from me and wove itself forward into the air, pulling me the rest of the way out of my body.

As soon as I was completely out of my body my sense of vision changed. The silver fires and phosphorescences my powersight had revealed to me were gone, as was the darkness underlying them. The Naga was still its luminous green but everything else, even my sleeping self, was bathed in a sourceless radiance that showed things with an impossible neutral precision, as though I were moving through an infinitely detailed three-dimensional pencil drawing.

I had only an instant to stare down at my body, the bracelet still clasping its left forearm, before the Naga was pulling me smoothly through the air. There was a barely perceptible sense of resistance as we passed through the solid oak door and then we were gliding down the hall towards the staircase, flying at what would have been shoulder height had I been walking and not streaming along behind the Naga like some sort of immaterial pennant.

At the bottom of the stairs the Naga twisted left and pulled me through a wall into the manuscript room, then through the closed door in its far wall and into my father's Oriental room.

The statue of Shiva burned with close-cropped green and white fires. We began flying in tight circles around it, circumnavigating it eighty-four times before plunging through the walls into the library.

A black sun burned in the fireplace, leeching the radiance from the neutral air and filling the room with flickering shadow. We dived into the flames and for an instant I was lost in endless darkness, in a sea of thirsty shadows, and then we were plunging through the rear wall of the fireplace and gliding down a hidden stairway.

The stairway meandered deeper and deeper into the earth, twisting and curving, doubling back on itself without apparent logic. Torches burned with colorless flames in holders on either side. At intervals skulls with burning shadows in their eye sockets were set in niches.

At last the stairs debouched onto a tiny landing high on the curve of a huge hemispherical cavern. A thick pillar of red-flickering shadow, like a column of burning blood, leapt from the dark waters of the small lake in the center of the cavern floor to the apex of the hemispherical vault; four slender columns of black flame rose to the roof from four dark pools ringing the central lake. The cavern was thick with drifting red and black shadows.

This must have been where father had taken Dara, where she'd been growing up while I'd been reading about Vlad the Impaler in the house above.

Steps spiraled down to the floor. We followed them. Below us I could see what looked like a pine or spruce forest, the trees clustered around the base of the stairs. A river divided the forested area from the rest of the cavern. As we got lower I could see two concentric circles of dark objects surrounding the central lake.

There was a photographic negative of a man descending the stairs ahead of us. We glided up to him, slowed, floated just behind him. I could hear his hard-soled shoes on the stone steps.

It was my brother Michael.

He turned right at the bottom of the stairs, following a path that took him a short ways into the woods, to a clearing where a stone altar stood. On stone tables surrounding the altar were all sorts of Catholic paraphernalia: holy water, vestments, sacramental wine, Communion wafers, crosses and crucifixes.

All the weapons that faithful Christians were supposed to be able to use to protect themselves against Satan and His creatures.

Michael paused a moment, studying the assortment, then took a single Communion wafer and sealed it in a plastic sandwich bag, put the bag in his pocket and proceeded on.

A stone bridge spanned the river. The cave floor on the other side was a tangled mass of ground-hugging black plants, fleshy bulbous shadows, creepers and fungi, all glistening with moisture. Some of the creepers sported flowers, dark drooping flaccid blooms. No plant grew more than two feet from the ground and there were no woody plants or briars.

The path cut through the growth. Beside it, perhaps a hundred yards beyond the bridge, its base concealed by a thick mass of flowering creepers, stood a great statue of Satan as a satyrlike man-goat clutching the traditional pitchfork in his right hand. The statue burned with smoldering red and black flames.

On the other side of the path, where it must have once stood facing the statue of Satan, was the shattered ruin of what had been a statue of Shiva. Though most of its chest was gone and its right arm was missing it still gripped its trident in the remaining hand. The three-eyed head lay on a pile of rubble at the statue's feet. Body, head, and broken stone all burned with green and white fires.

In front of the statue of Satan lay my father's open coffin. Its exterior had been coated with some glossy resin, as though to waterproof it, and a small squarish electrical device with a large two-pole switch protruding from it had been attached to the right side.

Michael paused a moment, staring down at father, then touched him lightly on the forehead with one black finger and continued on.

Coffins had been arranged in two concentric circles around the central pool. The resin with which they were coated seemed to drink the red-burning shadows. Every coffin had one of the electrical devices I'd first seen on my father's coffin attached to its right side.

Michael walked around the outer circle of coffins until he came to a gap in the arrangement. Leaving the path—I could hear the black vegetation squelching under his feet, sickeningly loud—he walked up to the last coffin on the right-hand side of the gap, lifted its lid and threw it back. The interior had been coated with the same glossy resin as the outside. Michael took the Communion wafer out of his pocket and placed it, still sealed in its plastic sandwich bag, on the floor of the coffin. Then he sat down to wait, a satisfied smile on his face.

Within moments vampires had begun to appear, men and women with Bathory faces returning to shut themselves into their coffins for the day. Some of them came walking up the path or across the black vegetation, others dropped from above as huge bats or swirling mists and only assumed human form after alighting. They came in perfect silence, without conversation or communication among themselves or with Michael before they closed themselves into their coffins.

A dirty gray bat with a wingspread of at least three feet landed in front of Michael. It shifted and changed, became a woman in white standing in a half crouch. She straightened and I could see that she was my Aunt Judith, her face pink and swollen, without trace of the stark beauty that had been hers earlier in the night.

"Did you feel well tonight?" Michael asked.

"Well enough," she said, dismissing him. She took a step towards her coffin, saw the holy wafer in its plastic bag, spun back to face Michael.

"You know why," Michael said. "Not while I still need him."

"Then keep him. But let me return to my coffin. I can feel the dawn."

"No. You disobeyed me."

She took three quick steps towards him but he held up an empty hand and she jerked to a halt.

"I have the power of three dhampires in me now," he said. "You cannot hope to defy me."

"And you'd kill me, one of your own?"

"Yes."

She stared at him a moment, her swollen pink face expressionless, then said, "Then let me return to my coffin and sleep. Let me be dancing with Satan in my dreams when I die. You owe that at least to the blood that we share."

Michael was silent an instant, then he nodded. "Very well." He lifted the Communion wafer out of the coffin and put it back in his pocket. He stepped back and Aunt Judith lay down in her coffin and pulled the lid closed over her.

Michael waited a few moments longer, then threw the switch

attached to the coffin and retreated a few yards. The coffin exploded into white hot flame. In less than a minute all that remained of it was a small pile of ashes.

Michael waited until the last sparks had died away and the vegetation had stopped smoldering, then turned his back on the coffins and took a path leading away from the river towards one of the columns of black flame.

We floated after him, followed him to Dara.

A circle within a five-pointed star had been cut into the bare rock, and at the center of the circle Dara lay naked and unconscious. She was on her back, her head to her side, as if she were asleep. Her skin was smooth and unbruised and I could hear her breathing, slowly but regularly. At each of the circle's five points a hand of glory stood upright. Four of the hands were lit and flaming: the hand I had seen at Carlsbad, each eyeball-tipped finger burning a different color; a black hand clutching a thick black candle which burned with a smoky blue flame; a six-fingered hand burning a sulphurous yellow; and the thumbless hand of an infant or a monkey burning a dull orange. The light from the hands flickered over Dara, pooled on her belly and thighs, in the hollow between her breasts.

One hand of glory was unlit. The palm and thumb were normal but all four of the fingers had been replaced by leathery gray upright cocks.

We were floating just outside the star, perhaps two yards above the stone floor. I tried to swim myself, drag myself down to Dara but I was anchored to the unmoving Naga like a balloon tacked to a wall.

Michael stripped off his clothes and dived into a pool of water to the right of the pentagram. His back and chest were covered with lines of small, long-healed scars. He emerged and dried himself carefully, then dived in again. After seven repetitions he rubbed his body with oil from a bottle on a stone table, then dressed himself in a skintight black garment that left his crotch exposed from the same table.

He faced the pentagram, gestured at it. All the hands of glory except the one with the eyeballs sewn to its fingertips went out. He gestured again and the hand with the leathery cocks for fingers burst into rose-pink flame.

And suddenly the Naga was pulling me back the way we'd come. I tried to resist it but there was no way to drag my floating feet, nothing to clutch at with my immaterial hands. I was dragged back to my room.

My body was still sleeping peacefully. The Naga slipped into my left arm like a hand going into a glove and the sourceless clarity was gone. I twisted around and lay down, feeling that slightest of resistances as I reentered my body and merged with it again.

I jumped up, grabbed the knives and yanked the bolt on the door. I got the door open, then had to grab the doorframe to keep from falling. I made my way down the stairs to the library.

Chapter Nineteen

THERE WAS A FIRE IN THE GREAT FIREPLACE, STACKED oak logs still burning fiercely from the night before. And hanging unsupported within and above the orange-yellow flames, partially obscured by them, was a ball of pale silver powerflame.

Confronted by the two fires, I realized that I had no idea how I was going to get through the hidden door that had to lead through the back of the fireplace to the stairway beyond. The mantelpiece was a smooth heavy slab of unornamented black marble and though three grinning wolf's heads were carved in high relief on either side of the fireplace, I had pushed and pulled and twisted them all often enough as a child to be sure that nothing I could do to them would produce any obvious result.

But perhaps the result only became obvious when you pushed on the rear wall of the fireplace and found a door swinging open; perhaps the only way to open the door was from within the fireplace itself. In either case I'd have to get to the door before I could use it, and I couldn't get to it as long as the logs were still burning in front of it.

I used a pair of brass fire tongs to try to drag the heavy iron grate with its load of burning logs out onto the hearth but was still too weak to move the grate more than an inch or two towards me. I ended up dousing the fire with buckets of water from the laundry room so I could wrestle the logs out of the grate individually.

When the logs had stopped spitting and hissing and the smoke and steam had cleared, I could see that the ball of powerflame was not the pure lunar silver I had thought it but veined with scraggly lines of reddish fire like a bloodshot eyeball. The veins would rise to the surface from somewhere inside the fireball, drift languidly around like strands of bleeding seaweed, then sink back into the interior, only to be replaced by new veins.

There was something purposeful about the way the veins drifted and clumped, as though the configurations they formed reflected in some way an awareness of my presence and movements. I put my hand in the fireplace, moved it slowly closer to the fireball, noticed that the veins seemed to be drifting in towards the point where my hand would have struck the surface.

I pulled my hand away and knelt down to wrestle the still-smoldering logs out onto the hearth, keeping my eyes on the fireball and carefully avoiding any contact with it. I had to catch my breath after each log and I almost passed out while dragging the grate out onto the hearth.

I squirmed in under the fireball, groping through the wet ashes in search of the hidden catch, then used my hands to explore as much of the walls and back as I could reach while keeping clear of the fireball.

Nothing. I wriggled back out and began searching the rest of the room. I ripped up the carpet and checked the floor underneath for loose boards or small holes into which keys could be fitted. I pulled the paintings from the walls and the books from their shelves. I checked the mantelpiece for pressure-sensitive areas, the light switches, desk lamps and electric sockets for hidden circuits. I pushed, pulled, prodded, twisted and banged on the wolves' heads in every way I could think of then crawled back into the fireplace and examined it again, all without finding anything.

I gave up, left the books and paintings heaped on the floor and sat down with the two carving knives in my lap to wait for Michael. But I was so weak from loss of blood and from the aftereffects of the drugs they'd given me that despite everything I could do to keep myself awake I kept drifting off.

"David." I started, opened my eyes. The knives were gone. Michael was sitting watching me from another armchair. I could feel the power in him like the sun on my skin; he blazed with silver and his eyes were cold stars, intolerably brilliant.

Wet footprints led from the fireplace to his chair, but there was nothing to tell me how he'd gotten through the fireplace, nor what he'd done with the knives.

"Where's Dara?" I demanded, trying to summon up the spurious charisma I'd used on the two cops in Provincetown and turn his attention away from the fear I couldn't keep out of my voice. But I was too weak, too sick.

"Below. As you obviously know. But the way you've torn this room apart proves that's just about all you know, so for your sake and mine, to save us both a lot of needless effort, I'm going to tell you some of the things you're going to have to know if you want to stay alive and safe."

He paused an instant, waiting for my response. I told him to go ahead.

"To begin with, there's no way for you or anyone else to force your way down to the caverns. None. Even if you could find your way past this door and its guardians—which you couldn't—you'd find the stairs beyond blocked to you by other guardians you could never pass.

"But you might succeed in getting yourself killed, and that's the last thing I want to have happen to you. Do you remember your encounter with Aunt Judith last night?

"Because of what she did to you—and because she disobeyed me in doing it—I was forced to kill her this morning when she tried to return to her coffin. As I could kill you, David. Or Dara. As all your undead ancestors will try to kill you the moment I quit protecting you from them. But as long as the two of you continue to be useful to me I'll keep you safe. And I may even allow you to live together with relatively little interference from me once I'm convinced that you've come to accept the fact that your lives are mine, and mine alone, to control."

"What happens when you no longer need us?"

"I no longer need you *now*, David. Either of you. I can use you, which is different. And I'll continue to be able to use you as long as I can make you obey me, but I'll never *need* you again."

"Then will you let Dara go? If we can't hurt you and we can't get away from you—"

"No. You *could* hurt me, David. You could even kill me: it's the traditional thing for a Bathory in your position to try to do and you're not as different from the rest of us as you like to think you are. What you can't do is hurt me in any way that won't end up being a lot worse for you than it is for me, and until you realize that, I'd be a fool to do anything that would let you think you had a chance to defy me safely.

"If you try to kill me and fail, you and Dara will be punished—and there, too, the family tradition is long and rich. And if you succeed in killing me—remember, as a dhampire you can only command the vampires of your parents' generation, and through them the preceding generations. You're helpless against a vampire of your own or a succeeding generation. Which means that by killing me you'd be creating a vampire over whom you'd have no control and whose greatest desire would be to add you and Dara to the long list of Bathory vampires."

"What happens if I kill myself?"

"Like Aunt Judith?" He was silent a moment, thinking. "It wouldn't do you any good. There are ways of dealing with the death of a nonreigning dhampire, the same ways father used to deal with Judith. Besides, your first victim would be Dara, not me. Which means that as long as you know that I'm keeping her alive I don't have to be afraid that you'll try to get at me by killing yourself."

"Unless what you do to her is worse than being a vampire."

"Perhaps—but by the time you're ready to make that decision you'll have learned that you're no different from the rest of us, David. You won't hate us any less, but you won't do anything to hurt the family, either."

He paused again, waiting to see if I was going to say anything else, then asked, "Do you have any other questions that need answering? I don't expect you to trust the information I give you but I'd hate to see you do something damaging to yourself or to Dara out of simple ignorance. Or because someone else was misinforming you."

"I don't have any questions at the moment, no, Michael."

"When you do, feel free to ask me."

The librarian found me asleep in the library, where I'd passed out while making a last attempt at finding my way through the hidden door. He pulled me out of the fireplace and shook me awake. I had him bring me some breakfast, then locked myself in my bedroom and went back to sleep.

I was awakened by a loud knocking.

"Who is it?" I asked.

"Nicolae, sir."

I looked out the window, saw that it was still a few hours till dusk. Besides, I had Michael's promise of protection, for whatever it was worth.

"Just a second." I unlocked the door, returned to my bed. "Come in."

"I'm sorry to disturb you, sir, but if you're feeling a bit better now your father's lawyer, a Mr. Abernathy, has been waiting to see you since noon, and since he has to be back in Chicago early tonight—"

I was feeling much better but I was still weak. And very, very hungry.

"Send him in," I said. "And as soon as he leaves have supper brought up to me. A sixteen-ounce steak, rare."

Mr. Abernathy was a tall, prudent-looking man with a rather florid face, a slightly receding chin, and blond hair running to gray. We shook hands and he took a seat, moving his chair close to the bed so we could talk more easily.

"I'm here to discuss your father's will, Mr. Bathory. I've already spoken with the other members of the family. But if you're feeling too sick today I can come back next Monday."

"Thank you, but I don't think that'll be necessary. I've been skimping on food and sleep for a few days and it caught up with me this morning, but I'm fine now."

"Good. In that case, Mr. Bathory, here's a copy of your father's will. Would you like to read it yourself before I go over it with you or would you prefer to have it read to you?"

"Just summarize it, please." I took the heavy manila envelope he'd handed me and put it unopened on the chair. "I'll read it later and get in touch with you by phone or in person if I've got any important questions."

"Well, the will states that you are to receive the sum of one hundred thousand dollars immediately, plus a lifetime income of four thousand dollars a month and two thousand dollars every year on your birthday. In other words, fifty thousand

112

dollars a year. In addition, you have cotenancy of this house, which was left to your brother Michael.

"Your uncles, Peter and Stephen Bathory, are to receive five hundred thousand dollars apiece, and there are various minor provisions for members of your father's household staff. Your brother Michael is to get everything not specifically provided for otherwise.

"However, your father also left three million, five hundred thousand dollars for the construction and maintenance of a temple to the Hindu god Shiva in downtown Chicago. Upon your death whatever money remains in the trust fund set up for you also goes to the temple, as does the total inheritance of any beneficiary attempting to contest this will in court."

"How did the rest of the family react to the last provision?" I asked.

"I couldn't tell what your Uncle Peter's reaction was, but both your Uncle Stephen and your brother were quite upset. Nonetheless, as you'll see when you examine the will for yourself, there's nothing either of them can do about it. I drew the will up myself and to the best of my knowledge it's airtight."

"How much was father's estate worth?"

"The cash and securities amounted to something a little over seventeen million dollars and the house and grounds are worth at least that, though they've yet to be completely appraised. I have the exact figures for the cash and securities here, if you'd like to look at them."

I said no and thanked him. He rose to go.

"There is one last thing—" He took a sealed envelope from the breast pocket of his coat and handed it to me. "Some weeks ago your father entrusted me with this letter. His instructions were to deliver it to you personally and confidentially as soon as possible in the event of his death."

I thanked him again. We shook hands and he left. I locked the door behind him, sat down on the edge of the bed and opened the letter.

Chapter Twenty

Dear David,

By the time you read this I will be dead, a suicide, and you and Dara will be in great danger. I will not try to pretend you owe me anything for having been your father, nor that the hatred you have felt for me for só many years is in any way unjustified, but I ask you to set aside your feelings until you have read this letter and verified the information in it with Dara. For many years both you and Dara have been under my protection but now that I am gone you will have to learn to protect yourselves, and to protect yourselves you will have to understand the dangers facing you.

You are in danger because you are both Bathorys and to survive that danger you will have to understand what it means to be a Bathory. What I tell you here I have learned for myself and I know it to be true, *though it contradicts much that the family has always believed.*

The Bathorys have been for centuries a family of vampires and dhampires. Dhampires are the living children and grandchildren of vampires; under certain conditions they can command their undead ancestors. All of my ancestors are now vampires, and so I am a full dhampire. When I, too, have become a vampire you will become a full dhampire, as will your brother Michael and your sister Dara.

A vampire is a life-thief, a parasite preying on the living. But he is also a dead man, and nothing he can do can alter the fact that he remains a dead man: the life he steals can never replace that which he has lost and for which he hungers. Yet he is incapable of understanding that the life he steals can never satisfy him; he thinks the answer is more, always more, and it is a part of his condition that he can never free himself of this delusion. It is a delusion that the living Bathorys have shared with their undead ancestors since the sixteenth century.

The vampire is no less intelligent than he was in life, but that abstract intelligence is limited by his total inability to imagine or care about anything beyond his present night's hunger. He is incapable of drawing conclusions from his previous nights' failures to satisfy his hunger, equally incapable of imagining the long-term consequences of his actions. Since his hunger is insatiable there is no point at which he can stop himself, and without a living dhampire to restrain him he will always overreach himself and betray himself by killing those whose deaths cannot help but lead others to first suspect his existence, and then to seek him out and destroy him.

Vampire and dhampire form one being, a being both living and dead. The life that the vampire steals from his victims goes to the dhampire, for only the living dhampire can truly assimilate the life the vam-

pire steals. The vampire has at most a brief taste of that stolen life before it drains from him into the dhampire.

The vampire hates the dhampire, since the dhampire takes from the vampire the life which the vampire has stolen to meet his own needs. The vampire believes that if he could drain the dhampire of life and blood he would regain that which he needs and which should be his and his alone; and though the satisfaction he would gain would not outlive the moments it would take for the dhampire's life to pass through and from him, he would at least have freed himself from the one person whose presence continually threatens the illusion upon which his existence as a vampire is based.

But the dhampire is the vampire's only true extension into the world of the living. How can the vampire, who so lusts after life, not love that part of his greater self which is truly alive? So the vampire loves as well as hates the dhampire. But the vampire is empty; he has nothing to give; he can only take; and his love is no different than his hunger.

Since it is the dhampire who receives and benefits from the life that the vampire steals it is in the dhampire's interest that the vampire not be stopped or destroyed. The dhampire can command the vampire, and he uses his power of command to limit the insatiable vampire for their mutual good—and for this, too, the vampire hates the dhampire.

Though the dhampire knows that the vampire hungers for his life and blood above all else, he also knows that whatever vitality the vampire possesses the vampire is in the process of losing to him, so that in a contest between them the vampire can only win by stealth or surprise. And to destroy the vampire would be to destroy the source of his own powers. So the dhampire is caught between fear and greed, as the vampire he fears had been caught before him, and superior though his strengths are, he has the limita-

tions of his living flesh, while the vampire has the strength of his eternal hunger.

A Bathory who is aware that he is a dhampire knows that he will someday become a vampire, so that what is in the best interests of the vampires he rules is also in his own best interest. But seduced by the stolen vitality he derives from his ancestors he is as incapable as they are of comprehending the insatiable futility of their hunger. If he does realize it, he either resigns himself to it, accepting it as the necessary price of his powers and pleasures or, perversely, he embraces it.

Yet in our family—and we are the only surviving vampires and dhampires in the world today, as the result of a process of extermination and intermarriage which has occupied us for hundreds of years—there are two further motives which animate living and dead alike: a sense of destiny and lust for power. For centuries the family has believed that it is its mission and its destiny to rule all mankind as, briefly, it once ruled Wallachia. As deluded as the vampires they ruled, sometimes eagerly awaiting the moment when they, too, could join their ancestors, the Bathory dhampires have sought for centuries to extend their dominion, working slowly, in fear of awakening new knowledge of their existence in a world that has forgotten that vampires are anything more than an outgrown and discarded superstition.

In each generation there is a single male dhampire who commands his undead ancestors. I was the reigning dhampire in my generation. To become a reigning dhampire you must first defeat your undead parents in a contest of will. Then, working through them, you must gain dominion over those vampires formerly controlled by your father, for each reigning dhampire becomes a sort of "focus" for the wills of his ancestors when he dies and becomes himself a vampire.

A dhampire can only control those vampires in his

*parents' and preceding generations; he has no power
over a vampire of his own generation. But there is a
period of forty days between a dhampire's death and
his resurrection as a vampire, and there is a way of
prolonging this period indefinitely. For years after
Judith's suicide I kept her in this state and so pre-
served my security and power, but your brother Michael has released her and though I can protect myself
from any physical attack she may make on me, yet
through her the massed wills of my ancestors are
driving me to suicide.*

*They are driving me to suicide not only because of
the hatred that they have for me, but because they
know me to be their enemy. I have been working to
defeat them, using my knowledge and powers and
authority over them to destroy them. With your help
I can still defeat them.*

*But if you reject my help, you will be the one
defeated and destroyed. Because you will be fighting
not only your family but the power behind that family,
and it is from Satan that the vampire derives the
strength with which he seeks to satisfy his hunger.*

*But I am no longer the willing and devoted servant
of Satan that I was when you learned to hate me. I
have renounced my allegiance to Satan and pledged
myself to Shiva and His consort Kali—or rather, to
the reality that lies within and behind Them.*

*Satan and His other half, His puppet Trinity, are
only one possible manifestation of the Godhead, and
an incomplete, fragmented manifestation in which
Christ and the Christian Heaven exist only as bait,
as lures which Satan uses to trap men within His
system. It is vital that you understand that all gods
are creations of the human mind, forms imposed
on . . .*

There was a knock on the door.
"Yes?" I said.

"Your dinner, sir."

"Leave the tray on the hall table," I said. "I'll get it in a moment."

"Certainly, sir."

I put the letter under my pillow, waited until I could hear his footsteps descending the stairs, then made myself unnoticeable and cautiously unlocked the door. The hall was deserted. I brought the tray back to my bed and gulped down the steak as rapidly as I could cut it into chunks, barely chewing it, eating as though I'd been a carnivore instead of a strict vegetarian the last five years.

I felt much better when I'd finished. I put the tray on one side and returned to the letter.

. . . the reality of the Godhead, but Satanism/Christianity is a particularly flawed and unbalanced creation. It is unable to grasp the reality of the world in the way which the worship of Shiva, who is both creator and destroyer, makes possible. The vampire is a creature, in some ways perhaps the ultimate manifestation, of Satanism/Christianity.

It is only by making a pact with Satan that a vampire gains the powers with which to try to satisfy the hunger for life and blood opened in him by the combined wills of the already existent vampires during the forty days of his transformation. And although I have as yet made no pact with Satan, I know that during that forty days I will lose whatever strength of will might have enabled me to resist Him. Once I have submitted to him I will become your worst enemy.

You and Dara could, perhaps, protect yourselves against me for what remains of your lifetimes. It is fairly easy to keep vampires away: garlic and wild roses of the type that grow here will do it, as will holy water, crucifixes, and any of a number of other religious objects which it has pleased Satan to make efficacious. It is somewhat harder to resist vampires when they have the help of human agents such as your brother Michael and your Uncle Stephen, harder still when they have the help of such persons as your late wife, who was your brother's lover before she was yours. But it is nonetheless conceivable that you and Dara could preserve yourselves from me as long as you live.

And it is not necessarily true that as a dhampire you, David, will become a vampire when you die. Certain conditions, such as death by suicide, a prior pact with Satan, or having been the victim of a vampire, must first be fulfilled. But the conditions of Dara's birth were such that as long as there are vampires to infect her with their hunger there is no way she can escape becoming a vampire.

Your mother, Saraparajni, was a Naga, one of a race of serpent people who live in an underground realm where they worship Shiva—or, rather, That which manifests Itself to human beings as Shiva—in the form of Shesha, Lord of Serpents. It was from your mother that I finally learned to free myself from my hereditary delusions about our family and its destiny.

But when Saraparajni left the Naga realm she became mortal, and soon after you were born she contracted a form of plague from the rats that live in one of the caverns beneath this house. When I realized that her sickness would kill her I arranged her death so as to ensure her rebirth as a vampire.

Vampires, like gods, are creations of the human imagination, and the laws which govern them were determined by the traditions and beliefs of the tiny principalities of what is now Hungary and Romania in which vampirism first appeared. As a result of those beliefs—and specifically, of the distrust and hatred of all foreigners which the people of these principalities felt long before they found themselves the West's shield against the invading Turks—a vampire confined to his coffin for seven years will regain his humanity for five years if he can emerge from his coffin onto the soil of a different country where a different language is spoken.

After Saraparajni's transformation was complete and she had emerged from her coffin a vampire, she allowed me to seal her back into her coffin for the required seven years. She accepted her confinement without protest, without having made any attempt to satisfy her hunger for life and blood: though the fact that she was a Naga did not prevent her from becoming a vampire, it gave her the strength to resist her vampire's hungers in a way that would have been impossible for a human being.

During Saraparajni's five years of renewed human life Dara was conceived and born. Then Saraparajni returned to the Naga realm and so escaped the death that would have been inevitable at the end of her five years of renewed life had she been human, though at the cost of eternal exile from all human realms. But because Saraparajni had been a vampire before Dara was born, Dara will become a vampire when she dies. That is, she will become a vampire if there are other vampires in the world to infect her with their hunger for life and blood.

If there were no vampires to force the transformation on her she would be safe, but it would be fatal to try to save her by killing the vampires who threaten her. A vampire whose body has been destroyed by fire, or who has had a stake driven through his heart is nether dead nor free, but only forced to reincarnate in a new body. By destroying the bodies of your undead ancestors you would not save Dara, but only succeed in thrusting your enemies beyond your reach and hiding them where you could never find them to defeat them. While the reincarnated vampires' new bodies lived, they would be plague vectors, spreading disease and pestilence; when they died, they would again become vampires.

Vampires can be neither killed nor destroyed, but

they can be made to change so that they are no longer vampires. If your undead ancestors can be made to understand that they have been duped by Satan, that the pact that they have made with Him, in which He promised them the means of satisfying their hungers in return for their submission to Him, is void because their hungers are incapable of satisfaction, then they can be freed from their condition. And once they have been freed, you and Dara will be free as well.

The first thing that you must do if they are to be freed is to perform a certain act of sex magic with Dara which will give you control over me and through me over the rest of your ancestors. The rite is necessary because Michael, not you, was my designated heir and he has knowledge and skills which you lack.

The rite must be performed in daylight, in a place of power above ground, preferably somewhere other than here at the family estate, where Michael's knowledge of the power flows could prove dangerous to you.

For four days before the rite is to take place you must abstain from all contact with each other. You must neither see, hear, nor touch each other. During this time you must wear only new clothing, which must be either entirely black or entirely white, and you must change your clothing completely every day. You must bathe seven times a day, the first, third, and fifth times in water to which an ounce or more of salt has been added. On the fourth day you must abstain from all food; on the day of the rite you must abstain from both food and water.

The day before the rite is to be performed one of you should go to the place selected and place a saucer of nitric acid on the ground, where it will begin to evaporate. You should then take a cord eighteen to twenty feet in length and soaked in a mixture containing two parts potassium perchlorate, one part bone charcoal, and two parts oil of garlic, and lay it on *the ground in as near a perfect circle as you can obtain with a single attempt. You should start in the east and continue around clockwise until you are again facing east. Then the ends of the string should be tied together.*

On the morning of the rite you should both rise well before dawn and bathe in fresh water, then put on fresh clothing and go to the site you have prepared. You, David, should approach the circle from the west; Dara should approach it from the east. You must not speak to each other. When you reach the circle remove your clothes and stand facing each other.

When the first rays of the sun touch the circle you should ignite it and step inside it before the fire dies. When the cord has stopped smoking you should begin having sex with each other, lying face to face with your heads to the north.

As the power builds in you visualize me in my coffin. Gradually you will become aware of my thoughts. You must reach out to them and with the aid of the power create, as it were, a vacuum in yourself into which they will be drawn. Once you have my thoughts in your own mind you will feel the urges and cravings that I will be feeling. They will be yours as much as mine. You must master them. I cannot tell you how to master them; for each of us it is a different process. But once you have mastered my cravings in yourself you will have obtained dominion over me and you will then command all the Bathory vampires.

Having gained mastery of me you will seal me in my coffin for the seven-year period. The coffin must be placed in a silver box filled with garlic and wild roses and hidden in a place where there is neither too much power nor any great danger of my discovery by the ignorant.

I will fight you with all my strength; I am no Naga to willingly accept such a fate. I will try to summon our ancestors against you whenever you relax your control over me or become distracted, and you will have to overcome me again and again. Your brother will try to steal mastery of me from you and use me against you: you must keep him from doing so.

As soon as you have my coffin safely sealed in its silver box there is a further rite which must be performed. The preparations and initial stages of this second rite are the same as those of the first, but as soon as you find yourself becoming aware of my thoughts you must visualize me collapsing in on myself until I am a small white ball clinging to the wall of Dara's womb. The ball will wait quiescent until nine months before I am to be freed from my coffin (and remember, I must emerge onto the soil of a foreign country where a foreign language is spoken), then begin to develop into a child. The child will be born at the same instant that I am reborn into the world of men.

The child and I will share one mind, though not one soul. If I am unable to complete my work before my five-year span is over, the child can carry on for me. Unlike me he will never have been defiled by direct contact with Satan, yet he will have all my knowledge of such contact. Even if I fail he will succeed.

But to be able to perform the rites in safety you must be able to protect yourself against the other members of the family. Your brother is a traditional Bathory and your enemy. My brother Peter is not a bad man, but he is weak: he should have been the reigning dhampire of my generation but he abdicated the position to me. He will be of little use to you. Stephen is another traditional Bathory. You may be able to turn his hatred of Michael to your own use but you will never be able to trust him.

Saraparajni cannot leave the Naga realm. Your maternal grandparents are Nagas and share the in-

difference of Shesha to the fates and desires of individuals: though their help would be invaluable, you cannot count on them for aid. You and Dara are half Naga, as is Michael, but I cannot tell you what, if any, value your mixed heritage will be to you.

Beneath this house lies the cavern in which your undead ancestors sleep by day. The entrance is through the fireplace in the library. A ball of fire is always burning in the fireplace but there must be a wood fire in the grate as well before entry is possible.

Inscribe the sigil on the palm of *your left hand, and on the palm of your right hand, the sigil. Stand before the fireplace with your right hand clenched and your left hand open, palm facing the fireplace. Visualize a unicorn and say, "In the name of Amduscias, Duke of Hell, I command you to let me pass." The door to the passageway will open.*

Then you must clench your left hand and show the sigil on your right palm to the flames. Visualize a leopard. Say, "Under the protection of Flauros, Duke of Hell, I pass these flames unharmed." You will feel great pain as you pass through the flames but you will not be harmed in any way.

There are skulls set in niches in the walls of the stairway leading down to the caverns. Each skull is a guardian and to each you must show the sigil on your right hand and say, "In the name of Flauros, Duke of Hell, I command you to take no notice of my passage." Otherwise they will destroy you.

Please show this letter to Dara as soon as possible. When she has read it the rest of the memories I arranged to have taken from her will return, and she will be able to confirm everything I have told you.

Then carry out my instructions immediately, without delay: the two rites must be performed as soon as possible. I ask you this not for my sake, but for your own, and for the sake of all those whom your actions can free.

Gregory Mihnea Bathory

Chapter Twenty-one

IT WAS JUST BEFORE SEVEN. SOON MY ANCESTORS would be rising to greet the night but I didn't dare wait until they were back in their coffins to try to get Dara out of the cavern. I had to act now, while Michael was still convinced that I was too ignorant to be dangerous.

I couldn't trust everything in my father's letter—the way he'd written around his responsibility for Alexandra's death while at the same time trying to justify it proved that he'd been only telling me those things it was in his interest to have me know—but he'd given me what looked like my first real chance to get Dara away from Michael, and if I let the chance slip I might never get another one.

I drew the two sigils on the palms of my hands with a black ball-point pen. Amduscias's sigil was relatively easy to draw but the best I could do at drawing Flauros's sigil with the pen held in my left hand was a crude approximation. I could only hope it was good enough.

I went over the formulas again, then folded the letter and put it in my shirt pocket.

Sometime in my attempts to get through the fireplace I'd lost the clove of garlic I'd had hanging from my neck, but there were more cloves in the room and I had plenty of twine. Still, a garlic necklace seemed little enough protection against the fifty or more vampires whose coffins ringed the lake, and I wasn't sure just how effective my brother's promised protection would be if he wasn't there to enforce it.

There were crucifixes and Communion wafers on the stone tables in the forest at the foot of the stairs. But could I use them effectively? After all, I was no Christian—and I had no proof that what my father had told me about the relationship between Christianity and Satanism was anything but more of his special pleading.

There had been something in the preface of my aunt's second book on the Church's persecution of witches . . . I had it. She'd been talking about the Waldensians or Albigensians, sects against which the Catholic Church had first levied the charges that they'd later used against those they'd accused of being witches and sorcerers: the slaughter of infants, mass orgies, and the like. But the Waldensians (or Albigensians) had believed that the Church's sacraments were useless unless administered by a priest who was himself in a state of grace, to which the Church had responded with the dogma that the sacraments were holy in themselves, not by virtue of the men administering them. So, if I accepted the Church's authority on the matter, crucifixes and wafers should serve me as well as they'd serve a Christian, or a priest.

I put the garlic around my neck, went out to the truck and hid the letter under the rock in the baby cobra's cage, then went back in, and into the library.

The two fires were burning; the librarian was somewhere out of the room, perhaps working in the annex. I stood in front of the fireplace with my right hand clenched to hide its sigil and showed my left palm to the flames.

When I tried to visualize a unicorn I got an unusually vivid picture of a slate-gray beast with white disease splotches, like patches of slime mold, distributed unevenly over its skin. The horn on its forehead had been broken off a few inches from the base.

Speaking slowly and carefully I said, "In the name of Amduscias, Duke of Hell, I command you to let me pass."

I could sense something dry and spiteful, like a malevolent

old woman, protesting my command. I repeated the words. A slab of marble behind the flames swung back and away, revealing the passageway beyond.

I clenched the hand with Amduscias's sigil on it and all sense of the spirit's presence vanished. Showing my right palm to the fire I visualized a leopard.

The leopard's image was somehow wrong, disturbing in a way I could not quite put a name to. I said, "Under the protection of Flauros, Duke of Hell, I pass these flames unharmed."

The fire in the grate flared up and I had an impression of childish laughter. I walked slowly forward, feeling the unnatural heat increase with every step. By the time I was standing on the hearth it was almost unbearable, more like what I would imagine the heat of blast furnace to be than like the heat of a wood fire.

The letter had said that the flames would be agonizingly painful but would not harm me in any way. But if the sigil I'd drawn was too imperfect to make the charm work?

There was only one way I could think of to find out. I thrust my right hand, the one with Flauros's sigil on it, into the flames.

It caught fire. My skin shriveled, went black, split open to reveal the muscles, ligaments, nerves burning like gasoline-soaked rags, beginning to fall from the blackening bone even before I could stop the forward motion of my arm.

I yanked it from the flames and the pain stopped and the charred stump was my hand again, whole and unharmed.

Without letting myself think about what I was doing I showed my open palm to the flames again, then repeated the formula and ran forward.

I slipped on a shifting log and fell sprawling. My flesh ignited, my eyeballs caught fire and burned, were gone, and I knew with a certainty that was worse than the pain that it was hopeless, pointless, to even try to escape, that I would spend the rest of eternity there, burning. But while I was surrendering to the pain my body's reflex action was bringing me blindly to my feet, carrying me staggering out of the flames and through the door at the back of the fireplace. I heard the laughter in my head again as the stone slab swung shut behind me.

I leaned against the cool stone a moment, forced myself on. The steps were slippery, uneven; the air was heavy and hard to breathe, as though it had had to pass through the diseased lungs of some huge animal to get to me. There were long stretches of darkness between the areas lit by the torches burning in their iron holders but the stone pulsed with power and I could see without difficulty.

At intervals skulls with eye sockets glowing the dull red of an almost extinguished fire were set in niches in the walls: seven on the left, six on the right. When I saw the eye sockets of a skull glowing red ahead of me I'd stop, pause a moment to make sure I had the formula right, then show the skull the palm on my right hand and visualize the leopard while repeating, "In the name of Flauros, Duke of Hell, I command you to take no notice of my passage." The fires would die away until after I was past, then flare up again, momentarily bright enough to turn the dark stone of the opposite wall a flickering orange-red.

I had no way of estimating how long it took me to reach the balcony overlooking the cavern. The pillar of flame leaping from the central lake was still red, but everything else below me was a burning silver, the images from my powersight so overwhelming my normal vision that the forest at the base of the stairs looked like nothing so much as a forest of gleaming aluminum Christmas trees.

There were only two other spots of color in the dazzling landscape. The statue of Satan glowed a dark red; the statue of Shiva a soft blue.

I turned to continue my descent, found my way blocked by a seventeen-headed golden king cobra with ruby red eyes. A Naga. About it a blue aura hung. Though it was coiled, long habit in appraising snakes made me estimate its length as between twenty and twenty-five feet.

I held my left arm out to it, showing it the golden Naga on my wrist, but it just hissed at me, its seventeen hoods flaring.

"Let me pass," I told it.

"No," it said. "You may not pass." It's voice was a sibilant whisper, the sounds of the different vowels and consonants coming out of separate mouths before being somehow orchestrated into coherent speech.

"Why?" I asked.

"Because the task your father set for you is impossible and would end in your destruction. Your father could never escape his hunger for personal immortality and his needs contaminated his knowledge."

"Who are you? Are you one of my grandparents?"

"I speak for them."

"Then will you help me?"

"No. I have done what I can by telling you to return to the surface."

I made a move forward but the cobra's hoods flared. "Be warned," it hissed at me. "I will kill you before I let you pass. Return to the surface."

I started to turn away, then turned back and asked, "My ability to make myself unnoticeable. Is that because I'm a dhampire or because I'm half Naga?"

The Naga tasted the air with its forked tongues, remained silent.

I climbed the stairs past the thirteen guardians and came at last to the door at the back of the fireplace. It opened at my command and I was again faced by the roaring flames.

I showed Flauros's sigil and repeated the formula, then retreated, repeated the formula again, and ran forward and leaped through the ball of powerflame onto the burning logs. I had only to step off of them onto the hearth. This time there was no malicious laughter as the door swung shut behind me.

The librarian was oiling his books, though it was long after dark. He hadn't even looked up from his work when I'd come hurtling out of the fireplace.

I used my power to direct his attention to make him believe me when I told him I hadn't been there and he hadn't seen me, but I had no way of eradicating his actual memories and no guarantee that Michael couldn't direct his attention back to what he'd seen as easily as I'd been able to direct it away.

I found Nicolae in the hallway and asked him who was still staying at the house.

"No one, sir. Your brother will be back very late the day after tomorrow, after midnight, I believe he said, and your Uncle Stephen will be back the next morning. But you're the only one here at the moment."

"You're sure?"

"Positive, sir."

I searched the house, found no one. If Michael didn't already know that I'd find a way through the fireplace he'd probably know soon after he got back. My only hope against him was Uncle Stephen.

But I wasn't ready to deal with Uncle Stephen yet. I was

still too ignorant, too easily lied to. I needed more information.

Perhaps I could get it from Uncle Peter.

I got directions to Uncle Peter's forest retreat from Nicolae. It seemed that despite my uncle's reluctance to tell me where he lived, everyone in the house knew how to get there. Nicolae even showed me the best route on a road map.

I suppressed Nicolae's awareness of having told me how to get to Uncle Peter's, loaded the truck with branches of wild rose from the cemetery and with garlic from the kitchen, and left for Pennsylvania.

Chapter Twenty-two

UNCLE PETER LIVED IN THE LAUREL MOUNTAINS, south of Pittsburgh, in an area that had so far escaped development. The last of the dirt roads that Nicolae had indicated to me ended in a locked metal gate with a big TRESPASSERS WILL BE SHOT sign on it. Uncle Peter's property.

I climbed the chain-link fence and followed the road a few hundred yards farther into the woods, to an unlocked garage containing a rusted white station wagon with four flat tires that looked like it hadn't been driven in twenty years. But there was no sign of any path, no matter how overgrown or disguised, leading away from the garage, and after a half-hour or so wasted looking for something better, I began following deer and game trails.

I was still following random game trails when night came. The moon was almost full and wherever the moonlight fell it blotted out the earth's feeble phosphorescence. Any hopes I'd had of locating Uncle Peter's cave by its powerlight soon died: these woods were almost completely devoid of power.

The sun was noon-high again before I saw the smoke of his

fire. I made myself unnoticeable, descended the hill I was on to his clearing.

He was squatting over a fire pit, roasting a piece of meat on a spit. He was barefoot and shirtless, wearing only a mud-stained pair of overalls. His gray hair and beard were matted with grease. I could see some blue smudges on his chest, part of a faded tattoo most of which was hidden by his overalls. He looked old, far older than he was, and when he moved it was with a hesitant jerkiness.

Maintaining my unnoticeability, I crossed the clearing to the cave. His attention never left the piece of meat he was roasting. Inside, the cave had a wood floor, on which three dirty red wool blankets had been spread as a bed. A crucifix in ivory and gold had been wired to the rock over the blankets. There was a fireplace of cemented natural stone, the chimney leading up through the roof, and, facing it, an ordinary pine dresser with an unlit kerosene lantern on it.

The gun rack leaning against one wall contained only three of the four rifles it had been designed to hold. Where the fourth rifle should have been was a silver scourge, the short, thick, ornately carved silver handle tapering slightly, the five lashes braided with silver wire.

I took the cartridges out of the rifles and put them in my pocket, then went back outside. Uncle Peter had finished cooking his meat and was sitting on a log gnawing at it. He was facing half-away from me; what I could see of his back and shoulders was completely covered by puckered scar tissue.

I walked over to him and allowed myself to become noticeable. He didn't notice me. I waved my hands in front of his eyes. Still no response.

"Uncle Peter—," I began. He started violently and dropped his meat but he still didn't see me: I could feel his attention swinging through me, past me and back again, never connecting with me. I picked the meat up out of the dirt and pressed it into his hand. He clutched at it.

"Michael? Michael, is that you?" His voice was higher than I'd remembered, thinner.

"It's David," I said. "What happened to you? Why can't you see me?"

"Did Michael send you?"

I considered saying that he had, decided against it. "No. I

came on my own, because I wanted to talk to you. What happened to your eyes?"

"I can't see now. It happens to me— Go away, David. Please go away. If Michael finds out you're here he'll hurt me."

"Why?"

"I can't tell you why."

"I won't tell Michael anything," I said, reaching out for his awareness, turning it away from his memories, his fears, away from everything he could have used to test the truth of what I was telling him, everything that could have made him doubt me. "You can talk to me, Uncle Peter. I won't do anything to hurt you and I'll keep you safe."

He hunched forward some more, arms tight to his sides, refusing. "No. He'll know that you're here. He has things that watch me all the time, just like Gregory did. He's always watching me."

It was possible: I remembered the albino bats outside our window in Carlsbad, remembered the cave insects crawling over the bodies, in through the dry puckered wounds, of the dead couple on the floor of the cave where I'd found Dara's shoe.

But though Michael might—or might not—have been able to penetrate my unnoticeability himself had he been here, I was sure I could conceal Uncle Peter and myself from anything he could have set here as a spy: Dara and I had had no trouble hiding ourselves from the vampires searching for us the night of my father's funeral. But I didn't dare conceal us until I was sure I could suppress Uncle Peter's memories of what I'd done.

I concentrated on his awareness again, focusing it on my words, away from his fears, bringing it back to what I was saying as I told him again and again that he could trust me, that he was safe with me, that I wanted to help him and protect him.

He finally began nodding, slowly seemed to relax. I wrapped us both in concealment.

He felt it. "What did you do?" he demanded, tensing.

"I made us both invisible," I said. "To protect you, so we could talk together safely."

He nodded again, straightened a little. "You can do that, can't you? I'd forgotten—"

"You can't make yourself invisible?" I asked.

"No, not like that, but your mother, I remember, she could . . . just disappear when she wanted to and you wouldn't even realize she was gone."

"Can Michael make himself invisible too?"

It was the wrong question. I had to soothe him again, detach him from his fears and convince him he could trust me all over again, but this time it was easier and he seemed more relaxed than before when I'd finished.

"Can Michael make himself invisible?" I repeated, testing him.

He ignored the question. "What do you want from me, then? Sex?"

I stared at him. He was gaunt and filthy, trembling, an ugly splotchy-skinned turkey-necked old man with a half-gnawed piece of greasy meat in his hand who looked like he was at least seventy years old.

"What do you mean, sex?" I asked.

"That's what they all wanted. Gregory, Stephen, Michael, even Judith one time, when I was already old. They came to me when they needed power."

"I'm not here for sex," I said, amplifying and repeating it until I was sure he believed me. "I'm just here because I need to know more about the family."

"My memory's bad," he said. "It started to go thirty years ago, when Gregory took the family away from me." He was speaking more easily, as though he was finally beginning to feel comfortable about trusting me. "Father taught me a lot about the family but it's gone now, and Gregory and Stephen never shared their secrets with me."

"Tell me what you can, anyway," I said.

"Only if you'll promise to do something for me in return. I'll help you if you'll help me."

"What kind of help?" I asked cautiously.

"Nothing evil," he assured me quickly. "Some farmers who live near here just had a baby daughter and I want you to protect her tonight."

"Protect her from what?"

"From me. It's not that—" He shook his head, continued unwillingly, "I don't want to hurt her or anything, but I'm a— A virolac. A werewolf. That's why I'm blind now. I'm always blind the day before I change."

He *was* blind, and he'd been perfectly able to see when I'd talked to him the day of the funeral, but— "I'll help her if I can," I said. "If you tell me the truth. But I'll need to know more about you to protect her from you. To begin with, what's a virolac?"

"A werewolf, I guess, but— Look." He undid the brass buttons at the top of his overalls, pulled the denim away so I could see the sigil tattooed on his chest.

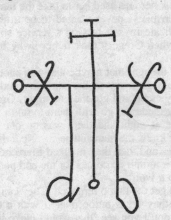

"You see?" he asked. The skin around the tattoo was red, inflamed, as though by some sort of allergic reaction.

"I don't understand," I said. "I can see that that's a sigil, but—explain what it means."

"Marachosias. He's a— A Marquis in Hell. A demon. But when father summoned him he came as a wolf with long black wings. You see, I was two years older than Gregory and father had trained me to replace him as the reigning dhampire when he died, but I wanted to be a priest and when Judith—"

"Start over again, Uncle Peter," I said. "You're going too fast for me. You're a werewolf because your father summoned Marachosias?"

"No, a virolac, because the vampires can take me and make me a vampire like them when I die even if I don't commit suicide or make a pact with Satan."

"Why?"

"Because father knew I didn't want to be a dhampire and

137

so he . . . just before he died he summoned Marachosias and made a pact with him to bind me to the family. Because, you see, I wanted to be a priest, I didn't want to serve Satan, even though I always knew that Satan can do nothing that doesn't serve God's ultimate purposes.

"I was older than Gregory, and when father died I was supposed to use Judith to build up my powers and take control, but Judith refused me and I couldn't make myself force her, so Gregory took her and used her to take the family away from me. It was horrible, I never wanted to be a dhampire, I just wanted to dedicate myself to God's service so I could go to Heaven, but when Gregory took father away from me it was like dying.

"But then I thought that maybe that was enough, that I was free and I could go away to the seminary and learn to be a priest, but they came and got me one night, Gregory and Stephen, and they made me go with them to this . . . tattoo parlor; it was late at night and there was no one else there but they seemed to know the man and he . . . put this on my chest with his needles and then they invoked Marachosias and made it so that once a month he comes for me and possesses me and makes me into a wolf. . . ."

"You could get the tattoo removed. They can do that now."

"No, what they do is tattoo over it with a different color ink, and that, don't you see, that would make it that I'd done it to myself all over again. This way, at least I know it's there and I can't lie to myself and pretend it isn't there; I can see it and fight it. Because that's why it's there, you see, God's testing me, He's giving me a chance to save my soul and not go to Hell. That's why He's given me to Gregory and Stephen and Michael, so He can see if my faith is strong enough to endure the pain and the temptations. I always knew that Gregory and Stephen were using the power they got from me to do evil, but that was the temptation, don't you see, to hate them for that and pretend that the evil wasn't in me too just like it was in them, to not be meek and forgive them for having used me to do evil, but I knew that if I could forgive them and resist the temptation and the pain, if I could let them use me without hating them and without ever honoring or worshiping Satan, then God would free me and save me. . . ."

* * *

Moonrise. Uncle Peter knelt naked on the wooden floor, the silver chains wrapped loosely around his wrists and ankles, praying.

I stood beside him, concealed from him, gripping the heavy silver handle of the scourge, ready to use it as a club if I needed to defend myself. He'd explained that any chains or manacles that he could get around his wrists and ankles were too loose to hold him after his transformation, but that it took him some time to regain control of his altered body after the change, and that during that time I could wrap the chains tight around his new legs and lock them tight.

He jerked and fell forward, began rolling around making snuffling noises. I stayed with him, ready to lock the chains into place as soon as he began his transformation. He got up on his hands and knees, lurched against the wall, and snapped at empty air with his stubby yellow teeth, then collapsed, unconscious.

I knelt by him, chains ready, waiting, but nothing happened. There was no transformation.

Uncle Peter wasn't a werewolf. He was only insane.

Chapter Twenty-three

IT WAS ALMOST DAWN. I'D SPENT THE NIGHT SITTING watching over Uncle Peter, waiting for him to awaken so I could turn him away from all memory of having seen and spoken with me.

As soon as I'd realized that he wasn't going to turn into a wolf, that he wasn't a werewolf or a virolac, and that the sins for which he'd been punishing himself for thirty years had never been committed, were only delusions, I'd tried to pull him from his trance and bring him back to a reality in which he didn't have to be afraid of killing innocent children. But his fantasies meant too much to him, were real to him, perhaps, in a way his waking life could never be, and his awareness was knotted tight to itself in some private region too deep within him for me to reach.

If that had been all that I'd learned—that my ability to direct and control other people's attention was limited, and could be resisted—it would have been enough to justify the trip. But though Uncle Peter's memory was bad—so bad that I was sure that Michael, and perhaps my father before him, had taken from him any memories he might have had which they'd thought could be dangerous to them—and though what little he did remember was colored and distorted by his obsessive need to prove to himself that by surrendering to Satan he was really purifying himself in the eyes of God, I'd still gained some information about the family that I thought I could trust.

While I waited for him to awaken I tried to piece together what I'd learned, sifting and rejecting, making connections between things I knew had to be connected even where Uncle Peter had been unable, or unwilling, to connect them himself.

My father's marriage to my mother had been arranged by his father, but had been planned generations before, as part of the same plan that had made the Bathorys the only surviving vampires and dhampires in the world. The Bathorys had survived because they'd taken those dhampires they could into the family by marriage while destroying the others, and they had hoped to extend their dominion in much the same way to the non-Christian world, where there were powers, such as the Nagas, that could oppose them and their plans. These powers, Uncle Peter explained, were in some way or another that he seemed unable to make clear ultimately not real because they owed allegiance to neither Christ nor Satan, but real or not they had to be dealt with if the family wanted to extend its dominion. So the Bathorys had planned to assimilate those of the non-Christian powers whose strengths and influences they thought they could turn to their benefit.

So father had married Saraparajni, expecting to make of her a willing servant of Satan, and had been himself converted to the worship of Shiva. Why he or the family had expected her to give up her previous beliefs and allegiances was unclear: Uncle Peter, with a missionary zeal worthy of the priest he had hoped to become, seemed to think that a simple exposure to Satanism—and, presumably, to Christianity as well—should have been enough to make its superiority self-evident.

Michael had been six when Saraparajni died and became a vampire, then allowed my father to seal her into her coffin. Father had been training him as a traditional Bathory dhampire, keeping whatever reservations he might have had about the family and its destiny to himself while preparing Michael to succeed him as reigning dhampire, and he continued this training during the seven years Saraparajni remained in her coffin. But after her rebirth he began turning further and further away from the paths he had trained Michael to follow and Michael, abandoned but unwilling to give up the destiny for which he'd been prepared, had gone in secret to Uncle Stephen to obtain the further training which had finally enabled him to force father to commit suicide and which had enabled Michael to take over the family.

Uncle Stephen was a black magician, a necromancer and an expert in the summoning of demons whom Uncle Peter blamed for the sigil on his chest that made him a werewolf. He was also an accomplished sadist, if I could trust the detailed descriptions Uncle Peter gave me of the things he had been forced to submit to whenever Uncle Stephen came to him for power.

And Uncle Peter himself— While waiting for him to awaken I'd been forced to think about him, about who he was and what the family had made of him, about, finally, the way I'd been planning to use him myself—and that, perhaps, was as important as anything else I'd learned.

Because he was too much like me. Like me he'd retreated to the woods, tried to live free from all involvement with, all responsibility for, the family, its actions and its victims. With the result that for thirty years the family had been able to use him at its convenience, and that the responsibility he had tried to refuse but never succeeded in escaping had driven him insane.

And it seemed impossible that it had been coincidence alone that had driven Aunt Judith to her isolated cabin in the Big Sur woods, even less likely that it had been another coincidence that had put Alexandra and me there in her place after she killed herself. We'd all been stored away until needed, like clothes in mothballs, or meat in a meat locker.

Even now—I'd been trying to get Dara to some vaguely imagined place of safety, some quiet secluded retreat where we'd have the leisure to study my father's plans for us at length before attempting to put them into effect. Like Aunt Judith, studying her grimoires in the Big Sur woods until the time came when the only option left her was suicide.

Uncle Peter turned over in his sleep, threw off the blankets I'd put over him. I covered him again, went outside.

Dawn was breaking. I'd have to leave soon to make it back to the house before Michael returned. I'd learned more reasons to be afraid of Uncle Stephen, and that I couldn't trust my ability to direct people's attention to give me the advantage over him that I'd hoped for, but I'd learned nothing that would have enabled me to deal with him from a position of strength or that would have enabled me to avoid the necessity of dealing with him at all. As far as I could tell, he was still the only person who could help me against Michael.

I went back inside the cave. Uncle Peter was awake and putting on his overalls. He smiled when he saw me.

"I didn't kill her! She wasn't there!"

"Tell me about it," I suggested. We walked outside together, sat down on the log by the fire pit.

"As soon as I began to change I sensed danger from you and from the silver you were carrying. It seemed to take me a long time to get control of my body, but it must not have really been very long at all, because while I was struggling for control you seemed to be moving in slow motion. Before you could pull the chains tight and lock me in them I got enough control over myself to slash you in the arm."

There was a half-proud look on his face. "Go on," I said.

"You dropped the scourge and backed away for a moment. I managed to get to my feet before you got your courage up to pick it up again. You threatened me with the scourge and tried to corner me in the cave but I was too fast for you and I ran around you and out into the woods. I ran for hours until I came to my neighbors' farm. They weren't home, but I was filled with my bloodlust and I killed two of their sheep. I might have killed more then, but their dog tried to stop me. He was a lot bigger than I was and a lot heavier, but he was slow and I tore his throat out.

"As soon as I'd killed him and partially satisfied my bloodlust I realized that there was a bitch in heat locked up inside the house. I could smell her. I broke in through a window. She was afraid of me but I snarled at her and she let me mount her anyway. Afterwards I killed her like I'd killed the other dog."

Regret and remembered pleasure fought for control of his voice. Regret finally won. "I'll send them some money," he decided. "I'll have to find out their names somehow."

"You don't know their names?"

"No. The only times I ever see them is when I go to their farm as a wolf. I can't make it that far on foot as a human being."

So they might not even exist. And it was obvious that, hate himself for it as he might, my uncle lived for these once-a-month nights of fantasy. But I still had to try to tell him the truth. I owed it to him in a way. Not because he'd trusted me—I'd forced that trust on him—but because having forced that trust on him, having forced him to believe that I wouldn't hurt him and wanted to help him, I owed it to him to do what I could to alleviate his pain. Otherwise I was no better than Michael or Uncle Stephen.

I didn't expect him to believe me, and before I went back to Illinois I was going to have to turn away any memories he might have retained of what I'd told him, but the information would still be there somewhere in his memory and perhaps someday he'd be able to face it and make use of it.

"Listen," I said. "Let me tell you what I saw you do last night.

"First you fell over and shook for a while. Then you got up on your hands and knees and began acting like a wolf. You weren't a wolf, you were just acting like you thought you were a wolf—"

I told him what I'd seen and what I hadn't seen, that for thirty years the family had been fostering his delusions so as to keep him in a position where he wouldn't dare resist the use they wanted to make of him. I showed him my arm, reminded him of how he'd remembered slashing it. I told him he could go back and live among people again, that he could return to the seminary if he wanted to.

He didn't believe me. I'd known he wouldn't. But at least for the first time in thirty years somebody had told him the truth, and it was there, waiting for him, if he ever wanted it or needed it.

He guided me back to the gate and unlocked it for me. We sat by the road just outside the gate for perhaps an hour while I turned him away from everything I'd told him or showed him or shared with him that could have been dangerous to either one of us to have him remember, then left him there and drove back to Illinois.

Less than five minutes after I'd walked in the door a servant I didn't recognize told me there was a phone call for me.

"Ah, David." Uncle Stephen's voice. "I've just rented a house near the estate and I was hoping you could drop by."

Which meant that he'd been following my movements, or at least had somebody in the house waiting to tell him when I returned.

"I'd very much like to talk to you," I said. "But I don't really feel like driving very far. Could I meet you at, oh, say the Howard Johnson's about three miles from here? In the dining room, in about forty-five minutes?"

I was eating my second cheeseburger when he arrived. He was dressed, as always, in black, and the fluid way he moved made him look almost as much younger than he was as Uncle Peter had looked older: he could have passed for a man in his late thirties.

He sat down next to me and ordered coffee.

"What did you want to discuss?" I asked him.

"I've got an offer to make you, but before I make it I think you should know that I already know that Gregory entrusted a confidential letter for you to his lawyer, and that after reading the letter you were able to pass the guardians and reach the landing above the cavern before you turned back."

"What makes you think so?"

"The whole house is bugged. Microphones, cameras, videotape, all the latest equipment. Installed by Michael at my suggestion."

"Does Michael know yet?"

"Not yet. He won't know until tonight, when he gets back. At which time, I might add, he will also become aware of your successful attempt at hypnotizing two of his servants, and of the fact that you've just returned from a visit to Peter."

He sat smiling, waiting, sipping his coffee, until I said, "You said you had an offer to make me."

"Yes. Because Michael hates me and will be giving me to Gregory as soon as he thinks he's exhausted my usefulness. With you I hope to do better."

"You still haven't told me what you're offering me. Nor what you want from me in return."

"First of all, David, I'm offering to destroy all record of the fact that Abernathy gave you that letter, of your trip to the cavern, and of your hypnosis of Nicolae and Thomas. Plus any other such records that it becomes necessary for me to keep from Michael, such as the record of the phone conversation that brought you here. More generally, I'm offering to do everything in my power to help you and protect you while you rescue Dara, and then make sure that you succeed in displacing Michael and taking his place as the head of the family. In return, I want you to transfer a share of your power over Gregory to me."

"Transfer it how?"

"Sexually, of course. I thought you knew."

Chapter Twenty-four

UNCLE STEPHEN SAT SLENDER AND ELEGANT IN HIS tight-fitting black, watching me. Waiting for my response. His eyes alert and ironic, a cool pale green, his dark hair cut close to his head, the hand gripping the white handle of his coffee cup deeply tanned, long-fingered, immaculate. Smiling. A Renaissance fencing master in clerical disguise.

He terrified me. I had no exaggerated fear of homosexuality—the early experiments at the academy that had convinced me that my interests lay elsewhere had also taught me that homosexuality as such was nothing to be afraid of—but the thought of having sex with Uncle Stephen, of being touched, penetrated, forced to submit to him, threatened me in a way that no physical pain or momentary humiliation could have. Perhaps because of the stories Uncle Peter had told me of his own pain and degradation, of the murdered children he claimed never to have seen but whose existence he'd known to be an essential part of some of the rites in which he'd been forced to participate. Perhaps because I remembered the way Michael had used me to rape Dara, and because of the way I'd recognized the self I had refused to be in him as he used me.

"I'm interested," I said, keeping my clenched hands under the table where he couldn't see them. "Maybe. But you're going to have to give me a lot more information, and a lot more reason to trust you, before I agree to anything."

A slight inclination of his head. "But you don't have much time left before Michael gets back, David. And once he's learned what you've done it'll be too late for me to do anything for you."

I shook my head, managed to smile at him. "No. Have the records destroyed now, before we discuss your offer. As a guarantee of your good faith, and to prove that you really can do the things you claim you can do."

He seemed pleased. "And what guarantee do you offer me of your good faith, David?"

"The fact that I need the help you're offering me as much as you need my help."

"More than I need your help, David. But, fair enough. If you'll excuse me—" He stood, made his way with stiff, almost military grace between the tight-packed tables, where families of six and eight were bolting all the perch they could eat for the special Wednesday-night price, to the pay phone in its half-shell by the door. I could see him dialing, see his lips moving as he spoke into the mouthpiece, but he was too far away for me to hear anything over the restaurant noise.

Which could only mean that Uncle Stephen had somebody on Michael's household staff, probably whomever Michael trusted to monitor the surveillance system. If there really was such a system, and Uncle Stephen hadn't gained his information about me through some other means. But in either case, it was further proof of his deviousness, of the fact that I could never be sure I'd figured out what he was really up to.

The waitress came by and refilled my cup of coffee.

"All right, David," Uncle Stephen said when he sat down across from me again. "You've got your proof of good faith and I'm ready to answer your questions. What do you want me to tell you?"

"How are you going to rescue Dara?"

"I'm not. What I'm going to do is help you rescue her. In two ways. First of all, by providing you with knowledge of a way to reach the cavern which Michael doesn't know about, and which he doesn't have guarded, and by arranging to make sure that he isn't in the cavern himself when you go to rescue her. Secondly, by providing you with the supernatural aid you'll need to free her and escape with her afterwards."

"What kind of supernatural aid?"

"A familiar spirit. Which is to say, a low-ranking demon or imp that's taken the form of a small animal, like a witch's black cat or a toad or a—"

"I know what a familiar is. And that you have to make a pact with Satan to get one."

"Rather, that you have to make a pact with any one of a number of demons to get one. But that, you see, is where I come in: I make the pact, I take the risks and I pledge whatever needs to be pledged, and you get the benefit of the familiar's services."

"And I won't be required to make any sort of pact, explicit or implicit, with any of the demons with which you'll be dealing, including the familiar itself?"

"No. The only explicit pact you'll be required to make is with me and that's what we're in the process of working out right now. As for implicit pacts— The operations I will be undertaking for you will involve the command of demons, true, but since they will not involve the submission of either of us to those demons they could be said to belong to what is traditionally thought of as High, or White, Magic. In any case your soul will not be jeopardized."

"Granting that for the moment, what assurance will I have that you'll live up to your share of our agreement?"

"What good would a share in your dominion over Gregory be if you had none?"

"But the familiar will obey you, not me."

"Yes. But you'll be present at the ceremony in which SUSTUGRIEL grants it to me, and you'll be there when I instruct it to obey you in all things not contrary to our agreement."

"What happens if something goes wrong while I'm trying to rescue Dara?"

"Nothing can go wrong, as long as you follow the familiar's instructions exactly."

"And if it asks me to do something impossible, or I make a mistake?"

"If you fail to follow its instructions you could end up killing yourself in all sorts of unpleasant ways. But you won't have to do anything too difficult, and if you pay attention you shouldn't have any trouble."

I took a sip of coffee, put the cup down. "Do you know why I stopped where I did, there on the landing, instead of continuing the rest of the way on down to the cavern floor instead?"

He was suddenly very still. "No. Why, David?"

"Because there was a Naga at the head of the stairs and it wouldn't let me past."

"Ah." His face lost all expression for a moment, as though he'd gone somewhere else to think. "The only reason the Naga was able to stop you was because you were wearing its token. That thing on your arm. Once you remove it the Naga will lose whatever power it has over you. And you'll have to remove it anyway, at least until you and Dara make it back to the surface, because the spirits with which we'll be dealing have a deadly hatred for Nagas. Michael wouldn't have been able to defeat your father the way he did if the spirits Gregory should have been able to call up hadn't been reluctant to obey him."

It was plausible, and Uncle Stephen had been the one who'd supplied Dara with the ointment that had enabled me to follow the Naga to the cavern that first time, but it was too quick, too glib. For all I knew the Naga on my arm represented the only chance Dara and I would have to ever break free of Uncle Stephen.

"But Michael and I are both half Naga," I said. "So is Dara."

"It doesn't matter. In dealing with spirits the symbol is often far more important than the reality behind it."

"Assume we've made it back to the surface safely," I said. "What happens then?"

"As soon as you've made it back I'll teach you how to take control of Gregory away from Michael, thus fulfilling my half of the bargain."

"And that will involve what? Another rite?"

"In a sense, but one which involves neither demons nor anything else you might find morally repugnant. It's a way of focusing and directing your personal power, nothing more."

"And in return you want what?"

"In return I want your participation—yours alone, David, not Dara's—in an act of sex magic that will join my power to yours in such a way that neither of us can command Gregory without the other's participation and consent. So that to command him you'll have to pass through me, and I through you. Think of a telephone system where each of us acts as operator for the other but where there is no other contact between us. So that you'll never be able to use your influence over Gregory to act against me, and so I'll be able to share in the power that you, as a member of the generation succeeding ours, have to command him. . . ."

When he'd explained the intricacies of the process I asked, "And what, exactly, will this act of sex magic involve?"

"Ritual sex—which is to say, anal intercourse, with you as the passive partner." Again the avuncular smile, the white teeth behind narrow lips. "Plus a ceremonial mingling of our blood, and a certain amount of mutual anger, hatred, fear and physical pain. The last as a result of a scourging, both for purificatory purposes and to obtain the blood we'll need."

"And that's all?"

"Yes. No murdered babies or sacrificed virgins, no castrations or mutilations or unexpected appearances by the Devil. You don't even have to jump up and down on a crucifix and swear to deny Christ forever. Just a lot of formal preparations and ritual acts and words—drawing circles, bathing, chanting the praises of God. That sort of thing."

Which left only the one real question: how much, if any of what he'd told me could I trust, and what could I do if he was lying?

I questioned him for three more hours without catching him in a contradiction or in anything I could be sure was a lie, finally agreed to meet him just before dawn at the house he'd arranged for us to use. I knew that he was lying somewhere, if only by omission, but I'd exhausted every other possibility available to me for rescuing Dara.

As he well knew.

I wrapped the golden Naga in a cloth, then put it with my father's letter in a heavy-duty plastic trash bag which I sealed and buried by the side of the road a short ways from the house where I was to meet Uncle Stephen, close enough so that I could get to it on foot if I had to. I spent the rest of the night driving around trying to think of a way out, or a way to protect myself. Unsuccessfully.

Chapter Twenty-five

THE HOUSE WAS SET BACK FROM THE ROAD, AT THE
end of a long looping potholed gravel driveway, half-hidden
by a small stand of maples. It was an old wooden farmhouse,
two-storied, big, with once-white paint peeling from its narrow-
boarded sides.

Uncle Stephen was waiting for me at the door, wearing a
robe of white linen and a cap of the same material. He put his
finger to his lips, reminding me of the instructions he'd given
me the night before, then motioned me to follow him as he led
me up a single-spiral staircase to a room on the second floor.
He motioned me through the door, closed it behind me.

The room smelled of paint. The ceiling and floor were
Chinese red, the walls white. The room contained a desk, a
straight-backed wooden chair, and a table on which a robe and
cap similar to those Uncle Stephen had worn lay neatly folded.
There was a thick book bound in red leather on the desk: Uncle
Stephen's grimoire, or rather, a copy of it, since he alone could
use the original. The pages alternated red, black, white; the
book lay open to one of the red pages.

An open door in the far wall led to a connecting bathroom,
also painted a spotless white, which contained a huge sunken
bathtub already filled with warm perfumed water. A piece of

parchment had been thumbtacked to the wall above the tub:
the Preparatory Orison. As far as I could tell it was identical
with the Orison I remembered from the copy of the *Grimoire
Verum* in my aunt's collection. I found myself wishing I'd done
more than skim through those grimoires in languages accessible
to me.

But so far, at least, everything had been as Uncle Stephen
had said it would be. I took off my clothes, setting them on
the floor to my right and a little behind me, then read the Orison
from the parchment:

"Lord God Adonai, who hast made man in Thine image and
resemblance out of nothing! I, debased sinner though I am,
beg Thee to deign to bless and sanctify this water, so that it
may be healthy for my body and soul, and that all wrongness
should depart from it.

"Lord God Almighty, all-powerful and ineffable, and who
led Thy people from the Land of Egypt, and has enabled them
to cross the Red Sea with dry feet! Accord me this, that this
water shall purify me of all my sins, so that I may appear
innocent before Thee! *Amen.*"

I lay down in the tub, submerged myself completely, then
rolled over twice before standing to face the wall and read the
Orison aloud a second time.

I stepped from the tub and dried myself with the new white
towel hanging on the rack to my right. Even dry I still smelled
of the perfume that had been in the water: the smell was faintly
sweet, resinous, not unpleasant. When I returned to the first
room and dressed myself in the white robe and cap I found
they smelled of cloves.

I knelt before the desk and read from the grimoire lying
open on it:

"Astachios, Asaach, Ascala, Abdumaabaal, Silat, Anabo-
tas, Felut, Serabilem, Sergen, Gemen, Domol, Dolos: O Lord
My God, Thou who art seated higher than the heavens, Thou
who seeth even unto the depths, I pray that Thou grant unto
me the things which I have in my mind and that I may be
successful in them: through Thee, O Most Puissant and Clement
of Lords, the Eternal and who reigns for ever and ever. *Amen.*"

For the next three days and nights I alternated kneeling to
repeat the prayer with sitting in the chair and studying the
grimoire. I was undergoing what was supposedly a purification:
I neither ate nor drank and I abstained, as best I could from

what the grimoire described as "all sin in thought and deed" while concentrating on my ends: on freeing Dara and taking control of the family away from Michael, on dealing with Uncle Stephen without being deceived, corrupted, enslaved or destroyed.

Much of the material in the grimoire seemed half-familiar: I thought I recognized formulas and procedures from the *Clavicule de Salomon*, the *Lemegeton*, the *Grimoire Verum*, and the *Dragon Rouge*, among others, but my memory wasn't good enough to tell me how exactly the formulas, procedures and diagrams I thought I recognized corresponded with those given in the grimoires I'd read, nor whether any of the operations in Uncle Stephen's grimoire had been altered or misdescribed so as to conceal the fact that their intended ends were other than those stated. Nonetheless I studied the grimoire intently, both because concentration on the ritual was a necessary part of the preparations and because I wanted to know if, and when, Uncle Stephen deviated from the stated rituals.

Uncle Stephen came for me shortly before noon on the fourth day, wearing a robe, cap and slippers of white silk on which various signs similar to that which Uncle Peter had had tattooed on his chest had been embroidered in red. Around his waist he wore a wide belt of what I knew from the grimoire to be lionskin, and he had a bag of the same material slung over his right shoulder. A white thread was tied around the finger of his left hand.

A man I had never seen before followed him into the room. He was pale but healthy-looking, sharp-featured, dressed as I was in a robe of white linen, but in place of my cap he had a paper crown encircled by signs like those on Uncle Stephen's robe. He was carrying a fresh linen robe and cap for me, and a pair of white sandals. The clothing smelled of aloes wood and musk, burnt amber and incense: sweet scents, which would serve to protect me somewhat in what was to follow.

Uncle Stephen changed the water in the tub and added to it an infusion of cinquefoil, the herb appropriate for magical operations ruled by the planet Mercury—as this operation, which would involve both the deception of Michael and the granting of a familiar would be. I didn't like the fact that the operation would be ruled by Mercury but had no choice in the matter.

I repeated the Preparatory Orison and bathed, then repeated it again and dried myself with a fresh towel.

"Now," Uncle Stephen said after I'd finished drying myself, "repeat after me: Through the symbolism of this garment—"

"Through the symbolism of this garment—"

"I take on the protection of safety—"

"I take on the protection of safety—"

"In the power of the All-Highest, ANOOR, AMACOR, AMIDES, THEODONIAS, ANITOR."

"In the power of the All-Highest, ANOOR, AMACOR, AMIDES, THEODONIAS, ANITOR."

"O, ADONAI, cause that my desire shall be accomplished, by virtue of Thy power."

"O, ADONAI, cause that my desire shall be accomplished, by virtue of Thy power."

So far there had been no deviations from the ritual laid out in the grimoire. "From now on," Uncle Stephen said as I was putting on the robe, "say and do nothing whatsoever unless and until I tell you to do so, and then do exactly what I say and only what I say. Your life will depend on following these and subsequent instructions without error. Now, follow me."

His assistant opened the door for us. A narrow strip of white carpet had been laid from the door down the hall and staircase, on through the kitchen and then down a second set of stairs into what must once have been a fairly typical basement rec-reation room, complete with acoustical-tile ceiling, fluorescent lights, knotty pine walls and parquet floor. There were no windows and the fluorescents were unlit: what light there was in the room came from the coals glowing red in two braziers, one in the far right corner, the other in front of the black-draped altar that had been erected against the far wall.

On the altar were the instruments of Uncle Stephen's art, burning silver in the semidarkness: a sheet of parchment, a quill pen, and an inkhorn, small bottles of stone and glass, folded pieces of heavy canvas, batons of blond hazelwood with squiggly characters running their length, an asperger like those used to sprinkle holy water in church services, and knives ranging in size from small letter openers to broadswords, some straight- bladed, some sickle-shaped, one with a blade of corroded bronze and another with both blade and handle of polished wood.

Uncle Stephen chanted some words I couldn't make out over three of the stone bottles on the altar, then handed them to his assistant, who began feeding the powdered contents of one of them to first one, then the other, of the braziers. The braziers began giving off a thick, resinous, overly sweet smoke with something astringent to it but I had no way of knowing if it was, in fact, the perfume the grimoire had specified for operations ruled by the planet Mercury: a mixture of mastic, frankincense, cinquefoil, achates, and the dried and powdered brains of a fox.

Uncle Stephen took the three folded pieces of canvas from the altar and laid them out flat on the floor: the pentacles in which we were to stand while the demon was being invoked. They were round, each rimmed with a thick red circle, with a second circle painted inside the first. Between the concentric circles were painted four six-pointed stars embellished with more squiggly characters and the letters *A*, *L*, and *G*. Each six-pointed star was surrounded by four smaller five-pointed stars. As far as I could tell the three pentacles were identical.

Uncle Stephen motioned me into the pentacle he'd placed to the left of the altar. His assistant had already taken up his place in the pentacle to the far right, from which he continued to feed the brazier in the corner. I hesitated an instant, then stepped into the pentacle.

Once I was standing within the inner circle Uncle Stephen took a small sickle-shaped knife from the altar and, kneeling, carefully cut the outline of the outer circle into the floor, then walked back to the pentacle he'd laid out in front of the altar, by the second brazier, and put the knife down in its center.

He took the asperger from the altar and carefully sprinkled me and the pentacle in which I was standing. I had no more way of knowing whether or not the water had contained the mint, marjoram and rosemary that it was supposed to than I'd had of knowing if the smoke was as the grimoire had specified. If it did, and if everything had been prepared beforehand as it was supposed to be prepared, and assuming that the grimoire itself could be trusted, I would be safe as long as I remained in the pentacle.

Which meant that there was no way I could leave until the ritual had been concluded.

Uncle Stephen picked up the sickle-shaped knife and carefully cut a circle around his assistant's pentacle, then a second circle around the brazier the assistant had been feeding, and connected the two circles with a straight line. He asperged the assistant with water from the same asperger he'd used for me.

He carefully set the asperger and knife down in the center

of his pentacle, then, turning to the altar, took the lancet from it and slashed his little finger, the one with the thread tied to it, with one quick motion, so that the blood spurted freely. He caught the blood in the inkhorn, spilling none of it; when the inkhorn was full he dipped the quill into it and began writing in blood on the parchment. I could see that he was drawing as well as writing, but from where I was standing could make out no details beyond the fact that the main design was diamond-shaped, with words and characters in each of the four corners, and that there was a lens-shaped form in the center.

The instant the quill touched the parchment the room was full of shouts and cries which grew louder as he continued drawing, were joined by the sounds of what might have been some sort of bizarrely distorted military marches.

Still following the ritual as it had been laid out in the grimoire, he pinned the finished design to the left side of his robe. He took two of the hazelwood batons and a small stone bottle and stepped into his pentacle. Kneeling carefully, he put the batons and bottle on the cloth beside him, then took up the sickle-shaped knife and cut the outline of his circle into the floor. He picked up the asperger and asperged himself and his circle, then put it down again and stuck the two batons in his sash and picked up the stone bottle.

In the corner his assistant was still feeding powder to his brazier; now, moving in such a way that only the neck of his bottle protruded beyond the confines of the circle he'd cut into the wood, Uncle Stephen poured the contents of his bottle into his own brazier. Thick smoke, sweet like rotting meat, poured from it, hid the room for an instant. When it thinned I could see Uncle Stephen tracing patterns in the air with one of his batons while he chanted Latin Psalms.

Finally he held the baton steady while he half-sang what I recognized from the grimoire as the invocation to Scrilin, the messenger who would carry his summons to SUSTUGRIEL, the demon he was invoking: *"Helon-tal-varf-pan-heon-mon-onoreum-slemailh-sergeath-clemialh-Agla-Tetragrammator-Casolay!"*

The voices and music were gone, replaced by a silent presence. The fluorescent lights flickered on, burned a violet red. Between Uncle Stephen and the altar an iron ring perhaps five feet across had appeared.

Uncle Stephen tossed the baton he had been holding into

the center of the ring and, taking the second baton from his sash and holding it pointing straight out in front of him chanted the invocation to SUSTUGRIEL: *"Osumry-delmusan-atalsoy-lum-lamintho-colehon-madoin-merloy-domedo-eploym-ibasil crisolay baneil-vermias-slevor-neolma-dorsamot-ilhalva-omor-frangam-beldor-dragin. VENITE, VENITE SUSTUGRIEL!"*

Nothing happened. Uncle Stephen took a thick seal of white wax from his sash and jabbed the pointed end of his baton through it. Holding it high over the brazier he shouted, "I invoke and command thee, O SUSTUGRIEL, by the resplendent and potent Names of your Masters Satanicia and Satanachia, and by the Name of their Master Lucifer, and by the Great and Unparalleled Name of JEHOVAM SABAOTH, our Lord, to come here to this place instanter! Come, from whichever place in the world thou art and give me that which I desire of thee. Come, then, in visible form, come and speak to me pleasantly and without deception, that I may understand thy words!

"I have thy Name and thy Seal, SUSTUGRIEL, and I hold them posed on this wand on which are written the Most Holy and Efficacious Names ADONAI, SABAOTH, and AMIORAM, and this wand I hold over this Fire in which I will destroy thy Name and thy Seal, and thus curse thee to the lowest depths of the Bottomless Pit, to the Circle of Everlasting Burning, unless thou appear to me immediately and in friendship, obedient of my every demand!

"Come, SUSTUGRIEL, through the virtue of the Most Holy and Efficacious Names ADONAI, SABAOTH, AMIORAM!

"Come, SUSTUGRIEL, and appear to me in this Circle of Iron! Come, I invoke and conjure thee in the name of ADONAI!"

He flicked the baton with the wax seal spitted on its tip through the fire and the room screamed, long and horrible.

A headless angel with black velvet-tipped golden wings was standing in the center of the iron ring. Blood and lymph dripped from its severed neck to stain its white robe, pooled on the floor below.

"What do you want from me, Magician?" the figure asked in a sweet, throaty voice that seemed to come from where its head should have been.

"A familiar spirit to do my bidding, SUSTUGRIEL. I bind thee to my services by thy Name and by the power of the All-Living God, ADONAI, TETRAGRAMMATON, PRIME-MATON, ANEXHETON."

"And what do you offer me for my service this time, Stephen Bathory?"

From the bag slung over his shoulder Uncle Stephen brought out a small brown puppy that could have been only a few days from its mother's womb. Its eyes were not yet open and it whimpered sleepily.

Uncle Stephen threw it to SUSTUGRIEL. The demon twisted around and caught it on its severed neck like a circus seal catching a ball on its nose. The puppy sank slowly into the red and yellow wetness. I could still hear it screaming after it had vanished from sight and the flesh had closed over it.

"It is enough, this time. You may have your spirit." SUSTUGRIEL held out its right palm. There was a swelling in the smooth ivory of the palm and something like a segmented gray worm encased in a membrane full of flabby pink jelly burst forth, inched its way out of the sheltering flesh. It lay on the demon's white palm six inches long, glistening, the pink jelly quivering. I could smell it, like a tiny gangrened limb.

SUSTUGRIEL dropped it to the floor, where it twisted and curled helplessly within its flabby sack.

"May I depart now, Magician?" the demon asked in its sweet voice.

Uncle Stephen described a circle in the air with his baton. "Go in peace, SUSTUGRIEL, without harm to man or beast. Leave, then, and be at my disposal whenever I shall call thee again. Leave now, I adjure thee! May there be peace between thee and me forever. Amen."

The demon was gone, and with it the iron ring that had held it contained. The parchment pinned to Uncle Stephen's robe caught fire and burned to ashes without singeing the white silk to which it was pinned.

"You can leave the circle now, David," Uncle Stephen said. "There's no more danger."

His assistant was already climbing the stairs. I hesitated a moment, then stepped out of the circle and walked over to where the demon had been, stooped down to examine the familiar.

The worm inside the quivering jelly looked hard and dry, more like some kind of root than like any sort of animal. At each end it had a tiny cruel half-human, half-reptilian face, the features blurred by the membrane and the never-still jelly but still clear enough for me to know that the thing was a parody of some sort of the Naga that had first taken me to the cavern.

The stench was unbearable. I stood up, backed away.

The thing lay there writhing, quivering, more terrifying than the demon itself had been.

"That's—it?" I demanded. "I thought familiars were black cats and toads, things like that, not—"

"They are." Uncle Stephen's voice was exhausted, wavering. He looked older than Uncle Peter now, feeble, half-dead. "This one just happens to be a worm. But keep away from it for the moment. I'll have to bind it to me before you can make use of it."

He stepped forward, stumbled, caught himself, took a deep breath and said loudly, "Spirit! In the Name of SUSTUGRIEL your Master and by the power of the Compact he has made with me I demand of thee thy Name!"

A deep bass rumbling, impossible to associate with something so small and soft-looking, came from the thing, became speech. "I am Monteleur."

"Monteleur! By the power invested in me by SUSTUGRIEL and by the power of thy Name I bind thee to my service and command thee to obey me at all times and to do no harm to me or mine, either through action or through inaction. I further command thee to cause no harm or unnecessary pain or suffering to David Bathory, he who stands here before thee, and to obey his commands except when they conflict with mine. Do you bind yourself to honor and obey this compact, Monteleur?"

"I bind myself, Master."

"Pick it up, David," Uncle Stephen said. "It can't hurt you now. Hold it against your belly, just above your navel. Disregard the pain. It will be over in a moment."

The rituals outlined in the grimoire had been followed to the letter, the instructions Uncle Stephen had given the familiar had been those upon which we'd agreed. I picked the thing up, held it against my flesh, gritted my teeth to keep from crying out as it burrowed into me. Moments later there was only a fading red mark on my skin to betray the worm's presence within me.

But I knew it was there. The pain had ceased when the flesh closed back over the wound it had made entering me but I could feel it moving around within me and I felt defiled.

Chapter Twenty-six

WE WERE BOTH DRESSED IN BLACK: HEAVY, BLUNT-toed black boots, black denim jeans, thick black wool sweaters, though the day was already hot. A two-seated sports car, dark purple and Italian-looking though of no make I recognized, had been left in the driveway the night before. I followed Uncle Stephen out to it, trying to ignore the worm squirming in my belly while he climbed in, reached over and unlocked the other door for me.

There was a wooden box the size and shape of a large shoebox on the passenger's seat. He handed it to me to hold while he drove.

"What's in this?" It smelled of cinnamon and cloves, with a faint mustiness to it that the stronger odors of the spices almost masked.

"A hand of glory, a very special one. The only one of its kind in the world. It'll put Michael to sleep for as long as you'll need to rescue Dara. I made it from the hand of one of the last vampires we hunted down in Wallachia.

"And Michael won't be able to do anything to protect himself from it?"

161

"No. I arranged to leave certain crucial gaps in his education. He has no idea that anything of the sort exists, or could exist. Do you want to take a look at it?"

I hesitated a moment, suspicious, then said, "Yes."

"Open the box, then. It can't do anyone any harm until it's been lighted, and you'd have Monteleur to protect you in any case."

The hand was shriveled gray skin stretched tight over bone and tendon, a wrinkled claw on a white velvet cushion. I closed the lid.

"How long will it keep Michael asleep?"

"About twenty-four hours. Which gives you far more time than you'll need."

"What about Dara?"

"Monteleur will protect her from its effects in the same way he'll be protecting you."

It took a little over half an hour to get to the estate. Uncle Stephen left me sitting on one of the gravestones at the edge of the cemetery while he drove the rest of the way up to the house to plant the hand where it would be the most effective.

He was back about five minutes later. "Michael's below, but he's unconscious. You won't have any trouble with him."

"You said you'd make sure he wasn't in the cavern."

"That was before I'd decided to use the hand, when there was still some possibility he could be a danger to you." He took an orange nylon backpack from the trunk and strapped it on, then led the way into the woods, following what seemed at first to be just another of the many deer trails that crisscrossed the forest floor. I hung back, staying as far behind him as I could while still keeping him in sight.

The trail dead-ended at a gnarled and tangled wall of intertwined rose bushes at least ten feet tall. Uncle Stephen waited until I'd caught up with him, then pushed his way through the bushes. I followed him through, found myself in a large grassy clearing completely cut off from the surrounding forest by the wall of rose bushes that encircled it. I'd never seen it before, though at one time I'd thought I knew everything there was to know about the forest. At the far end of the clearing, perhaps five yards away, was a single weathered gravestone bearing the name of RADU BATHORY but otherwise blank.

Uncle Stephen took some cloth-wrapped packages from his pack and set them down carefully in the center of the clearing.

Then he took a length of thick black cord, and laid out a circle with it, placing incense braziers from the pack just inside its circumference, one at each of the four points of the compass. He lit the braziers and, stepping back outside the circle, applied the flame from his lighter to the cord. A ring of fire sprang into existence, burning a few inches above the cord without seeming to touch it. The braziers were giving off thick clouds of sour-smelling smoke, almost none of which seemed to be escaping the confines of the circle despite the faint breeze that had made its way through the encircling wall of bushes.

Uncle Stephen took two withered brown things—dry roots, perhaps—from an envelope and held them out to me. As far as I could tell they were identical. I took one from him, waited until he'd chewed and swallowed his before taking mine. It was tough, but unexpectedly sweet.

"Take off your clothes and leave them here outside the circle." He began to undress. He had neither body nor pubic hair and when he'd finished removing his clothes he startled me by peeling off first his eyebrows and then the close-cropped wig I'd always thought to be his natural hair. He was deeply and evenly tanned, scalp as well as body, so thin I could distinguish the individual muscles and tendons. He looked like a man who'd been skinned and then dipped in walnut-brown dye.

He stepped over the ring of fire, looked back at me and gestured me after him. I told myself that nothing he could do to me could be as bad as having the worm in me and took off the rest of my clothes, stepped in after him. The smoke was a greasy fog, hot and rancid, as though made up of thick drops of some ancient cooking oil in atmospheric suspension. The drug was beginning to make me dizzy. I could no longer distinguish Monteleur's thrashing from the churning and twisting of my own bowels and intestines.

Uncle Stephen began chanting, long strings of precisely enunciated nonsense syllables. His shape was shifting, melting, becoming unrecognizable.

He handed me the scourge. I took it, whipped his chest and genitals until the blood flowed. It was mechanical; he wasn't real; I felt nothing.

He held up his hand and said, "Enough," and was Uncle Stephen again as he took the scourge from me and told me to turn my back to him.

I turned, screamed as the braided leather cut into me again and again.

He put the scourge aside and unwrapped a vial full of some heavy aromatic oil. He shook the bottle vigorously before applying it to my back, buttocks and ass, then rubbed himself with it.

"Lie on your stomach with your legs apart," he told me. "Concentrate on the pain you're going to feel, on your sense of being violated, on the fact that you don't know whether or not I'm going to live up to my half of our agreement after I've finished with you. You don't want me fucking you, you hate it, the very touch of me puts you in a rage, makes you so angry you could vomit or kill me right now—"

And then he'd grabbed me, opened me, and I could feel my sphincter muscles tearing as he thrust himself into me. I tried to struggle, to throw him off, but I was too weak, too dizzy, was back in that other clearing on the night of my father's funeral was Dara being raped by Michael in my body while Uncle Stephen thrust the cock that Michael had stolen from me into my ass as I vomited and he held my face down smeared it in the vomit so I couldn't breathe and there was a lead pipe in my hands I was bringing it down on his head in an ecstasy of hatred and loathing, and his broken head was falling away in shards of brittle plastic to reveal the severed neck of an angel with black velvet-tipped wings singing with a sweet throaty voice that had a screaming inside—

And Monteleur's laughter was spasming through me as the familiar sucked the power out of me, bloated itself on the pain and the ecstasy and the loathing. And it was over.

Uncle Stephen pulled himself out of me, left me lying there with the worm twitching in my guts as he walked over to the orange backpack and got two white pills out of a bottle.

"Here." He took one, handed me the other. "This'll counteract the drug I gave you earlier and put you back in shape to go after Dara."

He stood smiling at me while I dressed.

Chapter Twenty-seven

"IT'S BEEN TWO HOURS," UNCLE STEPHEN SAID, handing me the long straight knife in its jeweled silver sheath. "With Monteleur to help you you should be ready by now."

I nodded, glad to have an excuse to look away from him while I attached the sheath to my belt. My back and buttocks still hurt from the scourging and my sphincter muscles felt bruised and torn but the dizziness was gone and I felt well enough to function.

"Good. Monteleur will have taken care of the rest of the pain before you reach the cavern." His voice once again full of its overrich self-mockery, the archnesses and ironies that hid the greater falsehoods. "Remember, don't touch each other and don't speak to each other except through Monteleur. And don't do anything to harm the sexual hand. We'll need it later."

The avuncular smile, the clean white teeth, the eyes their cold startling green in the tanned face. I nodded again, unwilling to speak and let my voice betray me.

He'd explained that if we touched, or even spoke to each other before beginning the final rite we'd need an additional three days of ritual preparation before we could start over, and that during those three days Michael would be able to destroy us. Without Dara's knowledge, the memories she might or might not have regained, I had no way of judging how much of what he'd told me was truth and how much was lies—but what he'd told me was too consistent not only with what I remembered from my aunt's grimoires but with the instructions in my father's letter for me to see any alternative to doing what he had planned for me.

The entrance was under Radu's tombstone. The stone was heavy, far heavier than it looked, and it took all our combined strength to push it aside. Uncle Stephen had explained that the entrance was rarely used, and then only when it was necessary to take a human being or something of similar size below without passing through the house; he'd pointed out the holes, little bigger around than pencils, in the surrounding ground which the vampires themselves used.

Just beyond the entrance was a straight drop of about fifteen feet. Uncle Stephen lowered me on a rope. From there the passage continued level for a while, then angled sharply downward, beginning to twist and coil like some subterranean intestinal tract. The silver-burning rock was slippery with slime molds, chill to the touch; the air hung heavy and fetid.

"To the left." Monteleur's voice was a mocking bass rumble that I felt as much as heard, as though my heart and lungs, stomach, liver and intestines had all become sounding boards for the familiar's voice.

"Now right, and then left again. Now left again, and then down." The passageway had become a labyrinth of narrow twisting tunnels, some so low that I could barely crawl through them. There were deep pits that had to be leaped or skirted, crevices in the walls and ceiling where spiders as big as my head lurked. There were foot-long scorpions and nests of giant ants, pockets of poisonous gases, more pits, false tunnels, deadfalls. Once the way opened out onto a large cavern filled with heaped human and animal skeletons, thousands of bright-eyed rats staring at me from their nests among the silver-shining bones. But with Monteleur to guide and protect me it was easy, too easy, and I passed the traps and guardians unharmed, in no more danger than I would have been had I been strolling through a zoological garden or playing miniature golf.

Even the cavern when we reached it was too bright, too

clean. The pillar of burning blood at the center, the four pillars of black flame ringing it, the drifting clots of shadow—everything burned a brilliant silver, gleamed chrome and antiseptic.

Monteleur guided me along a path that skirted the center, avoided the statues of Shiva and Satan, the vampires in their concentric circles and my father in his open coffin.

"To your right." I turned, saw Dara lying naked in the center of a pentacle cut into the rock beneath her. A pool of water, a huge rectangular fishpond, behind her. Her legs spread, one twisted partially under her, and Michael, wearing his black costume with the crotch cut away, lying sprawled on her, his still erect cock buried in her. They were both unconscious, their breathing slow and regular.

Only two of the hands of glory were burning; Monteleur had taken care of the other three while we were still making our descent. The master hand with the eyeballs sewn to the tips of its fingers, each finger burning with a different flame, controlling Dara in a different way. And the sexual hand, burning rose-red, the leathery-looking cocks rising from the edge of the upright palm like the long necks of those huge clams you find along the beaches in northern Washington.

I laid out the six cloth pentacles Uncle Stephen had given me, forced myself to pause, take a few deep breaths and then check to make sure I had them in the right order. I put the white leather glove Uncle Stephen had given me on my left hand, carefully drew the knife from its sheath with my right. The blade was some sort of silvery alloy, incredibly sharp, inlaid with thousands of tiny gold sigils that caught the light, shimmered, seemed to float just above the white brilliance of the blade.

The master hand, the eyeballs sewn to its fingertips, their gaze focused on Dara. The little finger slightly bent, the skin stained and wrinkled, burning green: Dara's heartbeat, her other involuntary life functions. I held the hand steady, severed the little finger from it with a single blow of the silvery blade, caught it as it fell, its flame extinguished, and put it in the smallest pentacle.

The next finger, burning orange-red: Dara's voluntary muscles. The third finger, the index finger, the flames a rose with darker eddies: her perception of her body and of the world around her. The final finger, a brilliant cobalt blue: her physically based emotions, her anger, her fear, her pleasure and her pain. I severed them all, caught them in my gloved left hand, put them in their pentacles. The eyes sewn to their tips swiveled to watch me as I attacked what remained of the hand.

There was a livid design consisting of three large circles and a number of crosses, arrows, lines and smaller circles burned onto the palm: the sigil of FORNEUS. The thin yellow fluid was eating its way through my glove, beginning to burn the hand with which I held the mutilated hand of glory steady as I carved first a circle around the sigil, and then around that a pentangle, the flesh falling away from the blade like over-cooked stew meat. While I was still cutting the circle the sigil blurred and shifted and something part fish, part reptile, part human looked out at me, tried to reach me before I could complete the design, but Monteleur kept it away from me until at last I cut the last line of the pentangle into the palm and it vanished.

I put the hand in the pentacle Uncle Stephen had provided for it. I realized I'd been holding my breath again, forced myself to exhale.

And suddenly I was seeing Michael and Dara lying there in front of me for the first time, Dara's hips grinding beneath his sprawled unconsciousness as his erect cock writhed and wriggled deeper and deeper into her, a thick purple worm feeding, and yet I could see that they were neither of them moving, that it was I who was moving as the swelling waves of my need beat through me, as I let the knife fall and grabbed Michael by the arm, the black rubber or plastic of his sleeve a confusion of chromed reflections, taut and slippery as raw liver in my hand as I yanked him off and out of her—

A burning, an explosion of fire and agony in my groin and the lust was gone. In its place only shame, and an anger beyond all reason as I straightened, as my hand found the knife, hacked the flaming cocks from their hand of glory and I ground them under my bootheel into the rough stone floor of the cave, smearing the gray pulpy flesh across the darker gray of the floor—

This time the burning went on and on.

"You have violated your compact," Monteleur said when the pain ceased. "My master wanted that hand."

"I lost control." I tried to stand, found I could. I seemed to be undamaged. Dara still lay limp and unmoving in the center of the pentacle. A few feet away from her Michael lay curled around himself in a tight foetal ball.

"What's wrong with her? Why isn't she awake yet?"

"Because she's still under the influence of your uncle's hand. Stand behind her, where she can't see you or speak to you before we've had a chance to warn her. When she begins to awaken mouth the words you want me to say to her. I'll repeat them to her."

I moved around behind her, stood waiting.

"Now," Monteleur said.

"Dara. Don't say anything." Monteleur's voice rumbling from my belly. Dara opened her eyes and tried to sit up, saw me. "Don't try to talk. I'm speaking to you through Monteleur, a familiar spirit, but if we talk to each other directly or touch each other we'll lose any chance we have of escaping and taking dominion of the family away from Michael. But before we can leave we must immerse ourselves seven times each in the pool behind me. Do you understand?"

She nodded. I began taking off my clothes. The sweater ripped some of the scabs on my back open when I tried to pull it off. Dara sat the rest of the way up, stood. Michael lay curled at her feet. She stood looking down at him a moment, then stepped over him and made her way unsteadily to the pool. The leg that had been twisted under her was badly bruised. She hesitated a moment at the water's edge, her back to me, the silver fires of the place glowing on her rich dark shoulders, on her smooth tight buttocks and legs, shining from the hair falling black and thick to her waist.

She shook her head as though to clear it, looked back at me and then took a deep breath and dived in. The pool was not quite the size of a backyard swimming pool, but very deep: I waited until I was sure she'd be able to make it back to the edge without difficulty, then followed her into the water, making sure I kept far enough away from so that there'd be no danger of us brushing against each other by mistake.

Uncle Stephen was waiting for us at the surface. We climbed the rope, Dara first, and then I helped him move the gravestone back over the hole while Dara sat on the grass a few feet away, resting and massaging her leg. Behind her the circle was burning again, enclosing its cloud of thick smoke.

"The ritual part of what the two of you are to do is simple,"

Uncle Stephen said. "You are to rub yourselves with these aromatic oils and enter the circle from opposite directions—you, David, from the west, and you, Dara, from the east. You must find each other within the circle without speaking, and continue to refrain from speaking until the purpose of the rite has been achieved and David has established dominion over your father. Once you have found each other you must lie together with your heads to the north and begin having sex, with David, as the dominant partner, on top, and Dara as the passive, beneath."

I looked at Dara, trying to read her reaction in her face, but could see nothing beyond her exhaustion, her tension and fear.

"As the power builds in you"— he was speaking to me alone now, ignoring Dara—"your father's soul will be drawn to yours. You will find yourself becoming aware of his thoughts, beginning to share with him the transformation he is undergoing. As soon as you feel this beginning you must reach into him and take from him his lusts and his hungers, his needs and the strengths with which he intends to satisfy those needs, and make them your own: you must take the vampire within him and make it a part of yourself before you can command it, and through it, him.

"Remember, also, that you will be facing your brother as well as your father, and that you will have to defeat both of them to establish your dominion. But as long as the hand I've placed in the house continues to burn Michael will remain asleep, so that it will be only the productions of his will, and not that will itself, that you will have to overcome to defeat him."

And your part in this? I wanted to ask as he rubbed first Dara and then me with the proper oils and led us to our places. The smoke was so thick that I couldn't see Dara standing facing me, though she couldn't have been more than a few yards away.

At a signal from Uncle Stephen I stepped over the flames and into the circle. The smoke was aloes and musk, amber and incense, violets and vanilla and cinnamon, complex and exciting, so thick it was almost liquid, yet it was cool against my skin and eyes.

But I was blinded by it nonetheless. Dara and I found each other by touch, stood awkwardly afraid an instant before risking our first embrace.

Holding her at last, feeling her warm smooth oil-slicked flesh against mine, I knew that she was all and everything I had ever wanted, that I could ever want, and yet for a moment I held myself back, still suspicious of Uncle Stephen, still afraid of the worm curled inside me. But hope and desire overcame my fear and we sank down onto the grass and began to make love.

Chapter Twenty-eight

IN DARA'S EMBRACE I FORGOT ALL ELSE, FORGOT THE worm in my belly, forgot that I was engaged in a sexual rite for magical purposes. The spice-scented smoke coiled itself around us, sheltered and hid us as we rediscovered the smoothnesses and softnesses, the unexpected hollows and angularities, of each other's bodies. And as we touched and tasted and held each other, long before I knelt between her legs and she guided me into her, our fears and needs began to slough from us like the clouded skin an emerald tree boa sheds when the time has come to reveal the glittering beauty of the new skin underneath. We were there, with each other, making love: there was no need of anything else.

The power built in us, was us, united us with the living earth and the forest around us. We shared in the jiggling dance of the smoke molecules in the air above us; we drew water up from the roots of the grass on which we lay to satisfy the thirst of its green blades; we quivered in the wind with the trees surrounding us, drifted gently to earth with a falling leaf. And as our union evolved towards ultimate violence, ultimate stillness, we wove more and more of ourselves into the forest and the earth, into the smoke and the wind and the sun.

Monteleur—no longer a worm, but a strange configuration of twisting darknesses—wove itself into the pattern we were creating, were becoming, never a part of it yet always remaining in somehow harmonious counterpoint to it.

Below us, far below us, was the jeweled palace of the sun where the Queen sat in glory on her throne of ivory and as we sank our roots ever deeper into the living earth we could feel its warmth coursing through us, melting the frozen diamonds that covered our eyes and blinded us, opening us to the solar wind—

And we were trapped in the congealed wax of my father's corpse, lying dull and heavy and dead in his coffin as his hungers erupted like a sudden cancer in our lovemaking and we died, broke apart into a David and a Dara struggling to keep themselves from fragmenting even further as they fought against their newborn lust for each other's blood, their terrible need to violence, and then we were Gregory Mihnea Bathory and we were falling through the insatiable dark that his hunger had opened within him, through the endless frozen void and the icy wind that scoured the flesh from his body, gouged it particle by frozen particle from him and whirled it away into the hungry darkness. Soon the naked bone would jut from the crystalline tatters of his flesh, soon the bone itself would be gone, eaten by the wind, and all that would remain of him would be an ever-thinner cloud of ice crystals.

Above me, lost in the dark, was the tiny spot of light that meant rebirth. There, if Satan accepted my submission and lifted me from the knife-edged wind, I would find the blood to warm my frozen soul, to reanimate the life-starved flesh lying limp and heavy in my coffin.

There was no transition. I had been him, had shared his hunger and his pain, now I was there with him, falling with him through the dark and cold.

Or rather, we were there with him, for I shared the body I inhabited with Dara. The right side was male, the left, female, with two sets of genitals crowded side by side between the unmatched legs and one full breast on the left side of the chest. A hermaphrodite. Yet though we shared a single body we were no longer a single being: we no longer shared each other's thoughts, knew each other's feelings.

Then, suddenly, we were fighting my father as he tried to use our body as a steppingstone towards the invisible light overhead. Struggling, a tangled mass of arms and legs, we fell together through the wind.

Through the cold that was not the absence of heat and motion which I had learned about when I studied physics, the cold that stops with absolute zero and the cessation of all motion and change, but was a force sufficient to itself, an elemental will, the enemy of heat and warmth and life and not just its lack. But my father was three weeks dead and I was in a body not my own: it could do me no real damage.

A glowing red potbellied imp, like something from a comic book drawn by a man with little imagination but a truly malicious sense of humor, suddenly appeared in front of me.

"Would you like some help?" it asked in Monteleur's voice.

"Of course," Dara said. It was strange to feel what seemed to be my tongue and mouth moving in response to another's will.

"Will you agree to bind yourself to my service in return?"

"No." This time it was I who answered. The imp vanished.

My father was standing on our shoulders, stretching futilely towards the vanished light. I was supposed to vanquish him in a contest of will of some sort, but he seemed to be in the same situation I was in and, if anything, more terrified by it than I was: he was the one making the futile attempt to climb over us to safety.

"Do you understand what's happening?" I asked Dara, shaping the words and then letting my mouth go lax as I waited for her reply.

"Yes. We're trapped on one level of father's mind. This is a stage all the undead go through during their transformation."

"What do we do?"

"I don't know."

"If we're trapped in his mind, perhaps we can escape by willing ourselves back into our bodies. Try to project yourself back."

I summoned up all my own powers of concentration and tried to visualize myself back in the smoke-filled circle.

"Give up?" Monteleur asked. This time it was a great purple parrot with a huge yellow cock covered with warts and spines.

"No," I said. "I thought you were supposed to be helping me."

"I don't seem to be much help, do I?"

"Monteleur, I command you to help me."

"No. Not unless you bind yourself to my service."

"Why? Is this darkness your idea, or something Uncle Stephen planned for us?"

"No. It's a trap laid for you by your brother. And unless you find your way out of it before he reawakens he'll be able to keep you trapped here forever."

"Go away," I said. The familiar vanished again.

"Was that true?" I asked Dara.

"I don't know. But from what father told me I thought that the only thing involved in taking dominion was a straight contest of will power."

"You're sure? Nothing more?"

"Nothing that I know about."

We continued to fall.

"Perhaps if we can find a way to make love we can generate enough power to do something," I suggested. But our hermaphroditic body wasn't structured so that we could have sex with ourself and the cold so numbed our flesh that we were totally unresponsive to our attempts at cross-body caresses.

Father shifted his weight on our shoulders again. I reached up and hauled him down by the ankle, held him so that we were facing each other, though there was no way I could see him in the darkness.

"What do you want?" he asked. His voice was toneless, hollow yet somehow still as arrogant as it had been when he'd been alive.

"Tell me why you wanted to be on top."

"So that Satan will know I'm doing everything in my power to reach Him and surrender myself to Him." I was holding him so that his face was no more than a few inches from mine but I couldn't feel his breath on my face when he spoke.

Dara was trying to use our mouth. I surrendered it to her. "You've pledged yourself to Satan?"

"I have offered myself to Him but He has not yet accepted me."

"Do you believe him?" I asked Dara.

"I don't know."

"What's in store for you if Satan accepts you?" I asked.

"Blood," my father said. "Satan will send a river of flaming blood streaming down to me when He takes me for His own."

"Why would you want that?" I asked.

"It would bring me back to life."

"You'd still be here, wouldn't you?"

"No. This is death, the space between lives."

"Then Dara and I are dead too?"

"No. You're just here with me. I'm dead."

"What if we drink your blood?" I asked. "Will that get us out of here?"

"Mine?" he asked. "I have no blood."

"And if we drink our own?" Dara asked.

"It wouldn't do any good. You're both already alive. I'm the one who's dead."

"So why are we here?" I asked.

"You came in search of me. You found me dead and now you're trapped here with me."

I waited a moment to see if Dara wanted to use our voice, said, "What you're telling us is that we'll be here until your resurrection."

"Yes."

"And if you were to drink our blood?" Dara asked.

"Then I would be alive and you would both be returned to yourselves."

"He's lying, David."

"Why haven't you tried, then?" I demanded.

He didn't answer. I grabbed his head, forced it back to expose his throat.

"Forgive me if I'm doing you an injustice, father," I said. Then I bit him. It took me a while to rip his throat open, but when I did the blood he'd denied having began to ooze forth in a sluggish stream, thick, cold and bitter.

At first I had to force myself to swallow it. But it was warm inside me, heady and exciting, and as its warmth spread through me the taste changed, became shot through with sweetnesses, like bitter honey.

I drained him, hurled him away from me to float dead and dry forever in the cold and the wind.

And the forest was dark and chill around me, and I was lost. The wind cut through my thin cloak, and the thick branches overhead hid the moon from me, blocked its light as they had blocked the light of the sun during the days I had stumbled, ever hungrier, ever thirstier, in search of the way I had lost.

Ahead of me a clearing, with something bright shining from it. A fountain. I ran towards it, tripped over a gnarled root and picked myself up.

There was only a mirror, tall and narrow, standing upright in the moonlight. I could see myself in it, a child of perhaps ten, my eyes swollen from crying, my cloak ripped where I'd caught it on a branch the night before. Behind me the shadowed forest, the trees with their leafless branches like claws, reaching down out of the sky to rend and tear me.

But the image in the mirror shimmered, rippled, and the dark forest was gone from it, had become a child's bedroom, damask-walled, lit by the silver candelabra the mirror-me held in one hand as he smiled at me and beckoned me in through the mirror.

I stepped forward, felt myself shimmer and ripple as I stepped through into the warmth, and the mirror-me was no longer me but was my twin, my identical twin, and yet she was a girl, pale and delicate and lovely. She lay sleeping on her bed and I stood over her, gazing down on her, smelling the sweet freshness of her skin and hair.

I bent over her, kissed her gently on the lips so as not to waken her, straightened again. She smiled in her sleep, raised her hand to touch her fingertips to her lips, smiled again. And as her hand fell away the ring she wore on it, bright silver and razor-petaled onyx, brushed against the paleness of her throat and opened a soft rose, a bright wet flower, in her skin. I stared at the welling blood, the thick fat trickle creeping down her neck to stain her pale hair and the silken pillow under her with widening brightness as she opened eyes like pale sapphires and laughed up at me, arching her neck in invitation to drink from the flower she had opened for me and me alone.

And yet I drew back from her, confused, the welling richness of her blood burning in my nostrils, in the cracked dryness of my throat, and yet I took another step back, and another, looked away from her and turned to leave.

"David." My father's voice, grave and resonant, with none of the hollowness it had had in the void. I turned back, saw a woman like my Aunt Judith step from the bed onto the floor, saw her become my father.

"You're strong, David, as strong as ever I was in life, as strong as a son of mine should be. But Michael too was strong, and Stephen, and the family cannot tolerate three reigning dhampires. So there is one more contest you must win to gain dominion over me."

"Stephen?" I asked. "Uncle Stephen?"

"Yes."

"This contest. What is it?"

"We must be joined, you and I, body to body, heart to heart, so that the same blood flows through both our bodies."

"And the contest?"

"Only one of us can control our heart. That one will have gained dominion over the other."

"And neither Michael nor Stephen have passed this test?"

"No. It is an ancient thing, rarely used."

We unbuttoned our shirts and took them off. He took a golden knife with a serrated edge from beneath the blood-soaked pillow and cut through the muscles and ribs protecting his chest, lifted them away to expose his naked heart. It did not beat.

He handed me the knife and I did the same thing to myself, finding to my surprise that there was no pain. When my naked pulsating heart was exposed my father moved closer to me and we pressed our hearts together so that the two organs fused.

"I can feel your blood," he said. "The warm blood of a living man, in my veins."

"And I can feel yours in mine," I found myself saying, "crying out for life."

While we spoke we fought for control of the eight-chambered heart we shared. His dead muscles resisted my efforts to spark them into life; my heart beat on despite his efforts to stop it. His thick, unoxygenated blood dulled my brain but I kept on fighting for control, kept on keeping my heart pumping.

At last he conceded defeat. "You have my heart and my life," he told me. I allowed the eight-chambered heart to fission, making sure I retained control over both halves even after they were separated. We put our ribs and severed muscles back in place and waited the few instants it took for them to knit.

"Is that all?" I asked.

"Yes."

He was a too-heavy shadow trapping me in the long narrow corridor in which I was free, where I was the master, the rough-cut stone walls of the corridor also doors, hundreds upon hundreds of locked doors to which I was the key, and I was free to range the corridor, to open any and all of the doors, to close them and keep them closed—

"And I'm the head of the family now? I have dominion over you and all my ancestors?"

"Yes. Michael and Stephen can still command me as long as their commands do not conflict with yours, but you have final and complete dominion."

The walls were doors leading to the souls and selves of my ancestors but it was not yet night and they slept there behind the walls. There, in their coffins in the cavern beneath the house.

"What about Uncle Stephen? How can he be a member of your generation and still have the power to command you?"

"Through you, David. Through you," he said and he smiled. "But why not look inside me and learn the answers to all your questions for yourself?"

I looked into him and I saw. And as my memory returned to me and I knew where and how and why Uncle Stephen had lied to me, knew how he'd used me and what he'd done to me I found myself back in the circle, found myself building to an orgasm it was too late to avoid, but even as I climaxed in an explosion of synesthetic ecstasy I could feel Monteleur twisting and squirming in my belly.

Chapter Twenty-nine

I TRIED TO WRENCH US OUT OF NOTICEABILITY, BUT the worm was there, pinning us to the world. I said, "Dara—" but the worm was in my voice and there was no way I could wrap my words with silence and warn her against Uncle Stephen without letting him know what I knew, nothing I could say to her that he wouldn't hear.

I had to find a way to tell her to make herself unnoticeable and escape. A way to warn her against him that he couldn't tap, so she'd have a chance to get away from him before he realized what she was doing. Until then I'd have to stall him, keep him from realizing that I'd remembered that other time in the forest, when he'd first used me to gain control of father. Hope that his sense of drama, the joy he took in cat and mouse games would give me the time I needed.

I reached through and beyond my father to the dark corridor, tried to find the door that would take me to Dara, but Uncle Stephen was there in the corridor with me now, a watchful shadow, inescapable as the worm even now roiling through the secret darknesses of my body, and though the corridor was mine my body was the worm's and the worm was Uncle Stephen. I would have to find another way to warn her.

It was dark there on the grass, beneath the sheltering smoke, though outside the circle I could sense that it was still bright afternoon. I helped Dara to her feet. She sagged against me, trembling and shivering, too weak to stand without help.

Too weak to escape. Unless I could stall him long enough to give her the time to recover.

"The Naga," she said, then had to pause for breath. "Where is it?"

"Hidden. Somewhere safe." And then, speaking as much to Uncle Stephen as to her: "I had to take it off to come after you. But there's some clothing you can put on outside the circle and you need to rest. Come on, we can talk about things later, when you're feeling better. Right now I just want you to get dressed and lie down until you can stop shivering."

I led her through the spice-scented darkness, helped her over the ring of fire and out into the light.

Uncle Stephen grabbed her by the arm, spun her away from me, and before I could react I was paralyzed, every muscle locked and straining and a pain that went on and on in my belly as he slapped something against her skin, just below her navel, and I smelled again the intolerable stench that I'd first smelled in that basement room where Monteleur had lain twisting and coiling in its envelope of jelly on the parquet floor.

And then Uncle Stephen had let go and she was falling, crumpling, but the worm was still in his other hand, gray like a segmented root in its glistening envelope of yellow-quivering jelly.

The pain in my belly stopped and I could move again.

"Go help your sister to her feet, David." Uncle Stephen's voice was dry, slightly amused, as though nothing had happened. The worm still in his cupped left hand. "There's a dress for her in the backpack. Get dressed, both of you, so we can pay a visit to Michael."

I got the dress out of the backpack—another velvet dress like the one she'd been wearing when I'd first picked her up by the freeway entrance—and helped her on with it.

"And Dara—don't try to make yourself invisible and escape. Because even though Bathomar's refused to enter you I was able to persuade Monteleur, an in-every-way-similar spirit, to take up residence in David. Which means that as soon as you defy me or in any way disobey me, David will suffer for it. And should you succeed in killing me, or if I should die for any reason whatsoever, Monteleur has been instructed to kill David in the slowest and most agonizing way he can devise. Do you understand me, niece?"

"I understand you." Her voice was weak, but level, unfrightened, though she was still trembling, still too weak to stand without my help.

"Good. Understand this, then. I am not overfond of women and I share Bathomar's distaste for Nagas. I tolerate you only for the use I can make of you—and for the ways in which you'll enable me to make better use of Michael and David—and that toleration will cease the moment your usefulness ends.

"And David"— turning back to me—"should it by any chance occur to you that the noble and heroic thing to do now would be to sacrifice yourself in some way or another so as to allow your sister to escape, let me remind you that, one, not only do you have as yet no idea of the nature or extent of the punishment you'd be bringing down on yourself, and on your sister if I recaptured her, but, two, that with your brother's cooperation I'd have no need of your help to recapture her. And I have no need of Monteleur's long experience and malicious imagination to devise for her a long, slow, and very painful death. Do *you* understand me, nephew?"

"Perfectly."

"Then we've laid the basis for what I expect will be a long and successful relationship."

He had us wait for him in the library while we went below to fit Michael with the other familiar. Dara sat with her chair turned away from the fireplace, so she wouldn't have to look at the bloodshot ball of powerflame hanging in it. I pulled my chair up next to hers and sat down beside her.

"How are you feeling?"

"Better. Not good—never good, here—but a little stronger. I'll be all right soon. I just need a while to recover." And then, without moving her lips, in the same sibilant whisper the Naga on the landing had used, "David. Don't let your familiar know you can hear me. It can't hear me, no one without Naga blood could, but with it in you there's no way for you to reply to me without being overheard. So just sit back and look away from me. Try to relax.

"As long as you have the familiar inside you there's no way you can escape, or even try to escape. It can't read your mind but for the most part it doesn't need to—it's aware of everything that goes on in your body, any tension or anger or fear, any words you subvocalize and anything you feel or think to which you have any sort of physical reaction. So it's going to be impossible for you to surprise it: it may not know what you're going to do, but it'll know as soon as you do when you're going to do something.

"And though it's not very intelligent in itself, it will report everything you do and say back to Uncle Stephen. So you can't count on its stupidity, or on fooling it by saying things with double meanings.

"But if you can get it to leave you, even for an instant, you can make yourself unnoticeable and escape. The golden Naga— the one I gave you, that you said you hid—might be enough to force it out of you, if we can just get it on your arm. It comes from Patala, the Naga Realm, and I think that the reason the other familiar refused to enter me was because I'd worn it all my life. But unless you've hidden it here in the house, or just outside, there's no way we can get to it, at least not now. We'll be too closely watched. And any instructions you could give me would lead Uncle Stephen to it first, and he'd destroy it. So in a moment I'm going to ask you a question in my normal voice. Answer yes if the Naga's somewhere you think I can get to it easily, no if it's out of reach."

She was silent a moment, giving me time to think, then asked, "Has it been very long yet, David? Do we have much longer before they get back?"

I shook my head, said, "No. They just left. So we've got a while."

"Good." And whispering again: "Try to think of a way to get it back, or some other way to force Monteleur out of you. But don't try to tell me anything unless I ask you: I have most of my memories back and I know what's safe and what isn't. When Uncle Stephen gets back ask him as many questions as you can get away with about the things you need to know. Not so he'll answer them, but so I'll know what you need to know, and what I should tell you. But be careful. Neither Michael nor Uncle Stephen is at all stupid."

We sat silent a half-hour or so more before she asked me again if I thought they'd be back soon. I said no.

It was almost dark before they emerged from the fireplace. Uncle Stephen motioned Michael to a chair, had us turn to face them.

Michael ignored us completely, sat staring calmly at Uncle Stephen. But though he managed to keep his face expressionless his body was rigid and I could see that his hands were trembling.

"David, Dara, I want you both to observe Michael very carefully tonight," Uncle Stephen said. "I've instructed Bathomar to keep him in some sort of minor pain at all times—a toothache, a backache, cramps, something of the sort. But for ten minutes every four hours Bathomar's been ordered to put him in as close an approximation to absolute agony as he can achieve without damaging Michael physically—unless, that is, I specifically command otherwise. And low-ranking though Bathomar may be, he is still a demon of sorts."

"Why?" I asked.

"Because it amuses me, and because I have a score to settle with him. But also to let the two of you see what will happen to you if you refuse to help me achieve my ends."

"Which are what?"

"To spread vampirism as widely beyond this family as possible, in as short a time as possible. Because, David, unlike your brother I am an idealist. A Satanist, working for my master's eventual triumph.

"You see, David, for generations our family has taken vampirism for our private property, a way of attaining personal immortality granted us and us alone. We have taken Satan, our proper master, for someone we can use. I like to think of vampirism as a disease and of all of us, dhampires as well as vampires, as plague carriers, and yet what have we done over the last few hundred years, we Bathorys? We've hunted down and destroyed all the other vampires in the world, then quarantined ourselves and begun the task of our own self-destruction. Gregory would have destroyed us all if he'd been permitted to, as would you and Dara now if I gave you the chance. While Michael cares for nothing but his personal immortality and has already, ostensibly as a demonstration of his legitimate authority, destroyed my sister Judith, attempted to kill you, and planned to kill me.

"I intend to end all that, to see that vampirism is spread as an end in itself, and not merely as a means of prolonging the lives of a few self-selected individuals. And the three of you are going to do everything possible to help me."

"To help you destroy everything we've worked for over the centuries," Michael said.

"Perhaps. It's a risk I'm willing to take. Which is one of the reasons why I, and not you, Michael, am now head of this family."

"They'll give themselves away as soon as we lose control of them," Michael said. "They'll refuse to file their teeth, leave marks on their victims' throats instead of sucking the blood through the unbroken skin. And then people will know us for what we are and destroy us. That was the price we paid for getting Stoker to write *Dracula* for us, and it's too late to change it."

"Too late for you, Michael. Not for me."

"You had Stoker write *Dracula* for you?" I asked. "Why?"

"For the publicity," Uncle Stephen said. "Because we derive power from mankind's belief in us. Before *Dracula* was published few people outside of Central Europe knew much about vampires or were afraid of us, and their lack of belief kept us weak. But with Stoker's book we were able to capture the imagination of the Christian world, and even part of the non-Christian world—and that without giving people the information they'd need to hunt us down."

"As long as you keep the vampires from giving themselves away," Michael said. "As long as you keep them under control."

"And what about the Nagas?" I asked. "If we're such a threat to you, even Michael, because we're half Naga, what do you intend to do about the *real* Nagas—and for that matter about any other gods or demons or whatever that may not like your ideas?"

"Ah, but you see, all the Powers derive their strength from their worshipers' faith in them, and that faith is dying. The various political ideologies that have replaced the traditional religions of the Far East leave their followers without any sort of supernatural protectors, and the fad for Oriental religions in the West is already giving way to various forms of fanatical Christianity which can only help us. With luck we can hope for new witch hunts, or a second Inquisition, by the end of the century. Judaism and Islam we can live with; their demonologies and infernal hierarchies are compatible with ours. And with atomic weapons we'll be able to wipe out whole populations of believers should any sort of revival of the faiths which oppose us render it necessary."

"But what about Christianity?" I asked. "If Christ still has all those worshipers—"

"But very few of them actually believe in Christ. What they *really* believe in is something very different: that the world and any afterlife which might exist would be too terrible to be endured without the protection and intercession of Christ or someone like Him. And it's that terror, their fear of death and pain and evil—of Satan—that's real, and important. Not their futile attempts to convince themselves that they're not afraid, or that there's nothing to fear."

I thought about that for a moment, said, "Granting that, what do you personally expect to get out of this?"

"For myself, nothing. For Satan, everything. And what He intends is nothing less than the total destruction of all life in the universe. The gods and other supernatural beings, then men and all lesser forms of life, and finally Himself. And when He too is gone the universe will have been swept free of all taint and filth, it will be clean and pure and empty and perfect."

"But Satan won't be there to enjoy its perfection."

"No. So why does He want to destroy Himself? Because His only joy is in destruction. And when all else is gone, what will remain for Him but to destroy Himself?"

"But you yourself will have been destroyed. So, why?"

"For the same reasons. To see it all die, and myself and my Master with it."

Nicolae entered and announced dinner. To Uncle Stephen, not to Michael or myself.

"Dara, David, you won't be eating with us here tonight," Uncle Stephen said as soon as Nicloae was gone. "David, I want you and Dara to take your truck and drive back to your cabin in Big Sur. I arranged to have it taken off the market just after you left it—I'm afraid I gave the real-estate people the impression that I was you when I discussed the matter with them over the phone—and you'll find that I've changed things around a bit."

"Why?" I asked.

"I'm preparing to hold the Grand Sabbat there this year. On

Lammas Day, August first. And getting you and Monteleur ready for the Sabbat happens to be part of the preparations. Which is why I want you and Dara to stop and make love with each other at Carlsbad and the Grand Canyon, just like you did on the way here.

"There's gas in the truck and you can leave in, oh, say about fifteen minutes. As soon as you've had a chance to appreciate Michael's first real experience of Bathomar's talents."

Chapter Thirty

IT WAS LONG PAST MIDNIGHT, AND WE WERE HALF-way across Iowa by the time I realized that Monteleur was manipulating my emotions.

Whenever I happened to glance at the baby cobra in its glove-compartment cage I felt a muted repulsion, a feeling compounded of fear and disgust and even hatred, but so far back in my mind, so attenuated, that had I not been watching myself constantly to make sure I did nothing that would let Monteleur know that Dara was whispering things it couldn't hear to me as I drove, I would have never realized what was being done to me.

And I knew that my feelings were neither spontaneous nor natural because I could visualize the cobra without looking at it and feel nothing, I could remember the bushmaster that had killed Alexandra and the coral snake that had almost killed me and feel nothing, yet as soon as my gaze fell on the cobra in its cage the repulsion was there, and with it the fear that snakes had never before inspired in me.

The next time we stopped for gas I visualized myself feeding the cobra. No reaction: I'd fed it innumerable times before and the thought of doing so again roused no special feelings. But then I turned to Dara and said, "I think the cobra needs to be fed. Would you mind giving me a hand with it?"

Sudden panic blossoming within me. Monteleur had given itself away.

"Are you sure?" Dara asked. "He won't really need to be fed for at least another week or two and he's very nervous from the drive. It would be better to wait until we get to California and he's had a few days to calm down."

I said I'd trust her judgment and my panic subsided. I paid the station attendant for the gas and got back on the highway.

Monteleur was trying to keep me away from my snakes, and trying to keep me from realizing that I was being kept from them. Which could only mean that it was afraid of them, or that there was some way I could use them against it.

Both Monteleur and the other familiar had struck me as in some way parodies of the Naga I'd seen on the stairs. And Bathomar had refused to possess Dara because she was too Naga. So perhaps the familiars' fear of Nagas—if it *was* fear, and not something less comprehensible—extended to their earthly relatives or reflections, the cobras and other serpents.

To free myself from Monteleur I'd have to either force it to leave me, or kill it somehow while it was still inside me. And the only way to try to kill it with the cobra while it was still inside me was to have the snake bite *me* in the hope that the venom in my bloodstream would reach the familiar and kill it before I myself died.

Dying, the worm might try to kill me—and I'd seen how that other one, Bathomar, had been able to hurt Michael without even doing him any real long-term physical damage. It might injure me in its death throes; dead, its alien body might poison me. And I had no real proof that it was vulnerable to the cobra's venom, no real proof in fact, that there was any way a spirit of its nature could be killed at all. Besides which, only the cobra-headed Queen's unexplained intervention, and then Loren's injection of the proper antivenin, had saved me from the coral snake. Though it might have been my Naga blood that had brought the Queen to my aid, that blood alone had provided me with little or no real immunity to the venom, and I had no way of knowing why the Queen had decided to help me that time, nor whether she'd ever do so again.

And finally, to be sure that I'd killed Monteleur I'd have to wait until I was certain that the familiar was dead or beyond recovery before injecting myself with the antivenin, or I'd be saving it along with myself. But for all I knew I'd be dead long before it was.

Trying to force it out of my body looked more promising. If it really was afraid of the cobra I could try to arrange to have the snake threaten to bite me, hoping that the mere fear of being poisoned would be enough to force Monteleur out of me. If that didn't work I'd have to allow myself to be bitten, hoping that Monteleur would leave me soon enough for me to save myself, and without damaging me too badly in its flight.

If it refused to leave me I could hope that the venom would kill it without killing me, or that the Queen would once more come to my rescue.

I spent the next hour or so trying to think of other ways to use the cobra against Monteleur, or to protect myself from the familiar. There weren't any.

"I'm feeling really depressed," I told Dara. "Or not depressed, exactly, but scared and . . . I don't know. Scared. I can't talk about it."

"You want to tell me something, something important, but you can't say anything with Monteleur listening?" Dara whispered.

"Could you get the coke from under the cobra's cage and give me some?" I asked. "I need to cheer myself up, not feel the way I do. Be someone else for a while. You press there—" I pointed—"and the cage swings up and out. The coke's not really in the cage, so you don't have to worry about the cobra."

"You want to tell me something about the cobra? About being scared of the cobra?" She got the coke out and held the spoon three times to each of my nostrils. I thanked her and she put it away again.

We continued on a few more miles while I waited for the exhilaration I was planning to use to mask my reactions from Monteleur to hit. When I felt myself starting to shiver a little I had Dara give me another six spoonfuls, then let my eyes come to rest, as if by accident, on the baby cobra in its cage. I looked away from it as soon as I felt the first stirrings of fear and disgust in the back of my mind.

"I know what it is," I said, forcing myself to look back at the cobra, then looking quickly away from it again. "What I'm afraid of. My snakes. All of them, but especially the cobra. I never used to be afraid of any of them, and I got bitten a lot of times without ever having anything really bad happen to me, but when I think about what happened to me in Chicago, when that snake tried to kill me the same way the other one killed Alexandra, I get scared. Really scared. The way it climbed up on my glove to get at me—"

"You want me to use the cobra to kill Monteleur. How?"

The more I talked about my fear the stronger it became: Monteleur had decided I was ready to accept the feelings it'd been fostering in me for my own. I continued babbling, snorting enormous amounts of coke every twenty minutes or so, talking about everything and anything but returning again and again to the new fears that my snakes, and especially the baby cobra, inspired in me. It took a long time to get all the details of what I wanted Dara to do across to her—the coke cut us off from each other at the same time that it hid my feelings and reactions from Monteleur—but she finally had it right.

"I'm tired," she announced a while later, "and I need to use a bathroom. Can we stop at the next rest area?"

I said yes.

The sun had just broken free of the horizon when we found the rest area. Any truckers who'd been there for the night were already gone and there was only one other car in the lot, a tan station wagon with curtains drawn across its windows. I took a space at the far end of the lot, snorted four more spoons of coke, then used the men's room.

Dara was already back sitting in the truck when I came out. I got in, closed the door, locked it behind me.

"David?" I turned to her, jumped back: the cobra was there in her hands, inches from my face, staring at me while it flicked its forked tongue in my direction, tasting me, deciding what to do to me.

The fear Monteleur had fostered in me, the jangle from the coke, fed each other, merged, became terror. I pulled my arms in tight to my body, tried to shield my face and neck with them as I huddled back against the locked door, screaming at her to take the snake away, not hurt me with it, too terrified to reach up and unlock the door, push it out and open, run.

"Keep your voice down, David," she said, bringing the snake just a little closer to me. It was coiled on her cupped hands now, shiny black, just beginning to raise its head and expose its satiny throat. "There's no reason to be afraid of him, David. You're a Naga, and he's one of your relatives. Just like you, David. Just like you. Nothing to be afraid of."

Her voice soft, almost crooning as she stroked the back of the snake's head with her finger, inched it slowly closer to me. I tried to yell at her to get it away from me but the fear had reached my voice, left me unable to speak. And then Monteleur had taken my mouth and lips from me and I heard myself croaking, "No! No! Put it back! Put it back or I'll hurt you!"

"Nonsense." She was smiling. The cobra was rearing, spreading its hood, starting to sway back and forth. Its lidless eyes staring at me from its shiny black head, the hood extended to its fullest extent, the tongue flicking in and out, in and out.

Monteleur heaved through me, ripping me. My screams caught in my throat, forcing my jaws wider and wider as they tried to force their way out of me. Monteleur bellowing and screaming in my guts, pleading, threatening.

And the cobra struck. There was a burning in my neck where it had bitten me but the pain of its bite was nothing compared to the tearing in my belly, where Monteleur thrashed and screamed and ripped. Yet there was no dizziness or confusion, no muscle cramps or backache, and the burning in my neck soon went away. And in my belly Monteleur quieted and the pain began to diminish.

Monteleur had survived unharmed, and the Queen had not come.

"Nothing of this world can harm me," Monteleur boasted. "Nothing. Your snake hurt me, David, but only a little. Not nearly as much as I can hurt you—"

When I stopped screaming Monteleur had me start driving again. Every few hours it had me pull off to the side of the road for a while.

It was a long way to Carlsbad.

Chapter Thirty-one

I STARTED TO FEEL BETTER WHEN WE REACHED
Carlsbad. Monteleur was still amusing itself with me—a flash
of agony like a knitting needle through my knee, a sudden
ripping in my kidneys, an explosion of molten metal behind
my eyes—but now that we'd reached the caverns I found that
I could take their energies, use them, if not to resist the pain,
then to endure it.

We switchbacked our way down through the singing and
the burning, working our way ever closer to the source, the
center, the pulsing heart.

A ranger in park-service brown was standing talking with
two grandmotherly women in faded dresses just in front of the
fluted drapery stalactites that hid the hole from which the waterfall of suns burst to fall alive and glorious through air and
stone, ranger and old ladies alike. But he was too close; we
would have had to push him aside to climb the cave coral to
the hidden entrance. And Uncle Stephen had forbidden us to
use our "Naga invisibility."

We hung around for a while, pretending to examine another
set of drapery stalactites while we waited for the ranger to

finish his talk and move on to another chamber, but by the time the two old ladies were ready to leave they'd been replaced by a middle-aged couple to whom the ranger was already pointing out the various rock formations with the beam of his flashlight.

"He's not going to leave," I whispered to Monteleur under my breath. "Get him out of here. We can't follow Uncle Stephen's orders with anyone here."

I was suddenly assaulted by an unbearably powerful sulphurous stench, a hot hissing sound like lava fountaining from the rock, flowing towards me; all around me I could hear the rock grinding and splitting, the walls collapsing, men and women screaming in pain and terror. Yet the rock was unmoving beneath my feet.

The ranger yelled, "Earthquake! Make for the entrance!" and sprinted into the next chamber after the two old ladies, while the couple he'd been lecturing turned and ran back past us and out through the King's Palace towards the entrance.

We were alone.

I followed Dara up the rough cave coral to the entrance hole, wriggled after her through the long, low tunnel leading to the caverns' living heart.

The chamber was as I had remembered it: large, vaulted, its far end a pool of chill water from the depths of which bubbles rose to burst with a soft plopping sound.

I could hear the echoing voices of the rangers investigating what had happened in the Queen's Chamber, but where we were there was only stillness, only radiance.

And Monteleur, a dark maggot squirming through the crystal transparency of my flesh.

I took off my sweater and shirt, had removed one sandal and was beginning on the other when a white-hot needle jabbed itself up through the roof of my mouth, pierced my brain. I kept myself from crying out, undid my other sandal.

"No more, Monteleur," Dara said. "Not now, while we're carrying out Uncle Stephen's orders."

"Not now," Monteleur agreed. "Later."

We finished undressing. The stone was cold beneath us, and damp, but the pain was gone and I was free for the instant to forget Monteleur, to forget everything but Dara and the fires singing through us. Not even the knowledge that Uncle Stephen would soon drain us of the power our lovemaking was generating could destroy the joy we found in each other, the excitement and the purity of our union. We made love as slowly, as teasingly and as gently as we could, trying to prolong our freedom and our communion as long as possible, spending hours in caresses which barely brushed each other's skin, in kissing and tasting each other, building with infinite slowness towards union.

The earth's flaming life flowed through us and even as we held ourselves back from total union with each other we were one with it, lifted out of and beyond ourselves on its tides. But all too soon our lovemaking had passed from restraint to union, and our union had impelled us beyond ourselves into the symbolic landscapes of my father's mind.

The cold wind bit into us—we were one body now, but androgynous and complete, rather than clumsily hermaphroditic—but we commanded the void to release us and it was gone. My temptation took on reality around us but we willed the bedroom and the bleeding girl gone and they disappeared. My father cut open his chest, exposed his gray unbeating heart, but we willed him gone and he vanished.

We were standing knee-deep in the salmon-pink mud of an endless swamp plain. Tuberous liver-gray plants floated just below the surface of the scummy pools that covered most of the plain.

We were settling slowly deeper into the mud. Sinking. Dara gave me control. I dragged first one leg, then the other, free. As soon as I quit struggling we began to sink again.

There was no sun. Above us an oversized moon pulsed through changes of phase as though its waxing and waning were the beating of some sickly heart. The air and mud were unbearably hot and a pall of steam hung over everything.

In the distance a single green hill thrust itself up out of the pink mud. I began wading towards it, dragging myself slowly through the sucking mud, skirting the scummy pools.

There was a great gray-green plant like a tendriled melon on the hill's crest. The thing rested on a tangled mass of interwoven roots like gnarled gray worms digging their way into the grassy hillside beneath it, and from somewhere within the tangle four twisting rivulets of blood-red liquid began, to make their way down the hill's steep slopes to the shallow lake which encircled the hill like a carmine moat.

Most of the tendrils drooped listlessly down and across the

hill slope, but at seemingly random intervals one or more of them would leap into the sky and attach themselves to something invisible passing overhead. The attached tendrils would stretch to two or three times their flaccid length, then snap back to their original length and collapse back onto the hill.

We were perhaps five hundred yards from the edge of the lake. I stopped, kept shifting our weight from one leg to the other to keep us from sinking too deeply.

"Dara, before we get any closer, do you know what that thing up ahead is? The hill with the plant on it? Or what it's doing?"

"No. I've never heard about this—level. This reality."

"Can Monteleur follow us here? Or Uncle Stephen?"

"I don't know, but—they're not here now. I can still feel Monteleur back . . . in your body and Uncle Stephen is, is not *with* Monteleur but connected with it somehow even though he's far away from it—"

"Can they overhear us if we talk to each other here?"

"I don't know, but— We're still somewhere inside father's mind. In one of his symbolic landscapes. So they can maybe learn anything we say to each other from him."

"But you're not sure."

"No."

"Can you teach me how to—do the things you can do? The things that I can't. Like how you knew Monteleur and Uncle Stephen weren't here. And anything else, any—"

"Like this?" A whisper, sibilant and silent. "I can't, David. I don't know how."

"Can't you just, I don't know, *show* me or—?"

"I *can't*, David." Still whispering. "I—I'm half Naga, David, and so are you, but that doesn't mean that we're . . . halfway human and halfway Naga, all mixed together; what it means is that we've each got two souls, a Naga soul and a human soul. And before my grandparents gave me to father I lived in the Naga Realm, in Patala, and that's where I learned, where my Naga soul learned, to do—the things you can't do. All I know, all my grandparents let me remember when I left Patala, was how to reach my Naga soul and make use of some of its powers. That's all, and I just know how to do it, not what it really is or how to teach you to do it for yourself."

"Can we go there? Do you know how to get there?"

"No, but—ι can find the way there. But not with Monteleur inside you."

When we reached the lake I bent down, lifted some of the red fluid to our mouth in a cupped hand, tasted it. I had half expected it to be blood, though it had none of the odor I would have expected had it been blood, but it was thin and almost intolerably sweet, like the nectar of some overripe tropical flower.

As soon as the liquid touched our lips the sky was full of naked men and women. They floated slowly through the air above us, their eyes closed, following intricate intertwining trajectories from which they never deviated. When one of the sleepers came too close to the hill one of the tendrils would dart to him, attach itself to him somehow and slowly drain him of his substance, leaving his shriveled and emptied body to continue as before along its predetermined path after the tendril had fallen away.

We circled the hill. As we moved around it a face came into view on the far side of the melonlike plant, a face at least eight feet tall. My father's face. The tendrils began just over his molded eyebrows. His eyes were closed.

"Father," I yelled but he gave no sign that he was aware of me.

"What do we do now?" I asked Dara.

"I don't think we're in any danger from him. Let's climb the hill."

We waded through the red moat, climbed the hill. The grass was slick and the slope was steeper than I'd realized; we made slow progress. The face seemed to take no notice of us.

We had to step over some of the flaccid tendrils, thread our way between others. Each ended in a red-lipped mouth above which was sketched the same simplified caricature of a Bathory face. None of the tendrils tried to attach themselves to us, even when I stumbled over one.

We reached the crest and stood directly in front of my father's blind green face but he still took no notice of us. Around us tendrils continued to leap into the sky, drain their victims, fall back again.

"Father!" I yelled again. His eyes remained shut. I hit him on the chin, the only part of his face I could reach. The flesh was soft, like an overripe tomato, but he still refused to respond.

"What do we do now?" I asked Dara. "He doesn't seem to be conscious at all. Like he really was a vegetable of some sort."

"Perhaps he isn't conscious, not on this level." And then, whispering, "But perhaps if I whisper to him like I'm whispering to you now I can call him to us."

I gave her control of our body. She stared up at the face a moment, without moving our lips or doing anything else I could feel with our shared vocal apparatus, yet soon the gray-green lids hiding my father's eyes lifted, revealing eyes that were pools of green-shot darkness.

"Hello, father," I said when I realized that Dara had returned control of our mouth to me. "What contest must I defeat you in this time?"

His great vegetable lips moved sluggishly. "No contest. I remain defeated."

"Then why are we here?"

"To gain power from me."

"How?"

"By drinking for yourself of that life which I take but which I cannot hold for myself."

"These red streams?"

"Yes."

"And how do we escape from here?"

"You command me to send you back."

"And if Dara had not been able to make you hear her?"

"You would have found a way to make me hear you. Do you wish to return now?"

"Wait," Dara said. "What is this place?"

"A subjective reality."

"Explain it."

"This plant is the undead part of our family; it wore my father's face before it wore mine. The streams that flow from beneath my roots are the lives of those we love. The plain from which this hill rises is the body of Satan, and this hill, this hill is you my children, all three of you."

"Michael is here too?" I demanded.

"Yes."

"How can we communicate with him?" Dara asked.

"You are all three this hill and you are all three within the hill. There is an entrance beneath my roots, to the left of the spring from which the streams flow."

A sloping tunnel led into the hill. It was tight and twisty, slimy-walled; we had to wriggle through it on our belly.

Inside the hill three faceless stone figures, two male and

one female, sat around a fire fed by drops of the sweet red liquid that fell from the roof overhead. Within the flames a tiny red figure lay in an open coffin: my father.

One figure must have been Michael; the other two were us. None of them moved or gave any other indication of life or awareness. I couldn't even tell which of the two male figures was me.

"Michael," I said. "Dara." And then, "David."

There was no sign of any kind of response. The figures remained immobile, lifeless stone.

"Can you whisper to them, make them hear you like you made father hear you?" I asked Dara.

"I'll try," she said.

"Michael," the flames whispered with my voice, "we need your help." The words were those I would have spoken but had not willed their utterance.

"We're all in this together," the flames insisted in Dara's voice. "The three of us. We won't hold what you tried to do to us against you."

"What do you want me to do for you? And what can you offer me in exchange?" Michael's voice asked.

"We offer you our combined strengths, and the chance to awaken your Naga powers. We offer you the help that Dara, the only one of us who is still free, can give you," my voice whispered.

"We offer you sanctuary in Patala, your ancestral home, if you can help us reach it," Dara's voice continued.

"What do you want from me?" Michael's voice repeated.

"We need knowledge, knowledge of Uncle Stephen, of SUSTUGRIEL and his familiars, knowledge of our own dhampire's powers and weaknesses. We need the bracelet in the form of a Naga which David hid near the house and which only you can find for us," Dara's voice whispered.

"I have no help to give you," the flames whispered back. "The bracelet has been destroyed and what knowledge I have I will keep for my own use. There is no point in further conversation."

The flames were silent once more. The stone figures had not moved. We crawled back out, paused a moment to drink from one of the twisting streams.

"Send us back," I told my father.

Chapter Thirty-two

WE WAITED UNTIL THE SUN WAS GONE AND THE LAST light fading from the sky before leaving Indian Gardens: we wanted to make sure no one saw us when the time came to leave the path and climb the loose rock to the cave.

The cave was as I had remembered it, elfin, beautiful, shimmering. We unrolled our sleeping bags and spread them out.

There was a last moment of utter agony as I finished undressing, and then I was free. Free until we returned to our bodies and Monteleur drained us as he had drained us at Carlsbad.

We tried to hold ourselves back as long as we could, keep to our separate selves, but it could have been only a few hours at most before the walls separating us from each other went down and we met and merged, melted into the living energies surrounding us. Only to be wrenched from our joy, find our androgynous body once again standing knee-deep in the salmon-gray mud.

Dara gave me control and we started for the hill.

"Is Monteleur here, Dara? Or Uncle Stephen?"

"I don't think so." Her sibilant whisper. "And father's still not conscious of our presence here yet. But they still might be able to listen in on us."

"What about Michael?"

"I don't know. He's here, under the hill, just like we are, and he's half Naga, but I don't know if he's conscious of being here, or if he can hear us out here away from the cave."

"We'll have to risk it. I've been thinking about what you were telling me. The last time. Where is it, exactly, Patala? And is there any way we can get there?"

"It's within the earth, under it, and beneath the ocean, but— It isn't anywhere, exactly, or not any one place. When I lived there we could, I remember, look out and see, see almost anything, but now— When they took me away to live with father we just walked through the gates and then walked a little longer, five minutes maybe, or a half-hour, through some sunny fields full of wheat, perhaps, or something like wheat, and then we walked into the shadow of a tree, and then down through a passage beneath its roots into the cavern beneath the house. But after they went away and left me with father I tried to find my way back and I never could, not even when they'd come to visit him and I'd try to follow them.* . . ."

"What about them? Our grandparents, or even the Queen I told you about, the one who saved me from the coral snake? Is there any way to get through to them, maybe get them to help us?"

"No. I don't remember anything about a Queen, but— They don't care. Or, no, they care, they care more than anyone, but it's not like— They don't do anything, or try to stop anything. That first time, when they gave me to father, they just stood there all beautiful and peaceful and smiling while he made me watch one of the vampires—his father, I think it was, or maybe his grandfather—kill a girl not much older than I was, and then he gave me to the other vampires to play with, not hurt, he stayed there and made sure they didn't hurt me, but they were all around me, staring at me and touching my face and all over my body and telling me how much they loved me and wanted me and wanted me to be like them— And *they* just stood there watching, they didn't do anything to try to save the girl, they didn't care how horrible it was for me, how frightened I was, or— But before they left me alone grandfather took one of the—serpents—from his . . . aura and gave it to me to wear on my arm—"

"And Uncle Stephen found it where I hid it and destroyed it. But you don't have any other way to find them, or—I don't know. Let them know you need their help."

"No. I tried. All those years, even with the . . . bracelet I tried to talk to them, get them to come back for me and take me away but they never did."

I would have held her, kissed her, done what I could to reassure her if we'd been in our own bodies. Here, there was nothing I could do. We waded the moat, began to climb the hill. Just before we reached the crest Dara had me kneel and drink from one of the streams.

"More, David. We may need the strength it gives us."

I swallowed more and had started to straighten when an idea struck me. I scooped some of the red liquid up in our cupped hands, climbed the rest of the way to the crest of the hill and splashed it on the green face. The face opened its eyes, stared down at me.

"How do we get to the next level?" I asked.

"There are no further levels," he said. "From here there is only return. Return to your own bodies, or to the bodies of those others who are joined in me."

"Which others? Michael, Uncle Stephen, the vampires?"

"Your ancestors. Those already joined in the communion of which I am the nexus."

"How would I return to one of their bodies—to my grandfather's, say? And what would it involve?"

"I would merge you with one of them. You would be passive, a passenger only, experiencing what your grandfather experienced without awareness of yourself."

"And how would I get back?"

"I would bring you back."

"And what would happen to this body while I was gone?"

"It would remain here."

"I don't trust him with our untenanted body," Dara whispered, "not even here. But perhaps it would be worth the risk if only one of us were to go while the other stayed here, in this body."

I tried to look into him, enter into his consciousness and find the passage whose walls were doors leading to my ancestors' souls, as I'd done when I'd first defeated him and obtained dominion over him, but was unable to find it. Perhaps it didn't exist on this level, or existed in a form I couldn't recognize.

Yet for all his impenetrability I still had dominion. "I'll go," I said, "if you're sure you'll be safe here."

"I'll be safe."

"Put me in my grandfather," I said. "Dara will stay here, in this body, to command you until I return. Bring me back here at dawn."

And I was Mihnea Bathory, beating wings of furred membrane high above the deserted streets of a small town. It was sometime after midnight. I had no awareness of myself as David Bathory. I was Mihnea.

My thirst burned within me, made me shiver with rage even as I flew, though I had drunk the blood of two young girls tonight. But I had not drunk deeply enough to satisfy my need, drunk them to death and beyond, till they were emptied and I could fill their emptiness with my love, make of them my other selves and share with them the love they felt for those they had cherished among the living. And they had been only strangers, my love for them only brief and trivial, their blood not that that I needed, that of Stephen, Peter, Michael, David, Dara.

Suddenly, there below me, at the edge of town, walking across the only bridge to the tiny island in the artificial lake that was this town's answer to the monotony of its countryside, I saw a girl crying softly to herself. She was thin and without beauty, but her tears made her infinitely desirable.

I swooped down at her from behind, coming so close to her head that she felt the wind of my passage stir her long hair. She looked up, startled, saw me climbing, my black skeletal wings clearly visible as I flew in front of the moon, wheeled, dived down at her again, blotting out the moon completely, and then halted, hovered just above her in a flurry of hairy wings, so close she could see the red fire in my eyes, smell my rank odor. She screamed, began to run. I climbed back into the sky, let her go perhaps a hundred yards, halfway across the island, then swooped down in front of her again, letting one of my wing tips brush her shoulder. She tried to turn back, stumbled, then picked herself up and ran for the bridge, but I was already there, hovering in front of it, red eyes gleaming.

I ran her until she collapsed, hysterical and sobbing, then came to ground on the other side of the bridge and resumed human form. I was dressed, as always, in clerical black, with only my unorthodox crucifix to betray my imposture.

She heard my footsteps on the bridge, heaved herself up off the ground, prepared for a last desperate attempt at flight, but the moonlight gleamed on my clerical collar and when she recognized me for a priest she collapsed once more, still sobbing, but this time with relief.

"What's wrong, child?" I asked, helping her to her feet.

"Thank God you're here, Father! I'm a, a Lutheran, but— Thank God you're here!"

"Why?" I asked. "What's wrong? Is it something I can help you with?"

"There's a giant bat—" She stopped, realizing for the first time how impossible her story was, then went on defiantly, "—a giant bat chasing me. It wouldn't let me across the bridge—"

"A vampire?" I asked. She looked eleven, perhaps twelve. She'd scratched her face in her flight; the scratch had already scabbed over but I could feel her warmth, see the delicate pink tracery of the capillaries just beneath the surface of her skin, the throbbing in her throat.

"Yes!"

"Surely you're joking," I said. "If there's something you don't want to—"

"You're a Catholic priest!" she accused. "You're supposed to believe me!"

"In evil, yes, but in vampires? Perhaps you did see a bat, or a big bird, maybe an owl, but—"

"It chased me. And it wasn't just a bird or something. It was too big, and it knew what it was doing. And I could smell it."

"Where is it now, then?" I asked reasonably.

"I don't know—it flew away. You must have scared it off."

"In that case it doesn't really matter whether I believe in it or not, does it?" I asked. "Do you think you can make it home safely?"

"Please come with me, Father," she pleaded. "I don't— want to be alone right now. If you could just, take me home—"

"I can't, child. Not now. One of my parishioners left a note saying she was going to drown herself here tonight. I've got to find her, and before it's too late."

"Could I, could I borrow your cross?" the girl asked, chastened. "I'll mail it back to you, or something—"

"My crucifix?" I asked, pleased. "All right. You can bring it by the church tomorrow. But be very careful with it, and make sure you bring it back tomorrow."

"Thank you, Father." She smiled hesitantly as I took the crucifix from around my neck and handed it to her. She started to put it around her own neck, then stopped, stared at it, seeing it clearly for the first time in the semidarkness.

"But—," she stammered. "But Christ is upside down!"

"That's right," I said, smiling gently, letting my eyes glow red as I held her with my gaze, forced her to lift her head, bend it back to expose her neck as I caught her in my arms, bent to her bared throat.

But I had no fangs, I could not bite into her, feel the thick rich blood spurting forth, I had to suck it painstakingly through the unbroken skin, and it was never enough, a pitiful trickle that only fed my rage, my need, and for the third time this night I hated my children for what they'd done to me, for what they had reduced me to.

I left her unconscious but still living, to recover with a story she would never dare tell, and flew back to the estate.

I lay down in my coffin, closed the lid over me, felt my consciousness begin to fade—

I was myself again, back atop the green hill, facing my father's great vegetal face. But I couldn't feel Dara's presence in the body we shared.

"Dara?" I asked, but there was no whispered response, and the muscles of my mouth and throat remained lax when I tried to relinquish control of them.

"Where's Dara?"

"She asked me to put her into father's mind as soon as you quitted him." My father's speech was slurred; his tendrils hung limp and flaccid. The blind-faced fliers passed unmolested overhead.

I decided I had no choice but to believe him, sat down on one of his roots to wait for her return.

"Son, you know I love you," he said presently.

"And?" I twisted around to stare up into the green darkness of his eyes.

"Merge with me. Submit to me. Let me fill my veins with

your blood, so that I can then submit to you as my own father now submits to me."

"But I already command you."

"It is not the same. Our souls are divided."

"No thanks," I said, remembering the unassuagable loneliness that had been so much of Mihnea's thirst. "But I suppose you made the same offer to Dara?"

"Yes. She refused."

"Has any member of the family ever accepted?"

"Many. My own great-grandfather—"

"And how does he feel about it now?" I asked.

"He had never tried to declare the Compact void."

"What Compact?" I asked, remembering the letter he'd written me just before his death.

"The Compact you make with Satan to become a vampire."

"Tell me about it."

"After you die the wind claims you. But if you are to become a vampire Satan offers you a chance to escape."

"And the terms?"

"They are not harsh. Satan offers you new life as a vampire, with immortality and freedom from Hell—"

"I thought death was just the falling and the wind."

"That is death. There is also Hell. But Satan offers you escape from both death and Hell, and will grant you the powers you need to satisfy the hungers of your new existence. In return He asks only that you worship no other god than Him, and that you spend your days in Adoring Him."

Which must be what Dara was experiencing now, unless she was just lying trapped in Mihnea's body while his soul was elsewhere.

"And what is it like, the Adoration?" I asked.

"My transformation is not yet complete, so I have not yet spent a day in Adoration. But I know from my other selves what it is like. They sleep."

"That's all? They just sleep?"

"They dream of dancing."

"Has anyone ever withdrawn from the Compact? Declared it void?"

His face wrinkled, as though he was trying to frown. "I don't remember," he said at last.

"What about mother?" I asked. "Saraparajni? When you sealed her back into her coffin for seven years?"

He seemed confused. "Saraparajni . . . underwent the transformation but— No. I don't remember."

I brought him some of the liquid from one of the streams, splashed it over his mouth. "Does that help?"

"I . . . before she had ever tasted blood she let me . . . I sealed her into her coffin and—"

"Tell me about that. About the seven years."

"It is part of being a vampire, part of our natures." He sounded more sure of himself. "If we are sealed into our coffins for seven years without being released or tasting blood before our release, and if we emerge from our coffins onto the soil of a foreign country where a different language is spoken, we become mortal again, though we only live for five years as human beings."

"And afterwards? After the five years as a human being?"

"We either become vampires again or we—die. Forever."

"And mother did this, you sealed her into her coffin and took her—where?"

"To Mexico. It seemed safer than trying to take her overseas—"

"Did you have friends in Mexico, people helping you?"

"No. There was no one we could trust."

"And after that. After she had Dara and her five years were over—?"

"She returned to Patala."

"Did she die there?"

He seemed confused again. "If she'd been human . . . That was one of the limitations, but she was never truly mortal. She was a Naga."

I splashed more liquid over his face. "Did she die there?"

Because if she was still alive Dara might be safe there, might be able to escape becoming a vampire when she died.

"I don't know."

"How did you meet her? Did you go to Patala and then bring her back with you, or what?"

"No, it was in a temple. A temple of Shiva. In India. We were helping pay for a mission there, and one of the missionaries wrote us and told us about a beautiful woman the people said was a Naga, a snake-goddess. She called herself Manāsa then, or that's what the people called her, I don't remember, exactly, but— She was so beautiful. So graceful. I'd never seen anyone so beautiful. And then when I learned she was really a Naga I wanted to marry her, so we could gain her powers for the family. I thought that with the Naga intelligence in my sons and daughters they might be able to become vampires who wouldn't need to be controlled by the living. . . ."

"Why did she marry you?"

"I don't know. I never knew."

"She converted you to her god, didn't she? To Shiva?"

"No. She tried, but— No. I worship Satan. Only Satan."

I continued to question him, splashing his lips and face with the red liquid from the streams whenever he grew sluggish or seemed confused, but learned nothing that he hadn't already told me, or that hadn't been in his letter to me.

I was sitting on his roots when I felt the subtle alteration in the rhythms of our shared body that signaled Dara's presence. My father's tendrils began darting up into the sky again, seeking out their victims. It must have been dusk in Illinois.

"Dara?"

"Give me time, David. Give me time. I've spent the day in Hell." She was using our mouth and throat to speak, too tired for her special way of whispering. I went back to the stream, drank some more of the fluid from it, sat down by its edge and waited.

At last she said, "I was in Hell, David. That's what they do when their bodies are asleep, they're in Hell, dancing the dance of torment. Satan feeds on their agony and despair, He taunts them with the knowledge of how He's cheated them and how He's going to do the same thing to them again, and how there's no way they can ever escape. He makes a Compact with them—"

"I know about the Compact," I said, then gave the use of our mouth back to her again.

"But Satan cheats. He has never honored His Compact. His vampires, all His other slaves and servants, spend their days in agony, in unending torture, but when night comes He makes them forget what's happened to them during the day so they don't know that He's broken the Compact—"

"Why don't they renounce it during the day?"

"I thought I told you— During the day they're all merged with Him, part of Him. His will is their will and He tortures them by torturing Himself. Their pain is His pain. . . . He has created a Heaven so the damned will suffer from their

208

knowledge of its existence but He Himself is all the damned, they are all part of Him the same way I was part of Him, I was Him, I was Satan—"

She broke off. We were shaking. I stood up, walked around a little, cupped us some more of the liquid and drank it.

"Some of the damned are there eternally, no longer have any existence except as part of Satan, but the vampires are only there during the day. They could renounce the Compact and free themselves at night, when they're themselves again, but at night they don't have the knowledge to free themselves, they've forgotten what they knew during the day."

"But you remembered."

"Only because I have not one, but two souls. The human soul endured Hell, was swallowed up by Satan, while the Naga soul looked on, and when Satan released the human soul and made it forget, the Naga soul remembered."

"And Christ?"

"What Uncle Stephen said: Satan's finest creation. The bait for His hook."

"Father," I said after she'd finished speaking, "did you hear what she said?"

"I heard it, but I don't believe it. It makes no sense."

"But you told me the same thing, or almost the same thing, before you died. In a letter. And you haven't signed the Compact yet."

"He can't believe it, David, not even if he knew most of it when he was alive. That's what happens in the forty days— the other vampires make him over, take away everything in him that would keep him from being exactly like them when the time comes for him to enter the Compact. He's one of them now, part of them already, even if he isn't wholly a vampire yet. And none of them will ever believe the truth."

"It's part of Satan's game, the way He tortures them, and Himself: they actually have the ability to renounce the Compact and escape Him at night, but they have none of the memories that would let them realize that they want to renounce it, and they can't believe the truth about themselves when someone else tells it to them."

"But if we could do what father said in his letter," I said. "Find some way of giving them their daytime knowledge at night, when they'd be free to renounce the Compact. If there was some way of sealing them all in their coffins for the seven years, and making sure that none of them escaped, and that Michael and Uncle Stephen did nothing to free them—"

"No. Unless you found a way of reawakening their memories of Hell it would be useless. Remember who they were when they were alive, who they'd be again. The Countess Elizabeth Báthory. Vlad the Impaler. David Mathewson, the one who had all those women hanged as witches in Scotland. All the rest of them. Even if we could bring a few of them to believe us and accept a death from which there'd be no returning, the rest of them would be only too glad to become vampires once again when they died."

"So we do what? Try to escape and hope I live long enough to put you in your coffin, keep you there for seven years, and finally let you out again, after you die? And that you can do the same thing for me if what Aunt Judith did to me's enough to make *me* a vampire when I die?"

"I don't know, David. Try to get free and stay alive long enough to find a solution if there is one."

Or to find our way to Patala. If there was a way. And if I could free myself of Monteleur first.

Monteleur, who was waiting for me back in my body. Waiting for me to recover consciousness so it could hurt me the way it had hurt me when I'd returned to my body in Carlsbad. And the longer I waited, the worse Monteleur would make the pain.

"Send us back," I told father.

Chapter Thirty-three

JOHN WAS SITTING BARE-CHESTED IN THE SUN ON THE front porch, his eyes closed. He'd lost a lot of weight. A great purple butterfly with blue eyespots on its wings and tails like a black swallowtail's, only much longer, was resting on his right shoulder, slowly opening and closing its wings.

He opened his eyes, stared up at us without moving. "Hello, David. Welcome home." There was no warmth in his voice or face.

"Hello, John. What are you doing here?"

"Waiting for you. Stephen said you'd be here sometime today or tomorrow: This is Dara, I take it?"

"Yes. Dara, this is John. An old friend. He's a painter— John, you said Uncle Stephen told you I was coming? Is he here now?"

"Yes. He's back in the cave, but he'll be out fairly soon. You're supposed to wait for him here."

"Is my brother with him? Michael?"

"No. He won't be arriving for another month or so."

"For the Lammas Day Sabbat?"

"Yes."

"John, how well do you know my uncle?"

"Meaning what, David? Are you trying to find out just how much he's told me? Whether I'm a friend and associate of his or just an innocent dupe?"

"All of that, I guess."

"A friend and associate, then. Alexandra introduced me to him about four years ago but I didn't join his coven until after the rest of you tried to kill her."

I thought about that a moment, said, "John, neither of us had anything to do with that. That was father and Michael, not us. But what do you mean, *tried* to kill her? She's not dead?"

"No. Stephen rescued her for me."

He twisted his head cautiously to the right, stared a moment at the butterfly fanning its wings on his shoulder. It was bigger than any North American butterfly I'd ever seen—it must have had an eight-inch wingspread—and though it was abroad in daylight it had the feathery antennae of a night-flying moth.

"That's her, David. Alexandra. She's a butterfly now. And she's mine, like she always wanted to be. You can't have her back."

The butterfly shifted position on his shoulder. Alexandra. But I'd touched her cooling skin, watched the coroner's deputy probe her wound with his thick red fingers, close her eyes.

Alexandra. And the dead rise up never, unless they're vampires and then they're still dead, and then they'll always be dead. And she couldn't be a vampire, not there on his shoulder in the hot sun.

"That's really her? You're sure?"

"Of course I'm sure."

"How did it happen?"

"She'll tell you about it herself, if you'd like her to. But we'll have to go inside, where you can hear her. Her voice is too tiny now for you to hear her over the wind and all."

We went inside, sat down at the table. I noticed that the bookcase against the far wall that had held my aunt's collection of grimoires was gone. John sat down across from us.

"Don't try to get too close to her, or even breathe on her too hard," he said. "She's very delicate now."

"We wouldn't want to do anything to hurt her," Dara said.

"Just don't. And speak softly. You're talking too loud already. Loud noises scare her."

"Alexandra?" I asked, leaning close and whispering.

"Yes, David?" The voice was so faint I could barely hear it. I couldn't tell if it was Alexandra's voice or not.

"Tell me about it. What happened, how Uncle Stephen saved you."

"After you and John left to go swimming your father took control of me and made me open the bushmaster's cage," the thin voice—Alexandra's voice?—said. "And then he kept me from doing anything to save myself when Michael and Dara—"

"Just Michael," I said. "Not Dara."

"—while they used the snake to try to kill me, and then to keep you from getting to me with the antivenin."

"You were still—alive?" I asked. "You knew I was there in the cave with you, trying to save you?"

"Yes. They weren't expecting you back so soon, not while I was still alive. But I'd been part of Stephen's coven for a long time—I always knew that Michael was just planning on using me and then getting rid of me, that he never meant to give me any of what he'd promised me—and so even though you weren't able to get past the bushmaster and use the antivenin to save me, Stephen was there, waiting to snare my escaping soul. He gave me this butterfly to use until Lammas Day, when the constellations will be right for him to give me a new human body."

"Whose body?" Dara demanded.

"Perhaps yours, perhaps someone else's. He hasn't told me yet," the butterfly said with a tiny tinkling laugh.

But it wasn't Alexandra's laugh, could never have been her laugh, no matter how physically altered she was. Unless she'd become a vampire, and it was still bright out, still early afternoon: the butterfly couldn't be a vampire. I knew Alexandra, knew her for all her lies, for all the ways she'd tried to use me: whatever she'd done would have been done to satisfy her hungers, her greed, never out of the cold passionless delight that rang through the butterfly's laughter.

And if Uncle Stephen, if any Bathory could snare escaping souls and give them new bodies the family could have had the immortality it sought in the flesh, without having to become vampires. Another lie.

The butterfly shifted on its six legs again, uncurled its thread-thin black proboscis and jabbed it into the base of John's neck. John held himself very still, careful not to dislodge the thing.

213

He looked proud, a bit shy. I could see that his neck and shoulders were covered with tiny red-brown welts, almost invisible against the tan. Not a vampire, but some other form of parasite.

And Alexandra was dead, finally and irrevocably dead, or Uncle Stephen would never have had to resort to the butterfly to keep John tied to him.

"I keep her alive," he said. He was keeping his voice low, looking away from the thing while he spoke. Protecting it. "She'd prefer to live outside where she could fly around drinking nectar from flowers like a real butterfly, but it's too dangerous. There are too many things out there that would like to eat her. Birds, spiders, lizards, frogs and toads. Even other insects, real ones. Blood's better, like a sacrament we can share between us."

He was looking at me as if to say, a sacrament that only the two of us will ever share, that unites us in a way you'll never know. Another victim. Like Uncle Peter, Aunt Judith. Like Alexandra herself.

The butterfly withdrew its proboscis, delicately recurled it. A new body on Lammas Day. Some other kind of familiar or demon, being prepared so that on Lammas Day it could take possession of Dara as Bathomar had been unable to do?

The door opened and Uncle Stephen came through it, followed closely by three men in dark-blue suits who looked like Jehovah's Witnesses.

"Don't bother to get up," Uncle Stephen said, playing perfect host. He smiled and as he smiled Monteleur jabbed knitting needles through my knees again. "How was your trip, David?"

"Why don't you just ask Monteleur?" I demanded, unable to put up with any more of his unending cat-and-mouse. "Since you're going to anyway?"

"Because I have no need to ask Monteleur anything. Ever. I keep in constant communication with him through my own familiar."

"That?" I jerked my head in the butterfly's direction. John scowled, hunched his shoulder protectively.

"Not at all. That's Alexandra there on John's shoulder, whether or not you want to admit it, David. But I carry my own familiar around inside me the same way you do yours. That way it can keep me young and healthy and free of disease, protect me from heart attacks and kidney failures, that sort of thing."

I ignored the implied threat, said, "Then you don't need me to tell you what happened."

"True. I don't. I know all about your attempt with the cobra, and I intend to punish you for it. Both of you.

"Your own punishment, David, is unfortunately going to have to be more symbolic than real, more of a demonstration of our respective positions than an attempt to actually hurt you for what you did. I have few illusions about my ability to outdo Monteleur in the infliction of physical pain.

"But in Dara's case, as I think you can see, things are a bit different. If for no other reason than that any pain I cause her will serve to provide you with a further demonstration of your own helplessness. So—

"Here." He picked up one of the cotton sacks I used to transfer my snakes, handed it to her. "Go back up to David's truck and get the cobra you used. Put it in the sack and bring it back here to me. David, you stay here with me while she goes after it."

Dara left, returned a few minutes later with the bagged snake.

"Stand over there. Good. Now, take it out of the bag and hold it where we can all see it. Then kill it. Twist its neck until it's dead. Do it *now*, Dara, or I'll see that Monteleur hurts David while I kill the snake myself in some way that'll be much more painful to it."

She held the cobra a moment longer in her cupped hands, staring into its eyes. The cobra stared back at her, absolutely motionless, making no attempt to escape.

She killed it.

"Very good. For the rest— Come along with me now, the two of you. I've got some things to show you. John, you stay here until we get back."

One of Uncle Stephen's assistants preceded him through the door, waited for him outside. The other two followed us.

There was a small stand of live oaks just outside the entrance to the herpetarium. The bushmaster was nailed to the trunk of the biggest of them, hanging from a single thick nail through its head. Dozens of other dead snakes—garter snakes, king snakes, rattlesnakes, all the commoner local varieties—were heaped in a rotting pile around the base of the tree.

Uncle Stephen had had the entrance to the cave enlarged: there was a new door blocking it, thick brass-studded wood, perhaps seven feet tall. It took three keys to unlock it.

While the Jehovah's Witness who'd accompanied him across the meadow was unlocking the door, Uncle Stephen turned back to us, nodded to indicate the hanging bushmaster and the pile of dead snakes and said, "All that training you gave John in the care and collection of snakes turned out to be of some real use after all. As you can see."

I didn't say anything, tried to keep my face expressionless. Uncle Stephen smiled again, as though that had been just exactly the reaction he'd been hoping for, and gestured us inside. The Jehovah's Witness with the keys locked the door behind us.

I'd left the herpetarium unchanged when I'd put the cabin up for sale, more as a demonstration of the kinds of things one could do with the cave than because I'd actually thought someone would have a use for the cages and tanks. They were gone now, replaced by racks of swords and lancets, quills and wands; cloth-covered altars; jars full of teeth and bones; other, larger, jars in which homonuclei floated in varicolored fluids; pentacles drawn on floors and walls and hanging sheets of parchment—all the apparatus and equipment of a magician's laboratory.

In the back of the cave, where the narrow fissure through which the bushmaster had tried to escape had been, a broad keyhole-shaped archway had been cut through the purplish-red stone. On either side of the opening a hand of glory was mounted on a slim stone pillar. Through the arch I could see a huge cavern, high-ceilinged and very deep, with a granite floor covered with small circular depressions in which wood fires smoldered. Men in dark shirts and tunics were feeding the fires, kneeling before altars, chanting prayers; others were constructing something massive in the center of the open space. The rock glowed faintly silver.

A man in black was sitting at a high table just our side of the archway, copying an old manuscript onto fresh parchment. Nicolae. He didn't bother to look up as we passed him.

We threaded our way between the fire pits, came to another brass-studded door set into the silver-glowing rock. Uncle Stephen's torture chamber. Even before the assistant with the keys had drawn back the bolt and unlocked the door I could smell the stench of the room beyond: blood and rust and urine, wood smoke and charred meat.

The room was twice the size of the cabin, full of antiques that Uncle Stephen told us had been in the family since our ecclesiastical ancestors had first used them in the service of the Inquisition. Thumbscrews, Spanish boots, the ladder. Instruments for ripping and cutting, burning, breaking and crushing.

The Jehovah's Witness with the keys locked the door behind us.

I was blindfolded and gagged, manacled to a post and whipped. My lesson in humility. Uncle Stephen wielded the whip himself—a nine-lashed scourge, like the cat-o'-nine-tails with which British sailors had once been flogged, only supple braided black leather instead of rope, knotted, with tiny iron barbs twisted into the knots. Another heirloom.

And each time the whip struck Monteleur hurt me somewhere else, hurt me worse than Uncle Stephen could have ever hurt me with the scourge alone, kept me jerking and twisting and trying to cry out in no doubt exquisite counterpoint to Uncle Stephen's blows.

When it was over he had one of his assistants remove my blindfold, then stand holding my head to keep me from looking away or closing my eyes while the other two assistants stretched Dara on a horizontal ladder—the rack, as it was sometimes called—and fastened her legs to one end, her bound arms to a kind of tourniquet attached to the other.

Uncle Stephen began tightening the tourniquet, methodically increasing the force that would soon yank her bones from their sockets, leave her crippled and disjointed, if he didn't stop. Dara gave a sudden, involuntary cry, then clamped her jaws shut, denying him the pleasure of hearing her cry out again.

I was still manacled to the post, still gagged; I could do nothing but watch, nothing but listen to the screams that I alone could hear.

Uncle Stephen continued to tighten the tourniquet. I began to hear the dry popping sounds that Dara's bones made as one by one they were pulled from their sockets.

When it was over we were returned to the cabin. Dara had remained silent, had only allowed her control to slip as she

217

was taken from the rack, and then only to the extent of a single short moan as she lost consciousness. I was led, she was carried, back out through the caverns to the cabin.

They put her on the bed, left us alone. She was quiet now, not even moaning any more, her breathing ragged and shallow. I didn't know if what Uncle Stephen had done to her would have been enough to cripple a normal person, and if it had been, whether her dhampire's ability to draw on outside forces or her Naga ancestry would give her the strength she'd need to heal herself.

I lay down beside her on the bed, afraid to touch her, afraid that anything I could do to try to help her would only hurt her more. I tried to stay awake, to watch over her and be ready to protect her or help her if she needed my help, but too many days of fighting my own fear and pain had drained me, and I no longer had even the strength I would have needed to keep myself conscious.

Chapter Thirty-four

WHEN I CAME TO THE NEXT MORNING MY BACK WAS already beginning to heal, but I was loaded and confused, stupefied, as though Monteleur had pumped me full of barbiturates while I slept. It was weeks before I was allowed to wake up completely again.

Most of what happened to me during that time is gone, forgotten or lost, or perhaps never comprehended in the first place. Only a few images, a few incidents, stand out clearly in my memory.

A cavern somewhere at the end of a branching corridor deep under the hills, where I awakened to find myself looking up at thousands of dirty-white bats hanging from the roof, more entering through a natural chimney somewhere off to my right.

Another cavern. Warm, silver-dark, half-flooded, filled with the hopping gray-brown toads and scuttling eight-inch reddish salamanders that John caught and on which Uncle Stephen and Nicolae were operating, setting pentangular plugs of iridescent fire opal into the amphibians' skulls so that the jewels glistened from their foreheads like third eyes. This, as I remember Uncle Stephen telling me, so that the members of the minor covens, those who had neither the right to attend the Sabbat in their proper persons nor the right to use the body of a vampire whose forty days of transformation were still uncompleted, could attend by possessing each a toad or a salamander.

And in the main cavern, one hundred and forty-four coffins slowly filling with the bodies of the men, women and children killed by the vampires Uncle Stephen had brought with him. The bodies that the members of the twelve lesser covens— those ruled by Black Men who were themselves the twelve lesser members of the coven whose thirteenth member, the coven's Black Man, was Uncle Stephen—would animate for the Sabbat.

I remember John returning from the Monterey airport with Larry, who'd been lured to California with a telegram signed in my name and fitted with a familiar while still being driven down the coast to the cabin. He spent what might have been a week, might have been two or three weeks, with us before Uncle Stephen sent him back to Provincetown. I remember watching him hold a spoon for Dara, remember him trying to help her walk what must have been some days or weeks later. I remember hearing him crying late at night, when he thought we were asleep and unable to hear him, remember the sounds he made when his familiar hurt him.

I remember times I was manacled to the post or to iron rings set in the wall and whipped with Dara forced to watch, remember a little of my desperate clumsy lovemaking with her. I remember the time I realized that she could walk and hold things again without too-great pain, remember the anger I felt at my inability to let her know how relieved I was that she was going to recover.

My other memories are less clear. The day my father's transformation was complete and he took his place among the vampires whose coffins Uncle Stephen had brought by truck from Illinois. The summonings in the main cavern, when Uncle Stephen obtained the familiars with which those members of the lesser covens who were to be made Black Men of their own minor covens were to be fitted at the Sabbat. A vampire— perhaps my grandmother, from her resemblance to my Aunt Judith—bending over me and drinking from my neck as before

Aunt Judith had drunk from me, while Uncle Stephen looked on.

I have a vague memory of Dara trying to convince father that his days were spent in Hell, an even vaguer memory of the two of us trying to convince John that his precious butterfly was only a familiar spirit and that Alexandra was dead. I remember fragments of conversations I had with Uncle Stephen and Nicolae in which, from what I remember, I seem to have been asking them questions and listening to their answers almost like a trusting child demanding the truth of his parents, and another fragment of conversation in which Uncle Stephen was telling me that he used drugs even though his familiar could easily duplicate any effect they might have on him because he preferred to feel himself the object of external forces, rather than the prime mover.

Midway through July Uncle Stephen had the road down to the cabin graded and paved. As soon as it was ready trucks began arriving with the equipment needed to further enlarge and furnish the caverns, with food and drink for the Sabbat, and with the coffins containing all but perhaps a half dozen of the vampires that had been left beneath the house in Illinois.

An altar had been constructed among the live oaks outside the entrance to the caverns, where it was invisible from the road and air: a flat black stone, roughly oval, perhaps two feet thick, three yards wide and a yard deep, supported by four pillars of red-painted stone carved to resemble the legs of some crouching beast. Every day, at dawn and again at dusk, a small animal of some sort was killed on the altar and left there. The bodies were always gone by the time of the next sacrifice.

Behind the altar three crosses had been erected, intricately carved and painted, each large enough to be used to crucify a man; to the base of each cross a black goat was tethered, its horns painted with gilt.

There was no way to keep the fact of so much activity completely hidden from my Big Sur neighbors and Uncle Stephen knew more than to try. For some weeks now John had been telling people that I'd arranged while I was back on the East Coast to sell my land to some obscure Eastern Orthodox monastic order that wanted to build a hermitage and retreat on it, but which was going to allow me to retain lifetime tenancy of my cabin. Now, with trucks arriving daily and construction well under way, I was allowed to awaken from my weeks-long half-consciousness so I could accompany John to the bars and restaurants, the baths at Esalen and the private parties, where I could support and confirm his story.

Even with Monteleur inside me to ensure my obedience I was never allowed off the property except in John's company. And while I was gone Dara stayed in the caverns, manacled to a wall of the locked torture chamber, a hostage and a reminder.

Chapter Thirty-five

It was July twenty-eighth, somewhere around midnight. John and I were sitting at a table on the terrace at Nepenthe with a girl he knew named Cindy. She was blond, pretty, maybe twenty-one or twenty-two years old; she worked in a massage parlor in Seaside. I'd met her once or twice the year before, at parties Alexandra'd taken me to. The night was cool, the almost-full moon invisible in the fog. The last few days' rain had kept the tourists away and most of the people were local. Everyone was either inside drinking at the bar or over on the other side of the terrace, by the fireplace.

"Do you want another drink?" John asked Cindy. He'd already managed to tell her everything he wanted to about the Eastern Orthodox monastic order that had supposedly bought my property. "We've got a good two, two and a half hours before the baths open."

"All right," Cindy said. "A Mexican coffee. With extra brandy in it, to help me stay awake."

"You, David?"

I shook my head. All I wanted to do was get back to Dara as soon as possible. "No thanks."

"You can drive, then. I'll be back in a moment."

He pushed his chair away, started to get up.

And Monteleur exploded inside me, ripped its way up through my heart and lungs, out through my stomach wall to flap wetly against the inside of my shirt. The last thing I was aware of was Cindy screaming.

And then I was Michael as well as myself. I fell through the cold and the wind to the cave beneath my father's roots, the cave where I was already sitting cross-legged staring into the fire fed by the sweetness dripping from above.

I could see my headless body, Michael's body, lying dead there in the center of the flames. And standing over it a woman, a woman with Dara's face and body and youth, but four-armed, terrible, her skin a blue so dark it was almost black, her eyes dead clay, wet and shining. Around her neck she wore a garland of severed heads, around her slender waist a sort of skirt made of dangling hands, boneless forearms. A slender golden cobra was coiled around each of her long legs, smaller darker-colored snakes around her arms, a seventh snake looped twice around her neck, staring at me from over her left shoulder.

With two of her delicate hands she was gently caressing her cobras' golden heads. Her third hand held a bloody sword. With the fourth she was holding my severed head to her face so she could lap the blood still draining from it with her long black tongue.

She was staring out at me, watching me, her image writhing and flickering with the flames, infinitely desirable, infinitely terrifying. Her black hair which was Dara's hair fell thick and smooth and shining down her back; the hands with which a moment before she'd been caressing the heads of her serpents were opening to me now in invitation, beckoning me to her, and I was falling, jerking closer to her with every dancing movement of the flames, closer to the midnight darkness of her skin, to the severed heads whispering her eternal love to me from their toothless mouths, to the cold shining clay of her eyes, and the sharp teeth behind her blood-smeared lips.

"Not yet, Mother," I heard myself say. "Not yet."

And then I was myself again, was David again, and I was lying bandaged and bloody on the jolting floor of the truck.

Cindy lay unconscious on the floor next to me. I could see John up front driving, and a small man in a black suit—one of the members of Uncle Stephen's coven—sitting on the floor behind Cindy. He had a doctor's black bag on his lap. Which must have been how he'd gotten us out of Nepenthe, posing as a doctor. Unless he really was a doctor. My whole body hurt but the pain was far away, a dull throbbing that merged in and out of the sound of the truck's engine, the vibration coming to me from it through the floor.

Monteleur had tried to kill me, had almost succeeded. I opened my mouth to ask the doctor what had happened, why, closed it again.

My mother. That had been my mother, Saraparajni, there beneath my father's roots. And she'd been more terrifying in her beauty and her hunger than any vampire could have ever been.

No. That had been Michael's terror I'd felt, not my own. I'd seen her through his eyes. Or maybe the terror had been my father's. It was his symbolic landscape. Maybe she hadn't been real, or no more real than the landscape itself.

But real or not, she was there for Michael. And Michael had to have been behind whatever had happened to make Monteleur try to kill me.

I could reach him there, in the cave, if he was still there.

Monteleur was keeping me alive while it helped me repair the damage it had done to my heart and lungs, to the other organs in my abdominal cavity, but the strength to heal myself was coming to me from my father.

I closed my eyes again, made sure I subvocalized none of my thoughts as I climbed the shadow tide to my father.

I was in the dark corridor, but Uncle Stephen could find me there, listen in to me there.

I abolished the corridor, fell through the cold and the wind.

I abolished the void. I was standing knee-deep in the salmon-pink mud. I seemed to be in my proper body, and I was far closer to the hill than I'd ever been on arrival before. Perhaps because this time I was there without Dara.

I crossed the red moat, climbed the hill to the entrance beneath the roots, crawled in through it.

Michael was there, sitting cross-legged in front of the fire. The three faceless stone images were there, at the center of the flames, just as they'd been when I'd been there with Dara. There was no sign of the figure Michael had addressed as our mother.

"Michael." He looked up, noticed me for the first time. "What happened? Monteleur almost killed me—"

"I tried to kill Uncle Stephen."

"Tried?" I sat down next to him. "You mean you failed?"

"Yes."

"Why?"

"Because he's going to kill all three of us on Lammas Day. As part of the Sabbat. That altar he set up, the three crosses behind it—those are for us. He's going to sacrifice us and end the family. Replace us all with members of his coven. Unless you can find a way to stop him that I couldn't.

"I've been spying on you all through Father's eyes every night. Watching and listening, making sure I saw everything Stephen did, heard every order he gave, knew everything that he had you or his followers do. While Monteleur kept you drugged, and Dara didn't do anything.

"He had our ancestors kill the parents and grandparents of all the other members of his coven, kill them all the same night, and in such a way as to ensure they become vampires. He timed it so that they're all finishing their transformations now. They'll be ready for the Sabbat. And then he won't need us or the family any more. His followers will be able to do everything he needs to have done by vampires controlled by the living. The rest of us—you, me, Dara, our ancestors—we'll be vampires, yes, but we'll be out of control, without a dhampire to protect us from the living and keep us from destroying ourselves."

I thought about it a moment, asked, "Are you still back in Illinois?"

"Yes."

"How did you try to kill him?"

"I used Father. Stephen isn't there, with the rest of us—" he indicated the stone figures—"and I knew I could use Father to act for me as long as I didn't do anything to arouse his suspicions. I waited for a time when he was alone in the cabin, when you were off the property and he had Dara chained up, so he wouldn't be worrying about either of you. Then I had Father get one of the heavy steel struts left over from the construction out in the caverns and had him station himself outside the door to the cabin, where he had a chance to surprise Stephen while he was coming out.

"And that much of it worked, worked perfectly. When Stephen stepped out of the cabin Father was right behind him, ready to smash his head in with the strut before he knew what was happening."

"But he managed to duck away or something?"

"No. Father hit him. And it should have killed him. It would have killed you, or me, or even Father himself if he'd still been alive, but it didn't kill Stephen. I don't know why. Father hit him with the thing with all his strength but it just glanced off his head. It didn't even knock him unconscious, and before Father could hit him again he'd had Bathomar hurt me so bad I couldn't stay conscious myself to keep control of Father.

"I've got to get back to my body, David. If they realize I can come here to escape the pain they'll do something to stop me. But you've got to stop him somehow. You and Dara. It's too late for me to do anything."

"Michael, wait. If you'd succeeded, what were you going to do about Bathomar? How were you going to keep it from killing you?"

"I was going to come here, and deal with it from here before it killed me. Make a new deal with it, offer to do more for it than Stephen'd ever done now that he was gone."

"And you think that would have worked?"

"I don't know. Maybe. But even if it didn't there'd still be you and Dara. Or at least Dara, if your familiar killed you. And Uncle Peter. Some chance that one of you at least would do what was needed to keep the family going. With Stephen there's no chance at all."

"Michael. Another thing. Right after, what must have been right after you tried to kill him, when Monteleur attacked me, I came here. The pain drove me out of my body and I, I was sitting here with you. Only it wasn't me, wasn't David, I was just you. Michael. I didn't even know that I was both of us."

"And?"

"And I saw—a woman. There, in the flames, where those three stone figures of us are now. She was gesturing to you, trying to get you to join her there in the flames . . . and you said, "Not yet, Mother. Not yet—"

"You want to know if that was really our mother?"

"Yes."

"Yes."

"But how—why was she there? Here? And what did you mean, not yet?"

"She was there because I was dying, David. And maybe because you were dying too, I don't know."

"To rescue you?"

"No. To consume me. Swallow me up body and soul, David, not just drink my blood while granting me immortality in return." And he was gone.

Chapter Thirty-six

THE PAIN WAS WORSE. MUCH WORSE. A BAND OF burning metal tight around my chest, a hot gnawing in my belly, something jagged stabbing me in the lungs every time I took a breath.

I opened my eyes. The moon was out and the truck was bright with its light, with the backwash from the headlights, the green glow of the dashboard instruments, the silver phosphorescence that spider-webbed everything in shadow. We were making our way down the far side of the hills to the cabin and every time we hit another bump it tore something new apart inside of me.

Monteleur shifted, sliding through the pain. And the pain was real, in a way that nothing before had ever been. The other agonies had been imposed on me from outside, something to face and defy and try to defeat, but this was me, my intimate self, telling me that I'd been too badly wounded to heal myself, and somehow that was very different and far, far more terrifying.

"Monteleur," I whispered. The whisper hurt, hurt bad. "Make it stop hurting. Help me. Stephen didn't tell you not to. Make it stop!"

Monteleur shifted inside me, remained silent. I lay motionless, getting my breath back as best I could, then levered myself up into a sitting position. For some reason it was very important to sit up. But I couldn't hold myself there, it hurt too much to bend like that in the middle, and I had to lie down again.

The man with the black bag on his lap was watching me. "Are you a doctor?" I asked.

"Yes."

"Make it stop hurting. So I can breathe. I've got a punctured lung."

He shook his head. "There's no need. Monteleur's already done everything necessary. Everything your uncle wants. You'll have to do the rest of it for yourself."

He was lying. A real doctor would've given me something for the pain.

"Why?" I asked. "Why did Monteleur—?"

He shook his head, told me to wait until we got back to the cabin.

I closed my eyes again, thankfully climbed the tides of my father's stolen strength up out of the pain to the shadow corridor, trying to reach through to Dara. But Stephen was there, watching, listening, and there was no way I could get past him to her.

I returned to my body, and to the pain.

They took me to the caverns, chained me to a wall a few yards away from Dara. My chains had enough slack so I could slump a bit, but not enough to let me sit or kneel, even with my arms over my head. Not nearly enough to reach out to Dara and touch her.

She waited until they'd left us alone in the stench and silver-glowing darkness before asking me what had happened. They hadn't hurt her, hadn't told her why she'd been kept chained to the wall. But Stephen stood guard in the shadow corridor, cutting me off not only from Dara but from the deeper landscapes where we might have met in safety, and Monteleur was still wriggling through my agony, listening, ready to punish me again: I couldn't tell her about Michael or ask about the four-armed woman who'd looked so like the statue of Kali dancing in my father's Oriental room. My body was out of control, would have given me away if I'd tried to answer her Naga-whispered questions in any way. All I could tell her was what Monteleur had done to me at Nepenthe and how I'd awakened in the truck.

Dara tried to get Monteleur to tell her at least why the pain kept getting worse and worse, but it refused to respond to any of her questions.

The pain continued to worsen all the next day—I knew it was day because my father had returned to his coffin and I could no longer find my way up out of the pain to him—but when at last dusk came and he reawakened I was able to draw on him once more for the strength my body needed to heal itself, that I needed to endure its agony.

It was enough, barely enough: if they did nothing more to me I would survive.

Hours later I heard footsteps outside the door, the sound of keys turning in the multiple locks. The door opened and the man who'd claimed to be a doctor entered carrying a lantern. He hung it on an iron hook jutting from the wall just above our heads, then examined us to make sure we were still securely fastened in place, finally took two gags from his pocket and fitted us with them.

It would have been pointless to resist. Neither of us even tried.

He was laying a fire in the open furnace at the far end of the chamber when Stephen entered with Michael and one of the men who'd put Dara on the ladder for him that first night. Michael was blindfolded, with his hands tied behind his back, and staggering, barely able to walk. Stephen and his assistant were dressed in black: the same uniform he'd had me wear when he sent me after Dara.

Michael's face was etched deep with pain and fatigue, marbled purplish-red with broken veins and capillaries like the face of some sixty-year alcoholic; his body and hands trembled and he kept shifting from one foot to the other, licking teeth and lips, swallowing.

Uncle Stephen took off Michael's blindfold, pushed him down into a cane chair the assistant brought forward. Michael sat awkwardly on the edge of the chair, blinking up at Stephen but unable to meet his gaze. He kept glancing over at the two of us chained to the wall, at the iron maiden standing half-open next to the horizontal ladder so he could just glimpse the spikes inside, at the benches along the walls where the various instruments were laid out and gleaming, at the fire roaring to life in the open furnace.

Uncle Stephen took a half step back, turned to face Dara

and me. Behind Michael's back the doctor was attaching a rope and pulley to the ceiling. "Michael tried to kill me," Stephen said. "Tried stupidly—it's been thirty years since my familiar would've let something like that hurt me. And for the wrong reasons, if I believe him when he says he thought I was planning to crucify the three of you."

He paused, staring at Michael, challenging him to contradict what he was saying. Michael looked away, jaws working, finally found the strength to meet his gaze and demand, "Then what are the crosses for?"

"For Lucifer and his two assistants, Satanichia and Sataniciae." Stephen turned back to Dara and me, pretended to ignore Michael while he explained everything to us. "So that when they found themselves in the goats' crucified bodies they could descend from their crosses to their worshipers in proper traditional fashion. The three of you were to have had no part in that—I was just going to use you for some ritual magic later in the ceremonies. Nothing all that different from what I've already had you do for me."

"You're lying," Michael said.

Stephen seemed delighted with his response. "You'll never know whether I am or not," he said. "Because three days from now I'm personally going to nail you to the center cross in place of one of the goats. And after Lucifer abandons you I'm going to tear your heart out and eat it, then burn what's left of your body. Not as a sacrifice, but to make sure you can never become a vampire. Because I want you dead and in Hell with no way you can ever escape."

He paused a moment, smiling, then added, "Though I intend to use your three remaining days to find out the truth behind that oh-so-pretty story you told me about how you decided to risk your precious immortal life for the good of the family."

"For all of us," Michael said. "Even for you."

"You'll forgive me if I don't believe you." Stephen walked over to a bench, picked up something like a rusty fisherman's gaff, turned back to Michael.

"I've always thought the art of interrogation reached its finest point with the Inquisition. The first step was always to familiarize the . . . *accused* . . . with the instruments which were to be employed on him later, so he could better imagine and anticipate what was to come.

"So . . . This, Michael, is an eyeball gouger. Though you

probably won't have to worry about it until tomorrow, or even the day after, since I'll want you to be able to see what I'm doing to you . . .

"And this"—a spiked cylinder—"is a spine roller, while *this* is a forehead tourniquet. We have Spanish boots, of course, thumb and toe screws, throat pears, burning irons and pinchers . . . everything you were so anxious to have me teach you how to use."

His smile was frozen, terrifying. "But I think we'll start with squassation. Do you know what that is? We hang you by your arms while we drop weights attached to your legs. Very heavy weights. You'll dislocate your feet, hands, elbows, knees, shoulders, hips. . . . And then, perhaps, while you're still hanging there we can begin with the toe screws, go from there—"

Michael slumped forward, unconscious, and would have fallen from the chair if Stephen hadn't caught him.

"It won't help you, nephew. Not now, not ever." And, turning to his assistants: "Finish preparing him. I'll awaken him when it's time."

They brought high wooden stools, put heavy metal balls with chains attached to them—like the ball and chain convicts wear in comic strips—on the stools, locked the manacles at the end of the chains tight around Michael's ankles. They undid his wrists, manacled them together behind his back, attached them to a hook at the end of the rope the doctor had prepared earlier, hoisted him free of the ground.

I could hear his shoulders scraping out of their sockets.

Uncle Stephen picked up the eyeball gouger again, prodded Michael's dangling body delicately with it, then closed his own eyes for a second. Michael jerked back to life, whimpering.

"It won't work, Michael. You can't hide from me there." With his left hand he was caressing one of the cannon balls. "And we haven't even begun dropping weights, so this is just strappado, no worse, really, than the ladder, especially for someone like you, with your dhampire's resistance to pain—"

He pushed the ball from the stool. It fell, jerked to a halt just above the ground, swung slowly. Michael began to scream and Stephen jabbed the eyeball gouger at his face.

Michael burst into flame.

Chapter Thirty-seven

MICHAEL HUNG TWISTING AND BLACKENING IN HIS cocoon of ever-brightening flame, his fading screams not yet lost in the greater violence of Bathomar's frenzied bellowing. Stephen and the assistants had retreated to the far corner of the room, stood huddled together with their hands over their faces. The heat beat against my face and hands, crisped the unprotected skin, was beginning to reach through my clothing to the rest of me as the flames climbed the spectrum through ever-brighter, ever-fiercer oranges to a yellow-white like that of the sun.

I held my breath, tried to keep the rich fatty smell of my brother's burning out of my nostrils, but it was hopeless, I could smell him anyway, and when I couldn't keep myself from breathing any longer and opened my mouth, tried to gasp air around the wadded mass of rags with which I'd been gagged, my mouth was full of the roasting pork taste of him. My stomach contracted, heaved, I could feel myself starting to vomit, but I forced it back down again, swallowed it before it'd had a chance to block my nose and throat, choke me to death.

A tongue of blue-green appeared where Michael's chest had

been, spread. Bathomar's bellowing rose to a bleating scream and was cut off. The charred flesh was crumbling, flaking from the bone, consumed even as it fell away.

The flames drew in on themselves, shrank to a single point of intolerable blue-green, winked out. What remained of Michael's skeleton slipped from the manacles that had been holding it suspended. The blackened skull hit the floor and split open to reveal the seven staring heads of a black Naga with eyes like bubbles of bright glistening clay, wet and empty, like the eyes of the four-armed woman Michael'd said was our mother.

The woman he'd said was only waiting for him to die so she could devour him, consume him, destroy him utterly.

The Naga pulled itself out of what remained of the spinal column, coiled in and around the charred fragments of bone, raised its seven blunt Chinese-dog-like heads and tasted the air with its many tongues. Michael, or the thing that had devoured him? There was a watchful malevolence to it, a sliding grace, but no intelligence, no humanity, nothing of my brother. It was at least six feet long, the thick base of its many necks tapering to a body no bigger around than Dara's wrist—slender for a serpent, but still too big to have ever been contained in my brother's spinal canal, in any human spine, just as the seven slowly weaving heads with which it was regarding the torture chamber could never have been contained by a human skull. And yet I'd seen it emerge from Michael's shattered skull, seen it pull itself free of what was left of his spine.

"Michael?" I tried to make myself heard around the vomit-sodden rags, choked on them without succeeding. But the Naga understood me.

It hissed sibilantly at me, a cold inhuman sound from its many mouths, nothing like my brother's voice. I was too tired, too confused, to try to make sense of the sounds emerging from the different mouths, orchestrate them into something meaningful.

"No, David," Dara interpreted for me. "That's Vasuki. Michael's Naga soul. Michael chose to die and forget. His soul has gone on to find rebirth in another body."

"Not—" I choked on the rags, managed to continue—"destroyed?"

"No." But the Naga's hissing seemed to have shocked Uncle Stephen awake. He grabbed some of the instruments he'd been heating in the furnace, handed two long-handled knives to his assistants, and kept a hooked pole like the eyeball gouger, only longer, with a triple-barbed tip glowing red, for himself. The doctor took up position on his right, the other on his left. They began to advance, spreading out so they could come at the Naga from three sides at once.

The Naga had all seven heads trained on them now. Dara was whispering something to it through her gag but I couldn't make out what she was saying. The heads were weaving back and forth on their short necks, hoods spread, and the raised body was beginning to sway.

Stephen halted just beyond the Naga's striking range—and Monteleur struck. But even as I felt it starting to rip through me again, before I could scream, the Naga had somehow come uncoiled and crossed the distance separating us with a motion fluid and effortless as an incoming wave, had flung a smooth cool coil around my left wrist and flowed up onto my arm.

The room flickered, imploded, lost all silver. There was a confused shouting from the other side of the locked door, a scream. Another scream.

But Monteleur was still within me, smooth and heavy and cold like a porcelain egg. The Naga had stopped it before it had had time to kill me.

The Naga touched two red-tipped tongues to my manacles and they fell away with a smell of hot metal. I stumbled, half-fell, felt something new rip free inside of me, and then the pain was too much and my legs gave way and I fell the rest of the way to the floor. Lying there I reached out instinctively for my father, tried to climb the shadow tides to his strength, but I couldn't find the way back to him.

I made it to my feet, lurched the rest of the way to Dara without dislodging the Naga still coiled around my arm. Steadied myself against the wall as it freed her the same way it had freed me. She plucked the gag from her mouth, freed me of mine, then put her arm around me to keep me from falling again.

"David." A whisper only I could hear. "They're going to rush us. You've got to bring your arm up, hold it out so Vasuki can strike at them—hurry, David! Now!"

I brought my arm up. The Naga anchored itself to it with a few tight coils around my wirst, lashed out in warning at all three attackers before any of them had had a chance to realize what was happening. It weighed almost nothing but even so I was too weak to keep my arm out straight in front of me.

"Dara, I can't . . ." She took hold of my arm, helped me support its weight.

"You can't hurt us now," she told Stephen. "If you try Vasuki will annihilate you as it annihilated Michael. But if you unlock the door for us and protect us until we're safely away we'll let you live."

"I can't stop you," Stephen said, lowering his hooked pole, "but I can't protect you either. With Michael gone and that Naga cutting David off from Gregory I've lost control of the vampires. They're waiting for us on the other side of the door."

"Then get Monteleur out of me."

"I can't, David. Not with that Naga paralyzing him."

"Is that true?" I asked the Naga.

"Yes." A sibilant hiss.

"Can they get in here?" I asked Stephen. "Force the door or come sliding under it as a mist or something?"

"Not until they break through it. There's a veneer of wild-rose wood on the outer surface and around the frame they can't penetrate."

"But they'll break in eventually?"

"Of course." A patronizing smile. "They're not stupid, David. Just limited in what they can think about."

"He's telling the truth," Dara said. Then, whispering again. "Vasuki can't stay here. Now that he's free of Michael he has to return to Patala and we have to go with him. Monteleur will kill you if we don't."

"I can't. Not without Father's help. . . . I'm not strong enough."

"You have to be. If he frees you to draw on Father Monteleur will kill you."

"Why can't he kill Monteleur? Or get my Naga soul to do it?"

"He can't. Not here . . . in Patala, maybe, I remember that— No. It's gone again. And you've been cut off from your Naga soul for so long it would kill you to contact it now. Like it killed Michael. But he can take us back to Patala with him."

Something heavy crashed into the door. The wood cracked but held.

"You see?" Stephen asked. "Not stupid at all."

Another crash and the door burst open. Beyond the four

vampires wielding the iron beam as a battering-ram I could see a confused struggle filling the main cavern. A few of Stephen's followers were still on their feet but most were down, dead or dying, Bathorys lapping blood from wounds torn with blunt teeth and nails in their victims' necks.

The vampires with the beam dropped it, stood aside. Behind them Father was crouched over John's twitching body, his cheeks working as he sucked at the gaping wound in John's chest.

I tried to force Father away, make him make them all stop, but I couldn't reach him. And the depths of the cavern were dark, shadow-filled, without trace of silver.

Father looked up, staring straight at me but not seeing me. His mouth and face were smeared with congealing blood, flecked with shredded skin and flesh. Like an infected wound with the scab torn off.

He got to his feet. John tried to hold on to him but Father pushed him effortlessly away. As Father entered the torture chamber another vampire bent over John, put his mouth to the wound in his chest.

Father made for Stephen without once glancing at us. Stood there before him waiting until at last Stephen closed his eyes, offered him his throat, moaned with what could have been pleasure or pain as Father took him gently by the shoulders and ripped open his throat with blunt teeth.

Dara said, "David, Vasuki can free you of Monteleur in Patala. He can take us there. But only if we swear to return value for value, to pay for what we are granted with something of equal value."

"Who decides what it's worth?" I was feverish, only half-conscious. I couldn't breathe. The hot gnawing in my belly and chest was getting worse. I no longer had the strength to fight it.

"We decide."

"Do you want me to?"

"Yes."

Stephen lay on the floor, his mouth open. His body was still arching, spasming more and more feebly as Father fed, lips clamped tight to the ragged hole in his neck.

"Then I swear."

And the caverns were gone.

Chapter Thirty-eight

THERE WAS NOTHING BUT THE VOID. INFINITE DARKness, limitless emptiness, without even the absence of color, shape and form to give it definition and potential. And yet the void was alive, was filled with a thousand swimming, gliding serpent shapes bleeding in and out of existence, in and out of emptiness, like color bleeding from new clothing into too-hot wash water and then, somehow, back again. The thousand serpents were one sole serpent, thousand-headed, its ivory scales and crimson eyes burning in the emptiness like a swarm of suns, and Vasuki, Dara, I myself were only three of its myriad heads. But even that sole serpent that was all there was or ever could be was only a coiling in upon itself of empty darkness, a curdling in the void.

And yet four grass-green elephants stood upon its ivory coils, and on their backs they supported the world-mountain.

The earth was a tiny protuberance, a minuscule boss, high on one of the mountain's four faces. We were within the mountain, in the network of caverns beneath its roots which formed a world vaster than a thousand earths, looking out and down and through the living stone into the void. The caverns were filled with fires the color of burning blood, with rivers of flowing gold and silver and platinum, with oceans of white fire through which winged serpents of turquoise flame flew and coupled. Vasuki was a river of liquid jade carrying us up and out through the world-mountain's iron crust to its surface, there to become a fountain falling as green rain into the infinite sea surrounding the world-mountain, in which it floated on the backs of four great turtles of blood-red copper.

Around us the waters were golden and cool, sweet-tasting. Indolent dragons with shimmering amethyst scales and long emerald barbels swam in the luminous waters, laired in drifting undersea ice palaces. Great ropes of shining pearls were looped around their necks, around their long fishlike bodies and short reptilian legs. We clung to the ropes of pearls wrapped around Vasuki's broad scaly back as he took us deeper, ever deeper, until at last we came to Patala, to the land beneath the sea, all jeweled palaces, groves, streams and gardens, through whose golden sky the great dragons drifted and swam like luminous purple clouds.

And yet behind it, or around it somehow, like shifting constellations of half-glimpsed afterimages, was the network of fiery caves beneath the world-mountain's roots, was the golden ocean that was at the same time all around us and visible overhead, Patala's sky.

And within and beneath them all, bleeding in and out of them as it bled in and out of the void, the thousand-headed serpent, coiling endlessly and alone in the dark.

It was too beautiful; I couldn't look at it any longer; I could feel myself dissipating, losing myself in the transformations, the multiplicity. I squeezed my eyes shut, concentrated on Monteleur, the agony in my ripped and torn tissues, but even the pain fled me, lost itself in the fires, the golden sea, the beauty of the world through whose skies we were gliding.

I opened my eyes and stared at Dara, trying to anchor myself to her. But she was looking around in wonder and joy and I was suddenly terrified that I was losing her to the landscape, to her memories, that the woman I knew and loved, who knew and loved me, would become strange and inhuman and lost to me forever.

"Dara—do you remember this? What it was like here, before they took your memories away?"

"No, I—I recognize it, David, I . . . remember it, being here, but—" There was a pain in her voice, a longing, that seemed to confirm my fears even while it told me she was still mine, that I hadn't lost her. "But that's all. I see it and I remember it."

We came to a cave in the world-mountain's fiery heart that was at the same time a milk-white chamber in an undersea ice palace and an open pavilion of carved jade in a garden, where Saraparajni awaited us on a canopied throne fashioned from a single great ruby.

Saraparajni. My mother. The cobra-headed Queen, the four-armed woman whom I'd seen lapping Michael's congealing blood with her long, black cat's tongue.

But there was nothing inhuman or frightening about her now. She was small, with eyes of liquid gold, lustrous brown skin, long flowing dark hair and a face that could almost have been Dara's but which was younger-looking and somehow more sharply defined. She wore a long, half-transparent sarilike garment of emerald green silk sewn with myriads of tiny pearls, and there was only the depth to her eyes, a sort of infinite still resonance to her every feature to indicate that she was anything more than an exquisitely beautiful girl just ripening into adolescence.

She gestured us to cushions and her movement was a window opening on memories I'd never known I had, memories of things no human could have ever known or experienced, memories that stretched back far beyond the beginning of the human race to the creation of the universe.

I remembered the void in which the thousand-headed serpent Shesha knotted Himself in and out of a darkness that was not absence but paradoxical fullness, that contained all meanings, all possibilities, even as it contained their negation—

Shesha was Patala and the Nagas, as Shesha was the universe and everything it contained. There was nothing that was not Shesha. Imagine Shesha breathing. When He exhaled, His breath, which was no different from His self, became the universe; when He inhaled, the universe was drawn back into Him. In a sense the universe had been created and destroyed, yet it had always been Shesha, and He had been neither created nor destroyed.

Yet though Shesha was One, He manifested Himself as Two, as Shesha and Devi. Seen this way, Shesha was pure, limitless, changeless consciousness, without form or qualities, while Devi was that power by which Shesha veiled Himself to Himself and negated and limited Himself in order to experience Himself as form. Devi was the Veiler, the Creatrix, the Womb of all things.

Devi had created the universe from Shesha's limitless substance; Devi would destroy it. Yet it was Shesha and Shesha alone who had created and who would destroy it, for Devi was none other than Shesha.

Their union-in-opposition was the basis of all creation: the universe was made up of paired opposites whose opposition reflected that primordial duality: male and female, life and death, good and evil, the static and that which was in motion. Yet these oppositions were only apparent: the static was merely that which was not moving, that which was in motion only that which was not static. Each was real, but real only in relation to the other, and neither had any existence beyond that granted by their union-in-opposition.

Man was a microcosm: whatever existed in the universe existed in him; that which was not in him was to be found nowhere else. But where men were microcosms, the Nagas were Devi, and Devi alone. First created, the Veiler, the Demiurge, the Power by which the One hid Its identity from Itself to become the many, they would be the last to be drawn back into Shesha when the universe ended. In a sense they *were* the universe. . . .

The concepts were too vast to grasp, yet in that timeless instant in which I remembered them I had no need to grasp them: I was one with them, experiencing them from within, directly. But then the memory was gone, I had only the memory of having remembered, the certainty that for a moment I had *known*, to animate a comprehension reduced to that which I could assimilate and fit into my limited conceptual system even as it showed me the impossible narrowness of that system.

My mother, the seemingly barely-adolescent girl smiling serenely at us from her canopied throne was Devi, the Demiurge, had created the universe. Even here in Patala it was beyond belief, beyond understanding: I could only accept, and trust in my acceptance. But I understood now how my father and his plans for us had gone wrong. He'd had only himself, only his life as a Bathory dhampire, to use to comprehend whatever truths Saraparajni had shown him . . . and the knowledge that was even now fading further and further from my understanding and taking on the abstract factuality of something learned secondhand from school or books, like the Special Theory of Relativity, could never have been fitted unmutilated into the person my father had been, the life he'd led.

I moved closer to Dara, took her hand, felt in her the same fading memory of the instant of total memory we'd shared.

"What about us?" I asked, retreating to something more comprehensible. "Are we immortal too, or will we die the way Michael did?"

The Queen opened us again to total memory, and we knew that what we'd been granted when we'd entered Patala was not immortal life, for there was no other kind, but the possibility of maintaining unbroken continuity of consciousness and memory until time ended and the universe was once again drawn back into Shesha. Yet though in Patala there was no death, if we returned to the world we would once again become mortal, could die and be reborn like any other humans. Yet with this difference: our Naga souls would be able to reanimate our cast-off bodies, return them to life and health. For their own use, or so that we could be reborn as ourselves, with our memories intact. As Michael could have survived the death of his body and been reborn as his renewed self, had he not fled in horror to a new body and forgetfulness from that moment of intimacy with his Naga soul, from the knowledge of who and what he was that his contact with his second soul had thrust upon him.

Death—true death, not a vampire's ignorant slavery to Satan—was nothing to fear, neither extinction nor loss, but only change, yet even that necessity could be transcended if we learned to live in intimacy with our Naga souls, so that with their aid we could shed our mortality like snakes shedding their worn-out skins, to emerge fresh and renewed from the discarded envelope.

Reduced to myself once more, I remembered Monteleur, my father crouched over Stephen's body, Larry in Provincetown with the familiar squirming through him. Remembering my father's face, seeing it smeared with blood and torn flesh, I knew it for my face, the Bathory face I'd always kept carefully concealed, even from myself, behind my outer masks. It was there, too, behind Dara's face, and as we stared into each other's eyes, our two selves fusing to form one self, our two minds one mind, we knew that we couldn't bear to see that face looking out at us from each other's eyes, from every mirroring surface, for all eternity.

We had to do whatever we could to keep the Bathorys from hurting and enslaving more people, from turning more of their innocent victims into what they themselves had become. Because we were both Bathorys, both alive only through the use we'd been able to make of our ancestors' stolen strength: the vampires we'd left behind to spend their nights in impossible hunger, their days in Hell, were not only our responsibility but part of ourselves.

We had to return to the world, risk not only death and forgetfulness, a new life in a new body, but an eternity of torture and degradation in Hell.

Even as our decision clarified itself within us the Queen allowed new memories, new knowledge to surface within us. I was submerged by my past, our past, all our Bathory pasts: the unending round of days spent with Satan in Hell, merged with Him, suffering the infinite agony of His self-inflicted torments.

Was submerged by the horror, the despair, of that eternally repeated realization that there was no satisfaction, no escape, no hope, that we were Satan's now and forever, that He would never let any of those whom He'd assimilated ever find an instant's peace or freedom again.

Any vampire we killed would only be reborn in another body with its potential for harm intact—as Michael, gone on to rebirth and oblivion, would only find himself Satan's once again when his new life was over. The only way to destroy the evil the Bathorys represented was to free them from Hell by getting them to renounce the Compact they'd made with Satan—but Satan was in them, was them, would no more allow them to free themselves than He would ever free Himself from Hell and the agony which was His very reason for existing. . . .

Saraparajni gestured again, opening me to understanding.

Satan was a god, a totally conscious being, self-created, self-creating, capable of becoming anything His consciousness-of-self could encompass.

And yet—the gods were mortal. Totally conscious, they had

only their consciousness-of-self to sustain their existence. Deprive them of that consciousness and they ceased to exist.

Satan was a god, and the gods could be destroyed.

We could destroy Him.

Not out of a desire for vengeance, or to punish Him. Satan had to be destroyed for the same reason the vampires and His other victims had to be liberated. Out of compassion for His suffering.

Because the balance had shifted. In the time of Shesha's Exhalation the Nagas had been ruled by the joy of creation, and though they'd destroyed as well as created (since the old must always be destroyed to make place for the new) yet it had been the will of the One to become many which had filled them. But Saraparajni's marriage to my father had marked the midpoint of the cycle, and with our births Shesha's Exhalation had ended and His Inhalation begun.

Again that transcendent memory faded back into factuality, and I was left with the knowledge that it was for this that Saraparajni had entered the world, for this that Dara and I had been conceived: so that we could attempt to destroy Satan.

Attempt only, because the Nagas no longer knew the outcome of the train of events they'd set into motion. They were not omniscient; they too were capable of forgetting; in pouring themselves into the universe they had taken on the limitations of created beings so that now, at the midpoint between the cycles of creation and compassion, they'd forgotten the future and knew only the role they'd chosen to play, the broad path of their destiny.

We could fail, be swallowed up and consumed by Satan as our ancestors had been, our sacrifice serving some purpose the Nagas no longer remembered.

"How can we destroy Satan?" Dara asked.

Saraparajni opened us yet again to Satan's memories, to His eternal present, in which He suffered His entire existence, His every torment, simultaneously . . . in which Aunt Judith's suicide, the agonies of those hundreds of thousands of men Vlad Tepes had had impaled when he'd ruled Wallachia, the way Michael had used me and Dara, Christ's tragic farce on the cross—the revelation granted him in the moment of his dying, that he was not the Son of God but only Satan's creature, that he had bought with his sacrifice only another means of increasing the deception and despair of those who would come to believe in him—all this was part of the process by which Satan had wrenched Himself into existence. . . .

Satan was at the same time the product of men's fears and the self-created cause of those fears. He had been created afraid—afraid of losing His individual identity and dissolving back into Shesha's undifferentiated Self. Every god creates itself in its own image, and Satan had chosen to create Himself from Shesha through fear and pain. Hell, where He was tormented, He had created from those torments as a prison and a refuge: Satan was both Hell itself, and its prisoner.

Satan had chosen to create His identity, find the definition of His self, through pain. Pain is the interface of the self and the not-self; pain delineates boundaries and limitations, defining the one experiencing it to himself while providing the ultimate proof of that experienced self's own reality. Nothing defines one's separation and distinctness from the rest of creation so sharply as pain and Satan, who as a god was a being whose very existence was dependent upon His consciousness-of-self, had been led by His fear of dissolution to adopt the sharpest possible definition of Himself.

But the opposite of pain was joy. Joy in all its forms breaks down the barriers separating consciousness from that which it experiences, thus threatening the fortress integrity of the barricaded self. So it was joy which Satan feared most, and because Satan was a god—a figment of His own imagination—joy was an objective as well as subjective threat to His existence.

Satan dared not share another's joy, for that shared pleasure would erase, however temporarily, boundaries upon which His existence depended. Yet when He caused pain to another, He imposed His proper reality upon that of His victim, and thus avoided the risk of dissolution. Satan found the pleasure He needed to survive in inflicting pain on others, then merging those He tormented with Himself. Sharing the vampires' insatiable hunger, Alexandra's death, even Uncle Peter's struggles to free himself of the werewolf he'd never really been, Satan was able to preserve His existence.

Yet His need to make those He tortured part of Himself rendered Him vulnerable. If He could be tricked into expanding His self-boundaries to encompass a human experiencing the purest and most intense of all possible joys, that of union with Shesha, then Satan would also experience that bliss and, experiencing it, would be freed of His self-inflicted, self-creating torments . . . and so cease to exist.

"What do we have to do?" Dara asked while I was still struggling to make sense of what remained of that transcendent knowledge, still overwhelmed by Satan's agonies.

Once again memory blossomed within us. I opened my mouth to protest, said, "No—" Fell silent again. Because I *knew*, and there was no way I could deny that certainty, pretend it was anything other than what it was.

Dara would have to die and become a vampire; I would have to remain alive so I could reawaken the vampire Dara would become to the memory of her humanity, then bring her to share with me the ultimate ecstasy of union with Shesha. There was no way I could take her place; I was too much a Bathory and a dhampire, too shut-off from my Naga soul to ever reawaken to my lost humanity once I became a vampire. Our roles were set, immutable, and had been ever since Saraparajni had allowed Herself to die and become a vampire so that the daughter She bore during Her five years of renewed human life would be marked by Satan for His own, destined from birth to become a vampire.

Saraparajni could never have contaminated Satan with the supreme joy of union with Shesha and so destroyed Him Herself, because She was a Naga and the Nagas, first created, would be the last to know that union once more: Devi could not return to Shesha's limitless consciousness until Shesha's Inhalation was complete and the universe ended. But Dara had already spent a day in Hell: Satan would accept her, would consume her, could be destroyed by her—

If I was strong enough to reawaken her lost humanity without succumbing to her first. If I could bring us both to union with Shesha.

I knew what to do, how it had to be done. Not whether I could fight back the Bathory and the dhampire in me long enough to succeed in doing it.

"What happens to Dara afterward?" I asked. "If we destroy Him?"

But that too was forgotten, lost here at the midpoint between the cycles. Perhaps Satan's destruction would release his victims so that they'd be free to go on to new rebirths—and in that case Dara's Naga soul would reanimate her dead body, so that she could be reborn as herself, with all her memories intact.

Perhaps Dara and all Satan's other victims would dissolve back with Him into Shesha's limitless formlessness, sharing His liberation and annihilation.

The task had been set for all time, but the choice was still ours. Whatever we decided, Satan would eventually be destroyed—if not now, then years or millennia or eons later—while other, equally evil, gods would survive His passing, still others come into being after He was gone. There was no one to force us, no one to reproach us if we decided to remain safely sheltered in Patala until time itself came to an end.

I remembered that first time Michael had taken control of me in the forest at my father's funeral, the way he'd used me to violate Dara, had used our shared pain and degradation to provide him with the power he wanted. As Satan needed not only His victims' pain, but even His own, to maintain His continued existence.

No one to force us. Only Satan's agony, our Bathory faces staring out at us through the masking flesh for all eternity.

"Send us back," Dara said.

Chapter Thirty-nine

SARAPARAJNI GESTURED AND I FELT A STRANGE SUD-
den emptiness within me where the heavy cool porcelain egg
Monteleur had become in Patala had been . . . saw Dara start
as the familiar passed from me to her.

Taking upon herself the death that should have been mine,
that I'd entered Patala to escape.

The space around us was filling with clotted red-black shadows, drifting darknesses. I took Dara's hand, held tight to it.
Around us I could still see the jade pavilion in its gardens, the
undersea palace of white ice, the fiery caverns beneath the
world-mountain's roots, but superposed on them was Uncle
Stephen's torture chamber, my father frozen motionless in the
act of gulping down the last of the blood spurting from the
severed jugular and carotid veins in Stephen's neck.

I took Dara in my arms, pressed her to me, held her.

At last we let go of each other, stepped forward together
into shadow.

Dara screamed—and within her Monteleur too screamed, a
terrifying frenzied bellowing as the familiar reawakened to find

itself in her alien, Naga-impregnated flesh. There was a sudden burning implosion in my belly, a horrible sickening internal slithering as my torn and damaged tissues were sucked in to fill the void where Monteleur had been . . . a frenzied thrashing visible beneath the taut skin of Dara's belly as she collapsed to the floor of the torture chamber, Monteleur still screaming within her, arched her back in a single, final bone-breaking convulsion, and died.

Monteleur was silent. Gone. Had deserted her body as soon as she was dead.

The pain from what the familiar had done to me before Vasuki had paralyzed it, from the wounds which would have killed any normal human, came rushing back over me, but I held it off, refused it: I was the sole surviving Bathory dhampire now; all the life the vampires had stolen from those they'd killed, those they were even now feeding upon, came flooding into me, a black burning tide . . . and I drank it, used it to keep to my feet, wall off the pain, begin healing myself even as I held back my father and all the others—their skin dull white, smooth and dry as polished bone, all of them reeking with their victims' blood, their own rotting graveyard sweetness—used the strength I drank from them to resist the insane hunger in their eyes like dead, glittering sapphires or emeralds, dilated black opals.

Dara lay dead and crumpled at my feet. Falling through the cold and the wind, the empty darkness, already beginning to forget me, forget everything but the hunger blossoming within her.

Perhaps Monteleur was there with her in the freezing void where I dared not follow him, taunting and tormenting her.

Around me the cavern blazed like burning metal. The family was bloating itself on the last remaining members of Stephen's coven, his other followers. I made no attempt to stop them, contented myself with forcing the vampires outside the cavern and back in Illinois to leave their innocent victims alive and healthy enough to recover, as I drained all the Bathory vampires of the life and strength they stole, used it to complete healing my body.

When at last I was strong enough I carried Dara back out of the cavern to the cabin, laid her on the bed I'd once shared with Alexandra. She felt light, empty, a hollow wax sculpture. I lay down beside her, climbed the shadow tides back to my father, took from him the knowledge which had enabled him to prolong the forty days of Aunt Judith's transformation for so many years.

The method was simple, involving garlic and holy water, thorns from the wild roses which grew in such profusion on the family estate back in Illinois. Stephen had a stock of everything I'd need. I waited until dawn came and I could relax the hold I was keeping on Father and the others, then treated the hundred and forty-four half-transformed victims in their coffins—all those who were to have been possessed by members of the secondary covens for the Lammas Day Sabbat—with the garlic and holy water, shoving the thorns in under the loose clammy skin of their chests, directly above their unbeating hearts.

I was interrupted by a delivery truck full of food and drink for the Sabbat, twice more by disciples of Uncle Stephen's arriving early to take care of tasks they'd been assigned. I accepted the delivery, using my power to focus the deliveryman's attention to pass myself off as Uncle Stephen . . . used the same power to deal with all but one of the others the same way I'd dealt with the two Provincetown cops what seemed like so long ago, turning them away from all possibility of disbelieving me when I told them the Sabbat had been rescheduled for All Hallows Eve and that Uncle Stephen wanted them to remain in seclusion, not trying to contact him or any of the other coven members, until then.

If we hadn't succeeded in destroying Satan before All Hallows Eve Dara and I would both be dead, and vampires, and nothing we could do now would keep Satan from repossessing them after we too were His.

The final man was the only member of Uncle Stephen's prime coven who hadn't been in the cavern when the vampires killed the others. An undertaker from Salinas. He was as easy to deal with as the others had been: Stephen had told them all to keep the locations of their parents' and grandparents' bodies secret, telling no one—not even him—where they were, but I kept the man from noticing that I wasn't Stephen and that what I was saying was in contradiction to what Stephen had ordered him to do, sent him back to Salinas prepared to treat the bodies he was keeping hidden in his funeral home with garlic and holy water and wild rose thorns.

There was no way I could force the dead coven members

to tell me where their dead parents were hidden, no way I could command the vampires they would become on Lammas Night, when their transformations would be complete and they'd emerge from their coffins for the first time, to converge on the cavern, reclaim their childrens' bodies. . . .

And kill me if they could, rip me open and drain me of all the life and strength the Bathory vampires had stolen for me, the force so strong within me now that I could see my skin blazing brighter than the caverns, the vampires, anything else around me.

When the undertaker was gone I took care of all the bodies of the victims from the night before, dragged them to a chamber deeper in the caverns which my father's memories had told me Stephen had kept as a refuge, its reinforced-steel door covered inside with layers of rosewood veneer, its stone walls protected by spells.

I built a bier for Dara from the stacked corpses, laid her out on it.

Kissed her chill lips one last time before returning to the outer caverns to clean up the remaining signs of the previous night's slaughter, make sure that all the familiars Stephen had summoned for his Sabbat were secure in their pentacles.

When night came I stationed a vampire over the pentacles, so I could keep watch over the familiars through his eyes and make sure they remained undisturbed, then used the rest of my ancestors to try to search out the places were the coven members' murdered parents had been hidden. A few I found— John's family were in their family crypt; there were three back-packers in a ravine behind Chews Ridge where their daughter had buried them after she killed them; another man in a fresh grave in the Monterey Cemetery, just across from the college— but the rest were too well concealed.

Would be emerging from their graves Lammas Night.

Coming after me.

Chapter Forty

THE UNDERTAKER RETURNED THE NEXT MORNING with everything I'd ordered him to get for me: a chunk of flesh from the newly dead corpse of a man who'd died of natural causes, the silver bowls and platters, pastes . . . everything I'd need to prepare for the night when Dara's transformation would be complete. I put the flesh in the freezer in the cabin, turned the undertaker away from all memory of ever having known Stephen or been a coven member, sent him away. Spent the rest of the day reinforcing the chamber in which Dara lay on her bier of unrotting corpses, beginning my preparations for the Ritual.

Uncle Peter arrived the following day, Lammas Eve, as did the Black Men from the lesser covens who were to have been fitted with their new familiars before the Sabbat. I turned the Black Men away from their memories of Stephen and their covens, sent them away, but it was harder to decide what to do with Uncle Peter. I finally turned him away from all his memories and fears, left him a child with only enough self-awareness to feed and clean himself. There'd be time to restore him to himself if Dara and I succeeded; if we failed he'd be doomed anyway. This way he'd at least be able to escape his fear and guilt for a while.

Lammas Day I dealt with the few other men and women who arrived as I'd dealt with the others. That night I locked myself in my secure chamber, stationed my ancestors outside the door to deal with any non-Bathory vampires or other intruders who might try to force their way in.

Three tried. I let them continue until I was sure that they couldn't make it past the door and protective spells, then had my ancestors capture them and hold them till dawn.

The following day I destroyed them with fire, then returned once again to the chamber. I spent most of the next thirty-eight days in the clotted shadows beside Dara's bier of stacked corpses, watching over her and remembering her, leaving only when I had to do something for Peter. Thirty-eight days watching the beauty drain from her face and body only to be replaced by something else, a cold aggressive parody of the person she'd been, an obscene exaggeration of her natural sensuality and sexuality. Watching her lengthening canine teeth push their way like slow-crawling ivory worms out from beneath her ever-redder lips.

Every night I stationed Bathory vampires outside the door, kept the other Bathorys from doing their victims any lasting harm. Two more non-Bathory vampires were caught trying to force their way in to me, a third escaped. We caught another when Mihnea surprised her killing a teen-age boy camped just off my property.

But though I could force the Bathorys to leave their victims alive, I had no control over the new vampires, and every night brought a dozen or more killings in Monterey or Carmel, or among the thousands of military men stationed at Fort Ord.

It was almost impossible to keep myself from climbing the shadow tides to Dara, prevent myself from using them to enter her consciousness as once we'd entered my father's together, but she was of the same generation as I was and I had no dominion over her. Had I joined her I would have been lost, swallowed up in her transformation, yet though I dared not open myself in any way to what was happening within her, I could still feel her transformation reflected to me through the others, sense the growing elation in all the vampires I ruled as the moment approached when her transformation would have reached its end and they would all be free of my dominion.

Even shut off from her as I was, I felt the change in her when her transformation was complete and Satan took her from her body for her first day of torment in Hell. On that last day of my dominion I sealed all the other Bathory vampires in their coffins while they slept to keep them from taking any physical part in what happened between us.

Then I knelt beside her bier and concentrated in the way which Saraparajni had revealed to us in that last instant of total memory, until I could see Saraparajni in Dara, see the All-Mother, the Creatrix, She who was simultaneously mother, mate, and daughter to all created beings. She held the body of an infant to Her mouth with one hand, lapping its blood with Her thick black cat's tongue, while with the other She held a second infant to Her breast, suckling it. Her hair and skin were glossy black, and around Her waist She wore a sort of skirt of dangling hands, boneless forearms, while cobras coiled and twined around Her neck and shoulders.

She was utterly beautiful, utterly horrible. Kneeling there before her I worshiped her until at last she shuddered on her bier of waxy-fleshed corpses, a convulsive trembling that twisted and contorted her body and face without touching the dead stillness within.

Her face was a mask of rage and pain and hatred, the Bathory face that lay hidden as well beneath my own features, yet it was still only a mask, and beneath it I could sense the hungering emptiness, the need to gouge me hollow, empty and consume me and make of me only another vessel for the hunger that had already eaten her.

In the weeks I'd spent watching over her I'd prepared everything necessary for the Ritual, readied myself as best I could. I put aside my fear, let it flow through and from me, waited.

She opened her eyes and stared at me, made a low inhuman glottal sound deep in her throat. Conflicting emotions, none of them truly hers, chased themselves across the smooth perfection of her face, never touching the hungering deadness beneath, and then she smiled.

Her teeth were shiny white behind too-red lips, her breath was foul, and yet the very foulness, the deadness of her drew me to her, awakened all my need for her. I let her draw me down beside her onto the bier, lay trembling with pleasure as she trapped me in the shimmering depths of her golden eyes, while she ripped open my throat and warmed herself with my living blood.

Through the door I could hear a muffled scream from Uncle Peter. It went on and on while she drank from me, suddenly stopped.

When she'd drunk enough to warm herself, feel my life flowing through her veins, I wrenched myself free of her eyes, used the stolen strength I'd taken against this day from my ancestors to hold her will and my need away from me long enough to open myself once more to that total memory I'd been taught to summon, just long enough to use the last of my stolen strength to send that memory flooding into her, superpose it on the dark tide of life she was draining from me, shock her into awareness, into readiness to receive her own lost memories, there where they'd awaited her in the keeping of her Naga soul.

She choked, tried to scream. Her hands fell away from me and her eyes lost their fascination, grew dull and confused as she fought against her body and its hungers, her vampire's inability to accept and believe the truth her Naga soul was showing her. She began to shake, barely retained enough control to keep from vomiting up the precious blood she'd drunk.

The blood that would lend her the life she'd need for the Ritual.

"David, I'm—I'm not strong enough." Her voice was ragged with need, and yet still a cold, angry monotone. Dead. "I'm afraid and I . . . need more blood, I have to have it to go on, but please, David, don't let me take too much—"

I helped her sit up, held her steady as she drank from my opened throat until I was too weak to let her continue, then pushed her gently away from me, over to the far side of the chamber where I'd set up everything we'd need for the Ritual, all the objects and symbols that would help reinforce and imprint the meaning of what we were doing on our consciousness.

"David, *hurry*, they've got Peter, he's letting them out—"

We cleansed ourselves in a pool of scented water with the appropriate rituals, rubbed each other with the scented oils and pastes proper to the first part of the Ritual, dressed each other with clumsy haste in robes of coarse red silk. The air around us was heady with flower smells, fragrant oils and spices, the rich greenness of tree saps and grasses, everything that was freshness and life.

We sat down facing each other across a low silver table set with platters of human and animal flesh, fish and dry hard bread, goblets of bittersweet nectar, with its trays holding the objects I'd chosen for us to contemplate during the Ritual feast: flowers and flower garlands, blades of freshly cut green grass, the skull of a weasel, grains of rice, water containers and a libation jar, a lump of kneaded clay with five aromatic eucalyptus leaves across its top. The points of departure for our visualization and contemplation of human existence in its entirety, everything we needed to partake of and cherish that existence.

The moment of total memory we'd been granted was beginning to fade back into empty factuality; I could see Dara trembling with her need, feel my own need to sacrifice myself to her hunger twisting inside me.

And outside the chamber, through the steel door, I could hear a confused din: Peter and my ancestors preparing to try to force their way in. But the door would hold; we had the time we'd need.

I thrust them from consciousness, dipped the fingers of my left hand into the shallow silver bowl of vermilion paste in front of me, drew an equilateral triangle on the silver surface between us, its apex pointing to Dara, then touched my paste-covered index finger to Dara's forehead, just above the space between her eyes. As I washed the paste from my hand in a second bowl Dara dipped the corresponding fingers of her right hand in a second bowl and drew a second triangle over mine, but with its base towards her and its apex pointing to me, so that the two triangles superposed formed a six-pointed star. Then she touched my forehead as I had touched hers.

It was as though an eye opened, but not an eye there in my forehead where she'd touched me with the paste, not an eye that was in me or was any part of me at all. But it opened and I saw:

In the center of the six-pointed star Saraparajni sat on a throne of burning diamonds, and everything about Her was golden. She had rich lustrous golden-brown skin, long flowing hair, golden eyes, the slim graceful body of a girl just barely adolescent, yet from the waist down She was serpent and She rested on Her golden coils.

Her coils that were Shesha's coils as She was Shesha, thousand-headed, bleeding in and out of the void, in and out of existence; and on Shesha's coils stood the four grass-green elephants who supported the weight of the universe on their backs. And within that mountain universe, in the caverns beneath its roots, She was a winged serpent whose feathers and plumes were bright-burning blue flame, a winged serpent burning Her way up and out of the ocean of white fire, up through the rocky core of the world-mountain to emerge as a flowering tree, the Tree of All Life, that was no other than the serpent twined around it and around the Cretan priestess who took it and held it to her bared breast, fed it with her own milk and then let it slip from her into the pool where the sacrifices' bodies were thrown, which led to the golden ocean in which Dara and I drifted and swam, indolent and purple-scaled, our garlands of pearls streaming and singing with the currents as we made our way up and out of the ocean into the waiting channels of our spines, as we began to ascend them—

We sat facing each other across the six-pointed star of drying vermilion paste. Dara raised her left hand, moved her hands in a remembered gesture, awakening my response. I bent myself to the appropriate position, made the corresponding gesture with my right hand, feeling the eons come alive in me as I began following the fiery red solar breath in through my right nostril, throughout my body, my many bodies bleeding in and out of the golden ocean in which we swam, followed the breath out through the same nostril. . . .

The Ritual had begun.

But the repetition of thousands of uttered and unuttered words, each with its own unique constellation of meanings and emotions, of memories it awakened, the description of the visualizations and contemplations and adorations, the taste of human meat or the feel of Dara's chill flaccid flesh against and around me when at last I entered her, the ways in which we bent and moved our bodies as we made love . . . none of this would tell you anything. There is no way to describe what we experienced except to say that for a time we were allowed to pass from the imprisoning darkness of our limited selves to the unbounded radiance of Shesha's infinite Self, from the joy of our lovemaking to the infinitely greater bliss of which it was a reflection.

There are no words. I will not even try.

And yet I have been permitted to realize, if only for a moment, my Oneness with Shesha, and the memory of that Oneness which I yet retain calms me as I sit here in the cabin watching over Dara's vacant body there on the bed where I put it when the stench of the decomposing bodies on which we lay drove me from the caverns.

I know that we succeeded, that Satan has been liberated and destroyed, because when I returned to consciousness of my limited self and surroundings I saw that Dara's canine teeth were normal human teeth again, and that the false parody of life with which Satan had animated her had departed.

As I stumbled with her body out of the caverns into the daylight, blind in the darkness beyond the lamp-lit chamber in which we'd lain now that I no longer had my powersight to show me the way, I stumbled over stiffening corpses, dry brittle bones already crumbling to dust . . . slipped in stinking pools of putrescent corruption: all that remained of my ancestors and their victims now that the normal processes of dissolution had resumed their course.

Just inside the entrance to the cavern I found Uncle Peter's twisted body, as though he'd been trying to crawl out of the inner darkness back to the day sky when he'd died.

The Bathorys are silent within me, drawn back with Satan into Shesha or freed to be reborn in new bodies, perhaps even to fall victim to the new evil gods which will rise to take His place, the others which have survived His destruction. Yet the dark tide no longer links me with them; both their strength and their hunger are gone.

She is so still. I press my hand to the cold flesh of her breast, touch her neck, but I can feel no heartbeat, no pulse. Dead. Yet I know that life will soon be returning to this, her body, that even if in liberating Satan and His victims she has been drawn with him back into Shesha, the Naga soul with which she shared her mortal body will reanimate it for its own use.

Liberation.

Annihilation.

There is a faint hiss of indrawing breath and her chest begins to rise and fall in a ragged rhythm that gradually becomes smoother. Once again I press my hand to her breast—her flesh is warm now, heated by returning life—and I feel the gentle flutter of her beating heart.

Who is she?

"Dara," I say but she does not respond. Perhaps she doesn't hear me, perhaps she is not yet strong enough to reply.

Perhaps she is gone, never to return for so long as the universe endures.

Her eyes are shut but I think I can see her eyelids beginning to quiver. When she opens her eyes I'll know who she is.

When she opens her eyes.

FOLLOW THE ADVENTURES OF "THE MOST EXTRAORDINARY HERO IN THE HISTORY OF THE HEROIC EPIC." —*Washington Post Book World*

Gene Wolfe's

magnificent four volume saga

THE BOOK OF THE NEW SUN

has captured the praise and imagination of Science Fiction and Fantasy readers all over the world. Be sure to catch up on any volumes you may have missed.

Just check off the titles you want and use the coupon below to order.

- ☐ 46398-5 The Shadow of the Torturer $2.95
- ☐ 41616-2 The Claw of the Conciliator $2.75
- ☐ 45450-1 The Sword of the Lictor $2.95

And watch for the final volume
The Citadel of the Autarch

Available now in hardcover from Timescape Books